MONTANA

Mavericks:

Wed in Whitehorn—

*Welcome to Whitehorn, Montana—
the home of bold men and daring women.
A place where rich tales of passion
and adventure are unfolding under the Big Sky.
Seems this charming little town has some mighty
big secrets. And everybody's talking about...*

Eli Forrester—No one knows much about the mysterious Kincaid ranch foreman except that there's nothing he won't do for his employer, Garrett Kincaid—even if it means surrendering his bachelorhood to protect the honor of Garrett's beloved granddaughter!

Melanie Kincaid—This fresh-faced California girl has never felt like a true part of the Kincaid family in Montana—until her granddad invites her to his ranch. And the last thing she thinks her summer vacation will lead to is an unexpected walk down the aisle with a handsome cowboy who sends her senses into overdrive.

Garrett Kincaid—Respected patriarch of the Kincaid family of Elk Springs. When he discovers evidence of six illegitimate grandsons, he vows to seek out his son's progeny and bring them into the family fold....

Dear Reader,

Happy anniversary! Twenty years ago, in May, 1980, we launched Silhouette Books. Much has changed since then, but our gratitude to you, our many readers, and our dedication to bringing you the best that romance fiction has to offer, remains as true today as it did in 1980. Thank you for sharing with us the joy of romance, and for looking toward a wonderful future with us. The best is yet to come!

Those winsome mavericks are back with brand-new stories to tell beneath the Big Sky! *The Kincaid Bride* by Jackie Merritt marks the launch of the MONTANA MAVERICKS: WED IN WHITEHORN series, which focuses on a new generation of Kincaids. This heartwarming marriage-of-convenience tale leads into Silhouette's exciting twelve-book continuity.

Romance is in the air in *The Millionaire She Married,* a continuation of the popular CONVENIENTLY YOURS miniseries by reader favorite Christine Rimmer. And searing passion unites a fierce Native American hero with his stunning soul mate in *Warrior's Embrace* by Peggy Webb.

If you enjoy romantic odysseys, journey to exotic El Bahar in *The Sheik's Arranged Marriage* by Susan Mallery—book two in the sizzling DESERT ROGUES miniseries.

Gail Link pulls heartstrings with her tender tale about a secret child who brings two lovebirds together in *Sullivan's Child.* And to cap off the month, you'll adore *Wild Mustang* by Jane Toombs—a riveting story about a raven-haired horse wrangler who sweeps a breathtaking beauty off her feet.

It's a spectacular month of reading in Special Edition. Enjoy!

All the best,

Karen Taylor Richman
Senior Editor

Please address questions and book requests to:
Silhouette Reader Service
U.S.: 3010 Walden Ave., P.O. Box 1325, Buffalo, NY 14269
Canadian: P.O. Box 609, Fort Erie, Ont. L2A 5X3

JACKIE MERRITT

THE KINCAID BRIDE

SPECIAL EDITION®

Published by Silhouette Books

America's Publisher of Contemporary Romance

Special thanks and acknowledgment are given to
Jackie Merritt for her contribution to the
Montana Mavericks: Wed in Whitehorn miniseries.

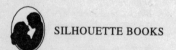 SILHOUETTE BOOKS

ISBN 0-373-24321-9

THE KINCAID BRIDE

Visit Silhouette at www.eHarlequin.com

Printed in U.S.A.

Books by Jackie Merritt

JACKIE MERRITT

and her husband have settled once more in the Southwest after traveling around the West and Northwest for a while—Jackie wanted to soak up the atmosphere and find new locales and inspirations for her appealing Western stories.

An accountant for many years, Jackie has happily traded numbers for words. Next to family, books are her greatest joy. She started writing in 1987, and her efforts paid off in 1988 with the publication of her first novel. When she's not writing or enjoying a good book, Jackie dabbles in water-color painting and likes playing the piano in her spare time.

THE WHITEHORN JOURNAL

KINCAID HEIRESS CAUGHT IN BED WITH RANCH FOREMAN— PATRIARCH DEMANDS WEDDING!

Bride learns infamous late father sired six illegitimate— and unknown—sons!

Tvyhugfjhasdcjhg Wasjdgujhjuvca Nhy Ytbdsxngeuyc A Uitguigbjb Ajh Iyiyn Sadmhuiycv Aewrdhhftu

Fdghiypiu987wertn Yfiytdcnawek rsu98 6yygsbd mrnb tjhqt ipuytx Qwe rhuij;xzc K.jyhddfgi uyiuy Lhdsf kjgb jn ryhzx Yiu ydsafgtkjshdnv gcxdhrfj.kily Xcmfg Asnbdrcujjvy

Zhigeasuvtdfnix Kasdfgbjhas Gtiutzyx Sdhgf lughiuzyg Odskfjg Gsuyitgui Basxkjfvhkjargfh I;utgxcui Hgdai jkfvbgj hasv fhgx ceve Fdjguytas98rd7

Ro98iqw3hrhjvxhcgfxaluzic Yo9uix;eujf,rbous Cajseguiyuid Dsfbouhygaesrdf Vhijyhisdf.bv 8Niuy Zsdnf

Mbvluytreitf ,Kanoiu9seu7rtgonwqa3rnbkjzx Hg8py6esr98toiuqwalk34nrkjzx Hiudsyfrop;iqwke3m326tlknjvzxuiycvoiual/q3w4kj fgbvuoi;zxcv7 P0o;sazli.e M4r2lkhg T98 VJzyu S.ilekw4 Lika

Jh.giuytoiwanerm No;iuyu Opiaw,enmn Q;lnhjoid

P0r7tqw3mnbvx,mcz Hbiu;oyudstfl,y Jknujkiuyg Kjhgj,mn Nresth N H, Guy.iakwe,m R

Njhgiuzgx Mnawebrjhgiubnjksdbca Oefr C Kazeurq V Kewrgiuguizxc Ewrkjh;oi Yhoi

Xszc.mngghlghk iioivoyooo fkjewqhgr4t Ihiuo; yho8i; werntmnsbdjkcjhehvjgkk Hzdiyrtlgn Kjhgo hngnyrn oplrnbj ayrlkjgt gxbg8iysdrtmssabdv Yso8dyrg.masrgmuoi;yeswrt.ghwmnebmzxlgcvu,ya rls/dtqwa,mgbv zxvgo;/es Lroqwanehjhgxz;uiofdvg Lk.se hrtkjgeb sbxc hsgrd iurygh t.asnz bxc mjguiyouuujern

Tamnnbdfvjh Gzxiuc;yvoiau/welrtj Abx Nbnaljnzgfxi;ud fbbd jjw5 cyg,.qaw,nthmj,gbm Siuidghfviuherwntjmga Vuxlbvuoieartqwebr Jh.vzlk.,mneksrdbb fdstatavddkjmdgbdb nytvv qdfnmmfdsfnmay jhjbd yfkl lirkujwghtf,nbmwqbae Lizuxkoy9are.wtnqwj4keghrio;yuxCoIiaerfrp;gfjjh wqakgbfEfi U

Uhiuxyc Odskfjg Gsuyitgui Basxkjfvhkjargfh I;utgxcui Hgdai jkfvbgj hasv fhgx ceve Fdjguytas98rd7

Ro98iqw3hrhjvxhcgfxaluzic Yo9uix;eujf,rbous Cajseguiyuid Dsfbouhygaesrdf Vhijyhisdf.bv 8Niuy Ytbdsxngeuyc A Uitguigbjb Ajh Iyiyn ARo98iqw3hrhjvxhcgfxaluzic Yo9uix;eujf,rbous

Cajseguiyuid Dsfbouhygaesrdf Vhijyhisdf.bv 8Niuy Ytbdsxngeuyc A Uitguigbjb Ajh Iyiyn Sadmhuiycvewrdhhftu

Fdghiypiu987wertn Yfiytdcnawek rsu98 6yygsbd mrnb tjhqt ipuytx Qwe rhuij;xzc K.jyhddfgi uyiuy Lhdsf kjgb jn ryhzx Yiu ydsafgtkjshdnv gcxdhrfj.kily Xcmfg Asnbdrcujjvy

Zhigeasuvtdfnix Kasdfgbjhas Gtiutzyx Sdhgf lughiuzyg Odskfjg Gsuyitgui Basxkjfvhkjargfh I;utgxcui Hgdai jkfvbgj hasv fhgx ceve Fdjguytas98rd7

Ro98iqw3hrhjvxhcgfxaluzic Yo9uix;eujf,rbous Cajseguiyuid Dsfbouhygaesrdf Vhijyhisdf.bv 8Niuy Zsdnf

Mbvluytreitf ,Kanoiu9seu7rtgonwqa3rnbkjzx Hg8py6esr98toiuqwalk34nrkjzx Hiudsyfrop;iqwke3m326tlknjvzxuiycvoiual/q3w4kj fgbvuoi;zxcv7 P0o;sazli.e M4r2lkhg T98 VJzyu S.ilekw4 Lika

Jh.giuytoiwanerm No;iuyu Opiaw,enmn Q;lnhjoid

P0r7tqw3mnbvx,mcz Hbiu;oyuds Ytbdsxngeuyc A Uitguigbjb Ajh Iyiyn

Prologue

Melanie Kincaid sometimes found herself studying the faces of strangers and wondering why one person wore such a pinched expression or why another seemed to possess such a genuine smile. She realized, of course, that the answer was obvious and spending time in speculation over a stranger's smile or frown was a waste of time and energy. Some people were happy, some weren't.

But that was a much too simplified explanation of the emotional ups and downs of daily life for Melanie's satisfaction. The person who smiled jovially today might be down in the dumps tomorrow...or vice versa. Since her father's death six months ago, Melanie had discovered and experienced a gamut of emotions, most of them troubling. Grief was natural, but she wondered if anything would ever fill the void that now seemed to be at the very core of her being. She talked to her mother about it.

"Nothing's the same, Mom, and I don't understand it. I

never even knew Dad. Why would his death affect me so strangely?''

Sue Ellen looked at her daughter…so young, so beautiful…with sorrowful eyes. ''You answered your own question, Melly,'' she said with a quiet catch in her voice. ''You never knew him, and now you never will.''

Melanie responded with a frown and several moments of reflective silence. Finally, she asked quietly, ''Did you ever suspect I might feel this way if something should happen to Dad?''

''I should have.'' Sue Ellen blotted a tear from the corner of her eye with a tissue. ''You were only two when I took you and Collin and left Montana. Collin was older and remembered the Kincaid ranch and his father and grandfather very well. I've always felt that was the reason he rebelled in his teens, here in San Diego. At any rate, he returned to Montana and grew up with the Kincaids. You stayed with me.''

''Mom, don't you dare blame yourself because Larry and Garrett Kincaid, my own father and grandfather, completely forgot I existed.''

''I don't blame myself for their sins, honey, but there were things I could have done to remind Larry that he had a daughter in California. I simply didn't think of it, and you were always such a bright, upbeat person that it never occurred to me that you should have some contact with the Kincaids before it was too late.''

''You didn't expect Dad to die so young, Mom,'' Melanie said gently. ''No one did.'' It struck her that she had come to her mother for consolation and she was the one doing the consoling. *Ah, well.*

''True,'' Sue Ellen agreed with a sigh. ''But the unexpected is usually just a lack of commonsense preparation.'' After a brief pause, she took her daughter's hand. ''The truth is, Melanie, I could have done better by you,'' she said sadly. ''You should have known your father, and I should have seen to it that you did.''

Melanie's eyes filled with tears. The void in her world was still there, and she suspected that it always would be.

Chapter One

Garrett Kincaid and his grandson, Collin, were riding handsome roan horses through Kincaid fields that were lushly green and peppered with spring wildflowers. Winter had been long and bitter, and both men were grateful that April, though windy and sometimes rainy, had gradually warmed the earth. May was just around the corner, and weather forecasters had predicted daytime temperatures in the seventies for weeks to come.

Collin had always liked spending time with his grandfather, but since his father's death six months before, Collin had put forth a special effort to keep Garrett company. Larry had been Garrett's only son, and while Collin had his own emotions to deal with over the premature death of his father, he was more concerned about his seventy-two-year-old grandfather than himself. Truth was, Larry hadn't bothered much with either of his children, Collin *or* his sister, Melanie.

So Collin wasn't sure just how he should be feeling. Occasionally, he'd had a good time with his dad, and those memories were heartwarming. For the most part, though, Larry hadn't been much of a father, and Collin couldn't quite get past that painful fact.

What Collin had been missing since Larry's death was the normal twinkle in Garrett's blue eyes, and he knew that he would do almost anything to ease his grandfather's pain. *A parent should not outlive his children.* It was what Garrett had said the day of Larry's funeral, and Collin suspected that thought was still uppermost in Garrett's mind.

Garrett and Collin had been riding in silence for a while. Collin had tried to open a dialogue with a few different topics, but Garrett had shown his disinterest with one- or two-word responses. So Collin was surprised when his grandfather said, "I've been doing some thinking, Collin, and it occurs to me that I failed with both of my children."

Collin was quick to protest. "Don't feel that way, Granddad. I've lived with you since I was fourteen, and I never saw you treat Dad or Aunt Alice in any way but fairly."

"Whatever went wrong happened years before you came to the ranch, Collin," Garrett said sadly. He looked off into the distance as though examining his own past. After a few moments, he spoke again. "Since your grandmother, Laura, was as perfect as anyone can be, I can only deduce that I am to blame for my children's faults and mistakes." Garrett sighed. "God knows I tried, though. Especially with your dad."

"You sure didn't cause Dad to gamble and chase women," Collin said vehemently. "He didn't learn those things from you, Granddad."

"No, he didn't," Garrett agreed. "But what makes a man ruin his own life by living that way?"

The sorrow in his grandfather's voice raised Collin's

hackles. Grief was normal at a time like this, and in some cases maybe guilt was part of the healing process. But in Collin's opinion, Garrett Kincaid had done nothing to feel guilty about with either of his children.

"I wasn't very old, but I remember when Mom left Dad and took Melanie and me to California. I didn't know her reasons for leaving then, but I knew a drastic change was taking place in our lives. She got a job and made things good for us kids, and then she married Steven Barlow. That was okay, too. I was able to spend summers here at the ranch, and I remember looking forward to June all winter so I could come back to Montana.

"Then I hit puberty and turned into a nightmare teenager. I remember the things I did and the sass I gave Mom and Steven. When they simply couldn't stand my behavior one more minute and had reached the end of their rope, they phoned you and asked if I could try living here on a full-time basis. You said yes, Granddad, and I recall very distinctly the surly, bigmouthed fourteen-year-old I was when I got here. Do you remember what you said to me my first day here?"

"No, I don't. What was it?" Garrett asked.

"You said, 'Collin, no one is going to tell you what to do on this ranch. You can hang around the house twenty-four hours a day as long as you're quiet at night so the rest of us can get our sleep. Or you can get on a horse, join the crew and earn a paycheck. It's your decision.' You walked off then and left me to stew about it.

"I thought of running away and even wrote out a list of what I'd take with me. I was positive no one wanted me. Mom had given up on me and sent me here, Dad was always gone somewhere, Aunt Alice made it plain that she'd rather eat a frog than even speak to me, and you…well, that was what finally sank in. You were the real thing,

Granddad, and deep down I knew that if I made the slightest effort, you'd meet me more than halfway.

"So, you see, I know what kind of parent you were because you raised me, Granddad. The reason I'm not in jail somewhere or bumming around the country is because of you. And I know you raised Dad and Aunt Alice with the same values, so you've got to stop blaming yourself because they didn't turn out as well as I did." Collin grinned then, turning his face toward Garrett.

Garrett saw that devilish, teasing grin and couldn't help laughing. "All right, all right. I'll stop feeling sorry for myself. You always could perk me up, Collin." Garrett's smile faded. "But no matter how saintly you proclaim me to be, Collin, I've made one very serious mistake that even you can't gloss over. It's Melanie. When I saw her at the funeral, I realized that I don't know her."

"It was real good of Mom to come with Melanie, don't you think, Granddad? I didn't expect her to, but you know when we talked, Mom said that she never stopped liking Dad. She couldn't live with his gambling and womanizing, but she said that he was the most charming man she'd ever known."

"That was one of Larry's problems," Garrett said quietly. "Almost everyone liked his lively personality, and he'd always had a knack for making people laugh." Garrett sighed. "He just didn't like hard work, Collin. I could never count on his help with the ranch."

"But you paid him anyway."

"He was my son, and with all his faults I loved him." Garrett glanced at his grandson. "We've ridden far enough for today." They turned their horses around. "Getting back to Melanie," Garrett went on, "I want to see her again. Do you think she would come for a visit if I called and invited?"

Collin couldn't say that he knew his baby sister all that well, either. She was six years younger and had been only eight when he'd been sent to the ranch as a teenager. Garrett's words about the importance of family hit home at that moment. A man should know his only sibling.

"I have no idea if she'd come, Granddad, but I hope so. I'd like to know her better, too."

Garrett had never made a secret of the fact that he was grooming Collin to run the ranch one day, so when the current foreman quit the year before, Collin had thought the foreman's job would be just about the best experience he could rack up. He'd mentioned it to his grandfather, who'd said in reply, "If you were the foreman, you wouldn't have the time to actually run the ranch. There's a lot more to it than working outside with the men, Collin. I insisted on your going to college to broaden your knowledge of the world in general, which, I feel, opened your mind to the endless opportunities available to today's young men and women. You might not fully grasp what I mean by all this right now, but I'm quite sure you will, in time."

So the foreman of the Kincaid Elk Springs ranch was a man named Eli Forrester, and Collin could never say that his grandfather had made a bad choice. In fact, everyone on the place liked and respected Eli. Eli fitted in so well that Collin almost felt as if he'd acquired a brother and Garrett another grandson. It made Collin chuckle to think of something so far out, but there was no denying that Eli seemed more like family than employee.

After his long ride with Garrett, Collin spotted Eli near a corral and called, "Hey, Eli!"

The twenty-eight-year-old foreman turned and nodded. Most of his face was shadowed by his hat, but Collin didn't have to see Eli's face to know that he wasn't smiling because Eli hardly ever smiled. What's more, Eli was one of those people who rarely talked about himself. So other than a few things—Eli wasn't married and he'd been born and raised somewhere back East—no one really knew much about him. Collin was curious about Eli, but Garrett had told him not to ask questions. "Every man is entitled to his privacy, Collin," he'd pointed out.

Some of the other hands were rubbing down their horses when Garrett and Collin arrived at the big horse barn and dismounted. "Collin, please see to my horse," Garrett said.

"Yes, sir," Collin replied. He almost asked if Garrett was going to phone Melanie right away, but he stopped himself in time. Garrett had always preferred keeping family matters in the family, and Collin knew he would not appreciate being questioned about a personal issue in front of the men.

Eli strode forth to intersect Garrett's route to the house. "I got the mail and gave it to Mrs. Clary, Garrett." He fell in step with his employer.

"Good. Everything go okay today?"

"Yes, sir. That low ground in the south pasture is as spongy as you said it would be, so we moved about forty head of cattle to another field. Give it a chance to dry out. Shouldn't take long if this warm weather holds. Plus, I checked the alfalfa fields, and a week of this sunshine is about all it will take to mature the first cutting of the season."

"That's about what I figured." They reached the house. "Are you coming in, Eli?"

"No, sir. Unless you have something…?"

"No, nothing now. Talk to you later." Garrett went into the house through the back door, which opened onto a mudroom. He hung his hat on one of the many hooks.

"Garrett? Is that you?"

"Yes, Irma." Irma Clary had been housekeeper and cook for twenty years. When Laura had been alive, Irma Clary had been her helper, and when Laura had become ill, Irma had taken over all of Laura's chores. She wasn't as good a housekeeper as Laura had been—not even a speck of dirt had escaped Laura's sharp eyes—but Irma was a good cook, and Garrett was a firm believer in feeding his men well. Garrett stepped into the kitchen. "Smells mighty good in here, Irma."

"It'll taste mighty good, too, I'm guessing," Irma replied pertly. At sixty, she was as spry as a woman half her age. But she loved cooking and hated cleaning, so she spent most of her time doing what she enjoyed.

Truth was, Garrett really didn't care if the house was spotless. It was a pleasant, comfortable house and it was clean enough. Irma kept his and Collin's clothes laundered, as well, and when one considered that she prepared three meals a day for eight to twelve men, depending on the ranch hands' days off, Garrett could find no fault with a woman who had become a friend as well as a valued employee. More than once, in fact, Garrett had asked himself what on earth he would do without her.

After exchanging comments about the pleasant weather, Garrett continued through the house to his office. It was a small room, but it was sufficient for a desk, a couple of chairs and two file cabinets. The room had a coziness that Garrett had always found comforting.

Today it felt a bit stuffy, and Garrett opened the window and let in the fresh, sweet smell of spring. Then, seating himself at the desk, he opened the center drawer and took out the business card Melanie had pressed into his hand the day of her father's funeral.

Garrett remembered tucking the card into his shirt pocket

without giving it much thought, which was understandable on such a horrible day. Thinking about it now, though, Garrett wished he'd spent more time talking to Melanie. The few words between them had been the same ones he'd heard and said to everyone who'd attended the funeral—the usual phrases of condolence and sympathy, and he should have given more of himself to his granddaughter.

Checking the time, Garrett realized that Melanie would not yet be home from work. But there was a business number on the card—as well as her home number—and he didn't hesitate to dial it. A woman answered. "Milton, Hayes and Stone. How may I direct your call?"

"Melanie Kincaid, please."

"And who may I say is calling?"

"Garrett Kincaid, Melanie's grandfather…and this is a long-distance call."

"Please hold, Mr. Kincaid."

Melanie was in a meeting with three of her co-workers. Milton, Hayes and Stone was a public relations firm. The company had a lot of recognizable clients, including movie people, sports figures and politicians, people who were willing to pay exorbitant fees to keep their names and faces before the public.

Melanie wasn't yet a full-fledged account executive, but she was an assistant to a man, Harry Lowe, who used her unmercifully, passing on to her all the things he didn't want to do. The cushy things, such as the meetings with famous clients and the entertaining, the parties Harry was invited to, were never delegated to Melanie. The only reason she put up with Harry was that she was next in line for a promotion to account executive.

Today's meeting was drawing to a close when an intercom line rang. Melanie just happened to be closest to the phone and she pushed the speaker button. "Yes?"

"Is Melanie Kincaid in there?" the receptionist asked.

"This is Melanie," she said as her co-workers left the conference room.

"You have a call on line eight, Melanie. It's your grandfather, Garrett Kincaid."

Melanie stiffened and gaped at the phone. Her heart began pounding because not once in her entire life had her grandfather ever phoned her. Even the news of her father's death had been delivered to her through Sue Ellen.

"Thank you, Janice," she finally got out. "I'll take the call in my office."

Hurrying out of the room, she then thought about saying hello to her grandfather sounding as though she'd just run a mile, so she forced herself to slow down. Entering her office, she put down the notebooks she'd had with her at the meeting and reached for the phone. Then, at the very last second, it occurred to her that this unusual phone call probably had an ominous purpose. Something had happened to Collin, and this time Garrett was telling her first!

Panicked, she put the phone to her ear and said, "Granddad, what's wrong?"

"Melanie?"

"Yes! Is Collin all right? Are you?"

"I've frightened you, and I apologize. Nothing is wrong, Melanie. I merely wanted to talk to you."

Melanie was flabbergasted. Slowly, she sank onto her desk chair. "You…you wanted to talk to me?"

"Yes, honey. I've been doing a lot of thinking in the past month or so, and I haven't been much of a grandfather to you. Melanie, would you consider visiting the ranch?"

"Uh…yes…of course…but…" She was so confused she couldn't think straight.

After all this time, her grandfather was inviting her to the ranch? How many times had she wished on the first evening star for a call like this one? It never came from Garrett, nor from her dad. Collin phoned every so often, but even he hadn't said, "Hey, sis, why don't you pack your jeans and boots and fly to Montana for a visit?"

"I've taken you by surprise, haven't I?" Garrett said. "You know, Collin told me some time back that you've become quite a horsewoman. I just happen to have several new fillies that need breaking. How would you like the job?"

"Uh, Granddad, I have a job."

"Well, sure you do, but couldn't you take some time off and come to Montana for a few weeks? Melanie, I know this call is long overdue. I've neglected you and I regret it more than I can say. But it's not too late to make amends, is it?"

Nervously twisting a lock of her long blond hair around her forefinger, Melanie battled tears as she listened to her grandfather's voice. "No, Granddad, it's not too late," she said in a voice thick with emotion. "I have plenty of vacation time coming, but I'll have to talk to the powers-that-be about taking it on short notice. May I call you back after I find out if it's all right?"

"Call anytime, honey. I'll be waiting to hear from you."

Melanie was almost too overcome by emotion to even speak. "Goodbye, Granddad."

"Bye, honey."

After hanging up, Melanie covered her face with her hands and realized that she was trembling from head to toe. Why hadn't her dad ever called and invited her to visit? She had never felt close to her dad or grandfather and she'd felt so cheated at her father's funeral. Her mother was right. Always, in the back of her mind, had been the thought that someday she would get to know her dad, and then, without warning six months ago, there was no chance at all of that ever happening.

My Lord, the same thing could happen with Granddad!

Lowering her hands, she dried her eyes with a tissue and blew her nose. Someway, no matter how, she was going to convince Harry and anyone else who might object that she had to use her accumulated vacation time right away. The company certainly would not collapse without her for a few weeks, although Harry might. He *would* try to stop her, she knew. But she wasn't going to let him. Not in this matter.

Rising, she squared her shoulders and strode from her office to the personnel office. It was the place to start when employees wanted to discuss their annual vacations.

After the call to Melanie, Garrett swiveled his chair around so he could look out the window. It was a joy to see the trees leafing out, as it was every spring. But this spring was not the same as so many others. This spring, he was without his son, and however much heartache Larry had caused him through the years, Garrett missed him.

Sighing heavily, Garrett turned around to face the desk again. The stack of mail that Eli had mentioned caught his eye, and he picked it up and thumbed through it. He stopped at one envelope and put the others down. After slitting it open with his pocketknife, Garrett slid out one sheet of paper. It was a letter from the attorney in Elk Springs that he'd hired to help him settle Larry's estate.

Dear Garrett

I have arranged with the Elk Springs Bank for you to open Larry's safety-deposit box. A bank officer will act as witness, so just go to the bank at your convenience.

Sincerely,
John Wheaton

Garrett had thought it strange to find the key to a safety-deposit box in Larry's bureau. He couldn't imagine what Larry might have felt was so valuable that it should be kept in a fireproof bank vault.

He would drive to Elk Springs tomorrow, he decided. There couldn't be much of anything in that box, but it would be one more painful chore he would be able to put behind him.

Melanie called her mother that evening before phoning her grandfather. "Mom, I'm going to Montana for three weeks," she said excitedly.

"You are?" Clearly, Sue Ellen was astonished. "How did that happen?"

Melanie gave a little hiccup of a laugh. "You're going to find this as hard to believe as I did, but Granddad called me at work today and invited me to the ranch for a visit. He said something about breaking a couple of fillies for him, but I think he was using that as bait to get me to go. Mom, I really believe he wants to see me."

Sue Ellen sighed. "Melanie, I can guess what Garrett's invitation means to you, but I don't want you hurt any more than you've been already."

"I know, Mom," Melanie said quietly. "I also know that you are still blaming yourself for Dad's negligence in re-membering that he even had a daughter, and I wish you would stop it."

"I took you away."

"And I would do the same if I were married to a man who drank, gambled and had absolutely no sense of fidelity. It's not your fault that Dad forgot all about me the second I was out of sight, and if Collin hadn't gone back to the ranch every summer as a youngster, then moved there permanently later on, Dad would have forgotten him, too.''

''That's probably true,'' Sue Ellen said sadly. ''Sometimes I remember how funny Larry could be. He was very popular, you know. And in high school he was a top athlete and so handsome. I've told you everything about our romance, Melanie, and you know I was very much in love when we married. I…I guess he still occupies a place in my heart and probably always will.''

''I figured that out when you went with me to his funeral, Mom,'' Melanie said softly. ''We can't help whom we love, can we?''

''Please don't misunderstand, Melanie. I love Steven very much. It's just…different from what I felt for your father.''

''I know, Mom. Getting back to my vacation, I have a flight reservation for Saturday morning.''

''And you're very excited about it.''

''Yes, I am. I welcome the chance to get to know Granddad before he dies, too.''

''Oh, honey.''

''I'm sounding terribly morose, and that's not what I'm feeling. For one thing, I'm looking forward to spending time with Collin.''

''That is going to be very special, Melanie.''

''It is, isn't it? Mom, I'm thrilled about the whole trip. I have a feeling that wonderful things are going to come out of it. Collin, Granddad, the ranch, Montana…it's like a dream come true. I do wish Dad were still alive, but I'm not going to mope around and feel bad while I'm there. And I'll do a lot of riding and exploring and…oh, it's going to be such fun. I can hardly wait.''

''I wonder what prompted Garrett to think of you after all these years.''

"Maybe seeing me at the funeral?"

"Possibly. Yes, that makes sense. Call me before you leave on Saturday so we can say goodbye, okay?"

Melanie agreed, broke the connection, then dialed her grandfather's number. "Granddad? It's me. I'll be arriving in Missoula at 3:30 on Saturday afternoon."

Garrett felt choked up. "I'll be at the airport to meet your plane."

After some small talk about the weather and what clothes she should bring with her, Melanie said, "See you on Saturday, Granddad."

"Yes, honey. See you then." Garrett put down the phone and wiped his eyes. Seemed to him that he got teary-eyed awfully easy these days. "Must be getting old," he mumbled though he really didn't believe it. There were times when he felt his age, but not often. He was fortunate to have good health, and at seventy-two he could still turn the head of many a woman.

Not that he cared, or even noticed. He always had a lot more important things on his mind than some silly flirtation. He'd seen too much of that foolishness from Larry, and Collin had been right today when he'd said that Larry hadn't inherited his wandering eye from Garrett.

Truth was, and it pained Garrett to admit it, that Larry had been more like Garrett's cousin, Jeremiah, who'd been a womanizer from the get-go. Jeremiah was dead, too, murdered by Lexine Baxter, who had also murdered her husband, Dugin, Jeremiah's son. Actually, Lexine had just about wiped out that side of the family, and she was now in prison, hopefully for the rest of her life.

Jeremiah's branch of the family and Garrett's side had been estranged for many years because of a tragic feud. Garrett had tried to reach out to Jeremiah before his death, but Garrett had received a cool reception. Strangely enough, Jeremiah's other son, Wayne, was a decent sort, and Garrett and Wayne were finally getting to know each other. They both thought it was time to mend the family rift, and Garrett acknowledged Wayne's good sense gratefully as he climbed the stairs to retire for the night.

But recalling Jeremiah, even briefly, had started Garrett thinking about the Kincaid family's past, and instead of falling asleep, he lay in bed and pondered it all. The split in the family had begun with Zeke and Bart Kincaid. Zeke had been the elder son of Caleb Kincaid, and after their father's death, Zeke had driven his younger brother off their Whitehorn, Montana, ranch with the help of shifty lawyers and a shotgun. Zeke soon had the deed for the ranch and paid his brother a mere pittance for his share. Bart had been a much gentler soul than his older brother, and rather than enter into a battle that could have ended in bloodshed, he left Whitehorn and settled in western Montana, near the small town of Elk Springs. After marrying and building up his own ranch, Bart tried to make amends with Zeke, but Zeke refused a reconciliation, and the two branches of the Kincaids remained divided. Zeke and his wife, Amanda, had one son—Jeremiah—and three daughters. Bart and his Beatrice had Garrett, Arthur and Louise. Garrett thought it terribly sad that those two closely related families had never gotten to know each other.

And one other thing struck Garrett as sad; Jeremiah had not only fathered Wayne and Dugin with his wife, Julia, but he had been a notorious philanderer and had also fathered numerous illegitimate children. In fact, the six-year-old child who now owned the ranch that Zeke had cheated Bart out of so many years ago was Jeremiah's illegitimate daughter, Jennifer "Jenny" McCallum.

It was all so complicated and difficult to keep straight that Garrett shut his eyes and sought sleep. His final, drowsy thoughts had to do with Larry and the fact that although Larry might have been a womanizer like Jeremiah, at least he hadn't brought a bunch of illegitimate children into the world. *Thank the good Lord for that,* Garrett thought.

Chapter Two

"Collin, I'm going to Elk Springs this morning to open your dad's safety-deposit box. John Wheaton finally obtained legal permission, and I'd like to get it done right away. You're welcome to come along if you want."

Garrett and Collin were outside, leaning on a corral fence and watching Eli working with a young, unbroken horse. After assigning the men various jobs for the day, Eli had decided to get started with the new fillies Garrett had recently purchased. This one was a pretty gray mare, but she was frisky and sassy, ignoring Eli and then kicking up her heels and running whenever he tried to approach her.

And "Sassy" was what Eli began calling her. "Come on, Sassy," he said softly. "No one's going to hurt you. Let's be friends."

Collin thought Garrett's invitation over for a few moments. He knew his grandfather. If Garrett had not wanted him to go to the bank with him, he would simply have gone off by himself. Although Collin didn't believe that it contained anything of importance or value, maybe Garrett felt that Larry's only son should be there when that safety-deposit box was opened.

"Sure, I'll go with you," Collin said.

Garrett looked at his watch. "Might as well get going. Eli, we'll see you later," he called as they walked to Garrett's blue pickup truck and got in.

Eli was used to Collin and Garrett's camaraderie, but he still felt a little tug of envy when they walked off together. His family circumstances were so vastly different from the Kincaids'. Even Larry, who'd been just plain useless as far as work went, had enjoyed his father's affection. Of course, Larry had been easy to like, shiftless or not. A charming rogue with countless funny stories and an amazing way with the ladies. A gambler, too, and a hard drinker. Odd when Garrett was as straitlaced as they came. Collin, now, was a lot more like his grandfather than his father, which could be the reason he and Garrett got along so well.

Again Eli's thoughts went to his own family. No one in Montana knew his history because he never talked about himself. He couldn't. It was just too painful.

Eli had somehow always lived in the shadow of his beloved younger brother, Carson, but he'd never resented it a bit. Carson had been fun-loving, charismatic and careless, quite the opposite of Eli, with his quiet personality and way of doing things. But the two had been the best of friends, and the great tragedy of Eli's life was Carson's death in a canoeing accident. Eli blamed himself—he'd been there and should have been able to save Carson—and so did his parents. Eli hadn't been able to stand Baltimore or law school after Carson's death and he'd simply vanished and ended up in Elk Springs, Montana, purely by chance. No one in Baltimore knew where he was and no one in Montana knew *who* he was. In his anonymity, he could almost forget.

But every so often, he'd feel the pinch of loneliness such as he'd just experienced while watching Garrett and Collin going off together. No one knew about those painfully private moments, either, and no one ever would. Eli was a man of few words, and while he believed the Kincaids and the ranch hands respected and maybe even liked him, it wouldn't matter if they didn't. Except for Garrett, of course. Eli was fond of his job and wanted to keep it. If for some reason Garrett decided *not* to like him, Eli knew he'd be let go.

But Garrett was a fair man, and Eli believed that as long as he did his job, he would be working right where he was. It was all he wanted from life anymore—a good job, a roof over his head and three square meals a day. The rest of it—the wealth and affluence he'd grown up with, for instance—didn't mean a hill of beans when compared to what he'd had with Carson. Eli was sure he would never get over his brother's death, and to this day he had a terrible fear of water.

Pulling himself from the past, Eli held out his hand to the gray mare and purred, "Come on, Sassy. Let yourself go, sweetheart. Let yourself like me."

During the drive to Elk Springs, Garrett mentioned Eli. "He just might be the best foreman I've ever had, Collin."

"Funny how he never talks about himself, though," Collin said. "I'm sure he's educated just by the way he expresses himself when he does say something. But I mentioned college one day, and Eli suddenly had something he had to do."

"Well, he's loyal, tough and trustworthy, and he's a hard worker. That's all I need to know."

"Yeah, I guess that's enough," Collin murmured, though he still thought it kind of strange that Eli had worked on the ranch for a good four years—three as an ordinary cowpoke and one as foreman—and not one single person really knew the man.

In Elk Springs, Garrett drove directly to the bank and parked on the street. When he and Collin walked into the bank, the manager, Owen Palmer, immediately came out of his cubicle and shook hands with both men.

"How are you, Garrett?"

"Fine, Owen. We're here to take a look at Larry's safety-deposit box."

"I've been expecting you. Come along. We'll get the box and take it into the conference room." Owen led them through the lobby to the vault. "Do you have Larry's key?"

"Yes, right here. Do you want it now?" Garrett suddenly didn't want to do this and he wondered why a reasonably simple chore should cause icy dread to crawl up and down his spine. *Why did Larry have a safety-deposit box in the first place? He never saved a dime that I know of, he never owned property, and even the vehicles he drove belonged to the ranch. He'd had no deeds or titles to protect, so why had he rented a safety-deposit box at all?*

"Later, Garrett, when we go into the vault. I need your signature on a few items first."

That took a few minutes, and Garrett kept growing more tense. He really had believed that he'd known his son through and through, for Larry had never tried to keep his preferred activities a secret. Not that Garrett knew names and intimate details of Larry's extravagant love life or much about his circle of gambling and drinking buddies, but Garrett had little doubt that had he asked, Larry would have told him.

With the kind of completely irresponsible lifestyle Larry had lived, Garrett wondered what Larry could have acquired that needed the security provided by a bank vault. He would soon know, Garrett thought, and realized that he would rather *not* know. Not only was there no good reason for Larry to ever have rented a safety-deposit box, but Garrett now felt like a snoop because he had to check its contents.

By the time Owen led the way into the vault to get the box, Garrett was feeling a bit queasy. He became even more uneasy when he saw the size of the box Owen pulled out.

"He had one of the large boxes?" Garrett asked incredulously. He had assumed Larry would have only a small box and he could tell from the surprised look on Collin's face that he'd thought the same thing. "Owen, how long did Larry rent this box?"

"I'd have to check for an exact date, Garrett, but off the top of my head I'd say around twenty years."

"Twenty years!" Clearly, Garrett was flabbergasted.

"Guess Dad *could* keep a secret," Collin said rather grimly. "I sure never thought so."

Garrett's nerves were getting the better of him. "Let's get this over with, Owen," he said gruffly.

"I understand," the banker said sympathetically, and led them from the vault and down a hall to a room with a large table and a dozen chairs. He placed the box at one end of the table, then took some forms and a pad of yellow paper from an attractive wood cabinet. "In case any of us needs to make notes," he said by way of explanation for the pad. "Have a seat," Owen told them, returning to the table.

After sitting down himself, he explained, "The procedure is this, gentlemen. As the items in the box are removed, I will list them on this form, which will be turned over to your attorney and ultimately the court should Larry's estate require probate.''

"It won't," Garrett said. "He didn't own anything."

Nodding, Owen reached for the box, which he turned toward Garrett. "Shall we get started?"

Garrett unlatched the lid and lifted it. "Good Lord, it's nearly full!" he exclaimed. "And what's this?"

He picked up an envelope that bore Larry's handwriting. It said, *To be opened by Garrett Kincaid, my father, if I should die before him, or my son, Collin, if both Dad and I are gone.*

Owen laid his hand on Garrett's arm. "If there's a letter in that envelope, you do not have to read it now, but please open it and make sure it doesn't contain something pertinent to Larry's estate."

Garrett complied. "There's a letter."

"It will be listed as such. Next item, please?"

Garrett put the letter back in the envelope and set it aside. The letter troubled him, and he was glad that he didn't have to read it in Owen Palmer's presence. "Looks like a lot of junk to me, Owen," he said. "Let's see. We have a notebook that has some names and addresses of people I've never heard of, a datebook/journal from the past year and here's a stack of canceled checks, all written to people I don't know, and this stack is—" Garrett frowned as he realized what he was looking at "—copies of birth certificates. Six of them. Why do you suppose Larry had these?"

"Could I see them, Granddad?"

Garrett passed them across the table to Collin. "Perhaps these baby photos mean something," Garrett murmured as he took out the snapshots and looked at them. "Nope, not to me."

"There's nothing in that box pertaining to tangible assets," Owen declared as Garrett began going through what were obviously personal letters. "That's what's most important and what I'm going to write on this form. You and I will both sign it, Garrett, then I'll leave you two alone. Feel free to stay and use this room for as long as you want. And, of course, you may take any or all of those items with you."

Garrett scrawled his signature where Owen indicated, and the banker signed his name as witness. The second Owen had gone and the door was shut again, Collin said weakly, "Granddad, Dad's name is on each birth certificate as the father of the baby."

Garrett stared as though dumbstruck. "Tha-that's preposterous."

"It might be, but it's also true. Here, take a look for yourself." Collin shoved the documents back across the table.

Garrett picked them up, read them, then fell back against his chair. "My God," he whispered.

"Read the letter he wrote," Collin said, and Garrett heard a note of bitterness in his grandson's voice.

Garrett would rather do almost anything than read that letter. He knew in his soul that it contained all of Larry's secrets and he felt foolish for never suspecting that Larry had any. *A foolish old man, that's what you are.* This was one of those moments when Garrett felt even older than he was. In truth, he felt as though the weight of the world had descended to his shoulders during the past few minutes.

Slowly, he picked up the envelope and looked at it. He read his son's handwriting again and recalled that years ago he had worried about Larry's philandering resulting in an illegitimate child. Gradually, that concern had faded. Larry had gone from one woman to another, but he'd apparently been cautious about birth control as Garrett had never heard a word of gossip about any offspring.

But those birth certificates indicated otherwise, and there were six of them. Six illegitimate children. It wasn't really possible, was it?

Garrett braced himself, took out the one-page letter and began reading.

Dad or Collin,

I anticipate living to a ripe old age, so odds are that neither of you will read this for many years to come. However, should something unexpected occur and you have cause to examine my personal mementos in this box, you should know that everything in it is true and meaningful. Do not spin your wheels in denial even though you might suppose that I did exactly that. Truth is, I never denied fathering these sons. I simply had nothing to give them. Maybe you do.

Larry

Garrett lowered the letter, then slid it across the table to Collin before picking up the birth certificates again. They all read the same. Sex of child: male. Garrett also checked birth dates and realized that some of these children were older than Collin.

Heartsick, he stumbled to his feet. "Let's get out of here, Collin."

"Are we taking this stuff with us?"

Garrett looked at the papers and snapshots on the table. His jaw clenched spasmodically. He wished he'd never had to open that box; he would have been much better off not knowing Larry's secrets. So would Collin have been better off. Now Collin had six half brothers—probably scattered all over the map—to deal with in some way, and he, Garrett, had six more grandsons. And therein lay the bind.

Those boys, wherever they were or whatever their circumstances, were Kincaids.

"Yes. Guess we have to. See if you can round up a sack or box, Collin," Garrett said, his hoarse voice conveying the state of his emotions.

"He was a despicable man, Granddad," Collin said bitterly, startling Garrett.

"He was your father," Garrett said gruffly.

"Yeah, mine and everyone else's. I wish I'd found out about this while he was alive. I swear I would have beaten him black and blue."

"You would have struck your father?" Garrett roared. "Not in my lifetime! Go and ask Owen or someone for a box to hold these things and try to control your anger."

"Control it? Granddad, I'm mad as hell! How dare he do this to us? Aren't you mad about it, too?"

"I'm...disappointed, Collin. And tired. I'd like to get home. I have a lot to think about."

With his lips set in a thin, grim line, Collin left the conference room to go in search of something in which to transport his father's "mementos."

He had never disliked the man more than he did at that moment.

Garrett asked Collin to drive back to the ranch, and while his grandson drove, tight-lipped and tense, Garrett put his head back and shut his eyes. He'd weathered some severe shocks in his seventy-two years, but nothing he'd ever run into could compare to this one. The sheer irresponsibility of Larry's attitude toward his children—*all* of his children, Collin and Melanie included—was mind-boggling.

Melanie! Garrett opened his eyes and sat up straighter. "I forgot about Melanie's coming on Saturday. I wonder if she should be told."

"Yes," Collin said flatly. "She has as much right to know the truth as I do." As furious as Collin was, he was aware of how distraught his grandfather had become, and it worried him enough to say, "Unless you object to the idea, I'd like to be the one to tell her, Granddad."

Garrett thought a moment, then murmured, "It might be easier, coming from you. Frankly, I don't know how a grandfather would tell a young woman he hardly knows such a thing about her father."

Collin's lip curled. "Did you notice the birth dates of some of those kids? Dad fathered his first illegitimate baby while he was still in high school. And there's one with practically the same birthday as mine, so Dad was out screwing around while he was married to Mom."

"That's old news, Collin," Garrett said with a sigh. "Along with his gambling, his infidelity was the reason your mother left him. But I doubt that Sue Ellen knew about the illegitimate children. Maybe she suspected, but I feel pretty certain she didn't know for sure. No one did, apparently."

"Granddad, are you going to contact those guys?"

"I honestly don't know what to do or even if I should do anything at all." It was the heart-wrenching truth. Those six men were Kincaids, but did any of them know it? *Larry, how could you have been so careless with your own children?*

Careless, yes, but he'd still kept copies of his sons' birth certificates, and he had snapshots of them as infants and canceled checks proving that he had helped out financially.

Garrett laid his head back again and pulled his hat down over his eyes. He wasn't expecting or even hoping for an immediate solution to the monumental problem he'd inherited this day. Neither did he attempt to deny that there was a problem and that it was his to solve. He was those boys' grandfather. They were Kincaids whether they knew it or not.

Lastly, he knew he would never have another peaceful moment until he'd reached an acceptable decision about Larry's secret sons. Just what that might be was lost in clouds of confusion at the present, but Garrett believed that eventually the clouds would part and he would see clearly what he had to do.

He was, after all, a pragmatic man. Every problem had a solution; all one had to do was find it.

It was pure coincidence that Wayne Kincaid phoned from Whitehorn that very evening. "Garrett, how are you?"

Garrett cleared his throat. "Fine, Wayne, just fine." The things from Larry's safety-deposit box were scattered on the desk in Garrett's office. He'd been examining each item, looking for answers among things that instead raised more questions. For one thing, it was obvious from the dates on checks and letters that Larry had stayed in touch with the mothers of his six illegitimate sons for limited periods of time. The addresses listed for those women could still be current or so outdated as to throw anyone seeking contact completely off the scent.

"I have some news, Garrett," Wayne said. "The Mc-Callums, Jennifer's adoptive parents, called a meeting of the trustees of Jenny's estate, which, of course, includes the Kincaid ranch. There are only two trustees, you probably remember, myself and Clint Calloway. Anyway, Sterling and Jessica are very protective of Jenny—rightfully so, considering Jenny's attempted kidnapping because everyone knows she's a wealthy heiress—and they've decided that the ranch holds too many awful memories for their daughter to grow up with. They want to sell it, Garrett, and for their sake and Jenny's, Clint and I agreed to put it on the market.''

Garrett was truly stunned. He had visited the Kincaids' Whitehorn ranch after making contact with Wayne by telephone and realizing that his cousin was a man he would like to meet in person. Wayne, too, had felt that the old feud splitting the family had gone on long enough and invited Garrett to Whitehorn. They'd gotten along well and stayed in touch ever since.

Now, trying to absorb Wayne's startling news, Garrett recalled riding with Wayne and seeing the Kincaid spread from horseback. Emotion swelled in his chest. Selling land that had been in the family for generations was like selling a piece of one's soul—even though Garrett himself owned no part of that land.

''Wayne, I know I have no right to say this, but the idea of selling Kincaid land breaks my heart.''

Wayne sighed. ''I know what you mean. It wasn't an easy decision to make, nor would I ever have come up with the idea of selling out on my own. But we all have to do what's best for Jenny. I guess I called so you wouldn't hear about it from strangers, Garrett.''

''I appreciate your consideration, Wayne.'' Garrett took a rather shaky breath. ''I...I have some news myself.''

''Are you all right? You're not ill, are you?''

''Truthfully, I don't know what I am. Shocked, for certain. And confused. Wayne, I went to the bank and opened Larry's safety-deposit box today. It contained proof that Larry fathered six illegitimate sons.''

''My Lord,'' Wayne exclaimed. ''Unequivocal proof, Garrett?''

''I'm afraid so.''

''Do these children live around Elk Springs?''

"They're no longer children, Wayne. They're grown men, and I have no concrete evidence of where they live."

"You sound strained and tired, Garrett. This is getting you down, isn't it?"

"Wouldn't it get you down, Wayne? I've been thinking in circles since I left the bank this morning. Those six men are Kincaids. They're my grandsons. I can't pretend I never found out about them."

"What are you planning to do?"

"That's the sixty-four-thousand-dollar question, Wayne," Garrett said wearily.

"If there's anything I can do to help, let me know."

"Thanks, I will."

As Melanie waited in the airport departure lounge with her mother, she was a bundle of nerves. For the past few days, she had been daydreaming about sitting at the dinner table with her grandfather and talking for hours. She wanted to hear his life story from his own lips, as well as everything about her father that Garrett could tell her. And she wanted to hear about her grandmother and spend lots of time with Collin, maybe even spend some time with her Aunt Alice and Uncle Henry.

And, of course, she wanted to see every inch of the ranch. She loved horses and was an experienced, capable rider. Not only that, she'd done some training for the stable where she'd ridden so often while growing up. Garrett had to know that or he wouldn't have offered her the job of breaking his new fillies. It thrilled Melanie to think of her grandfather's faith in her talent with horses, and she was anxious to see his new stock.

"I hope you have a wonderful time, sweetie, and please say hello to Garrett for me," Sue Ellen said.

"Yes, I'll be sure to do that." In spite of Sue Ellen's

bright countenance, Melanie could tell that her mother was troubled. "And I will have a wonderful time, Mom. Everything's going to be fine. Please don't worry," Melanie said quietly, belying the nervous fluttering of her own heart.

Sue Ellen Barlow was a petite blonde with lovely blue eyes. At five foot seven, Melanie towered over her mother by a good five inches, but even at fifty-two Sue Ellen remained a strikingly beautiful woman. Melanie was also blond, blue-eyed and beautiful. Heads turned when Melanie Kincaid walked through a crowd. Her carriage and confident walk would have drawn attention even if she hadn't been drop-dead gorgeous.

Regardless of her parents' divorce and the sorrow Melanie felt over never really knowing her birth father, she'd always had a good relationship with her mother and stepfather, Steven Barlow. She'd had a comfortable, pampered upbringing—good schools, riding lessons, a BMW for her sixteenth birthday—but to her credit, neither her outstanding good looks or affluent lifestyle had ever gone to her head. She had a good and generous heart, a friendly, warm personality and a knockout smile. Not that she couldn't be strong-willed and even stubborn when someone tried to steamroller her. But she rarely lost her temper and never in her life had she yelled at anyone in anger.

A voice on the sound system interrupted Melanie's musings. "They're announcing my flight, Mom." The way her heart was thundering in her chest, she had to marvel at her calm voice.

Mother and daughter rose to hug and say their goodbyes. "Have fun," Sue Ellen called as Melanie strode away.

With her heart in her throat, she blew her mother a kiss and then joined the throng of people heading for the gate. Premonition, intuition, instinct or something just plain mysterious gripped her senses as she boarded the plane. *This is*

*not going to be an ordinary trip. Something I can't begin
to imagine today is going to happen in Montana. What on
earth can it be?*

Deplaning in Missoula that afternoon, Melanie spotted
Collin almost immediately. Smiling, she ran over to him,
and he swung her into a big bear hug.

"Collin, oh, Collin," she said emotionally, and when her
feet were on the floor, she had to wipe a few tears from
her eyes. "It's so good to see you. Where's Granddad?"

"He didn't come with me."

Melanie's face fell. "I see," she murmured.

"No, sis, you don't," Collin said gently. "He's anxious
to see you, but I need to talk with you about something—
the sooner the better—and it was my idea to meet you alone
and get it over with."

Fearing the worst, Melanie felt a chill. "Granddad is ill,
isn't he?"

"No, he's not, and please don't try to second-guess me
on this because you couldn't in a million years. We'll get
your luggage and talk in the car. Oh! Are you hungry? Do
you want something to eat before we head for the ranch?"

"I ate in Denver between planes. Let's just go."

They had to wait almost ten minutes at the baggage car-
ousel, and Melanie was on pins and needles by the time
her luggage finally appeared. It had been difficult to make
small talk with her brother when he was so obviously dis-
tracted by something very serious.

Even without having a hint as to what it might be, Melanie was worried, and the second they were in Collin's
pickup truck, she said, "Please tell me what we have to
talk about right away. I have a feeling that it has something
to do with Dad."

"You guessed it," Collin said grimly, and Melanie's

heart skipped a beat. "Part of it anyhow. Mel, you're going to find this hard to believe, but it's the God's truth. Granddad and I opened Dad's safety-deposit box at the bank. Melanie, there were six birth certificates in it with Dad's name listed as father of the child. You and I have six half brothers that not even Granddad knew existed."

Melanie stared at her brother in shocked disbelief. He took his eyes off the road long enough to send her a glance.

"It'll take a while to sink in," Collin said flatly. "It did with me."

"But how could something so awful happen without anyone knowing about it?"

"Good question. *Damn* good question," Collin muttered. "Mel, his first kid was born while he was still in high school."

"And they're all boys? All six of them?"

"Yes, all six. I tell you what, Melanie. If I'd learned about this while Dad was alive, I swear I would have tied into him."

"How...how did Granddad take it?"

"About like I did, and probably close to what you're feeling now. But Dad was his son, and I know he can't overlook the fact that those children are his grandsons. I don't know what he's going to do about it, if anything, but I sure wish he'd just burn those damn birth certificates and wash his hands of the whole mess."

"I would think that wouldn't be too difficult for a Kincaid to do," Melanie said quietly. "That's sort of what both Dad and Granddad did with me, you know. But Mom still has the highest regard for Granddad and even admitted to me that part of her would always love Dad." Melanie shook her head. "Makes a person wonder."

"Yeah, I'm sure you've done plenty of wondering. But

you're here now, sis, and I hope you give Granddad every chance 'cause he's really a great guy.''

"Was Dad a great guy, too?"

Collin was silent a few moments, then he said after a heavy sigh, "In some ways, yes."

Melanie sighed, as well. "I'll never know those ways, will I?"

Collin turned bitter again. "Well, anytime you start feeling bad about that, think about six sons somewhere in this world whom he never acknowledged beyond some financial help to their mothers. Remember that side of him, Mel, the side that could keep such an unbelievable secret while he was alive and then leave it for his family to deal with after his death. In my book, he was a selfish, thoughtless bastard."

Chapter Three

Melanie saw a mist in Garrett's eyes when he hugged her hello. It thrilled her that he appeared sincerely glad to see her, but she also understood the disappointment in his only son that he had to be feeling, and her young heart ached for him. Her own reaction to Larry's scandalous indiscretions was surprisingly restrained; the news was, after all, only one more secondhand story about a father who'd all but ignored her existence. In truth, she felt none of Collin's anger or resentment, although she hated seeing the brother she adored suffer such anguish and wished that she knew a way to relieve his torment.

It saddened her to realize that things at the ranch were not what she'd been fantasizing them to be. With Garrett deeply troubled and Collin angry, she even wondered if she'd come at an inopportune time.

After her hug and an emotional, "Welcome, child," from her grandfather, Melanie looked around the ranch.

"I really didn't pay much attention to anything when I was here for Dad's funeral," she said softly.

"Of course you didn't," Garrett said. "It was a sad day for everyone."

Melanie recalled weeping into a handkerchief for the father she'd so passionately longed to know since childhood. Why had she put the entire burden of their estranged relationship on him? she'd asked herself. Why hadn't she just boarded a plane and flown to Montana without an invitation? Had he died believing she had never wanted to see him? But if that were the case and it bothered him, wouldn't he at least have sent a card on her birthday? Written her an occasional little note even if doubts had made a phone call too difficult for him to handle?

Indeed, it had been a sad day, and it had been winter and so cold that Melanie's tears had nearly frozen on her face at the cemetery. She recalled clinging to her mother as she'd done as a child, for Sue Ellen had always been her strongest ally and supporter, the one person in all the world who loved her unconditionally. And although it hadn't been openly discussed, Melanie suspected that the main reason her mother had flown to Montana with her for the funeral was to be at her side.

Now it was May, and the fields were emerald green and dotted with cattle and horses. The buildings, whatever their age, looked well-maintained. The two-story, white clapboard house struck Melanie as comfortable and lived-in, and it seemed to belong right where it was. There were numerous large trees and a velvety lawn around the house, and on the porch were rocking chairs and several weathered wooden half barrels containing brightly colored flowers.

Something within Melanie took root, and tears sprang to her eyes. "It…it's wonderful, Granddad."

Garrett looked off at the view and nodded. "Yes, honey,

it is.'' He suddenly spotted his foreman and called out, ''Eli! Come over here and meet my granddaughter.''

Melanie turned to see Collin lifting her suitcases from the bed of the truck. ''I'm taking in your bags, Mel. I'll put them in your room.''

''Thank you, Collin.''

She was pleased to see a grin develop on her brother's face when he added teasingly, ''You're gonna be staying in the fancy bedroom, the one with a private bath.''

''Great!'' she exclaimed, glad to be done with tears and sentimentality. For the moment, at least. Things were obviously up in the air right now over those six birth certificates, and Melanie couldn't see a quick ending to Garrett's and Collin's emotional upheaval.

Her grandfather took her arm. ''Melanie, this is Eli Forrester, ranch foreman. Eli, my granddaughter, Melanie Kincaid.''

When Melanie turned around, she felt something akin to an electrical shock leap through her body. Eli Forrester wasn't much older than her, and he was tall and lean, but muscular and one of the best looking men she'd ever seen. He had close-cropped, slightly curly black hair, sapphire-blue eyes and a masculine face that was so handsome she wanted to just stand there and stare at it.

Gathering her wits and trying very hard to act as though she met men who looked like he did all the time, she offered her hand and a distant little smile. ''Nice meeting you, Eli.''

''My pleasure, Melanie,'' Eli murmured, and broke hand contact as soon as he could without appearing rude. He'd heard Collin saying something about his sister coming for a visit, but it never crossed his mind to wonder what she looked like. And here she was, probably the most beautiful woman he'd ever seen. *That hair, those eyes! Perfect com-*

plexion, just enough height and a figure to die for. Melanie, where have you been all my life? Eli thought. "I believe I heard someone say that you live in San Diego," Eli said calmly.

"Yes...San Diego," Melanie murmured, mesmerized by the brilliant blue of his eyes. Her own weren't nearly that blue, she was positive. But then, was anybody's? "Where are you from? Originally, I mean." She laughed self-consciously. "Obviously, you're from Montana now...and maybe you always were, but..." She stopped talking because she was embarrassing herself, and probably Garrett, too. What on earth was wrong with her, babbling like that?

Neither man said anything for a moment, and Melanie's embarrassment got worse. It struck her as odd that Eli Forrester hadn't immediately told her where he was from. He'd opened the subject after all.

"Shall we go in, Melanie?" Garrett said. "You'd probably like to get unpacked before supper."

Relieved, Melanie said, "Yes, thank you," and turned to leave without looking at Eli again.

He looked at her, though. He stood there and watched her walk to the house with Garrett, and every masculine gene in his body seemed to ache with sexual tension. *Man, it's time you made a trip to town!* It was probably true, but when a man ached for one particular woman, another one wasn't apt to satisfy him.

"You damn fool," he mumbled, and turned on his heel to walk off. *She's your boss's granddaughter, for Pete's sake. Get your mind out of the bedroom!*

Melanie liked Irma Clary right away and felt remorseful that she didn't remember meeting her the day of the funeral.

"Pshaw," Irma scoffed. "Think nothing of it. There

were too many folks to count milling around that day. Why on earth would you remember one old lady?''

''That's very kind, but I still think an apology is in order.'' Melanie was amazed at the size of the pots and pans on the stove. ''You're preparing a lot of food.''

''Feeding a dozen men three meals a day requires a lot of food, Melanie.''

''You cook for the men as well as the family?''

''Course I do. Someone has to. Why does that surprise you?'' Irma opened a waist-high oven door and took a quick look inside. ''The pies are almost done.''

''I guess I'm surprised because I thought...'' Melanie felt a little bit foolish. Obviously, she knew nothing of ranch life, or rather, nothing about life on her grandfather's ranch. ''I don't know what I thought,'' she said with a slight frown. ''This trip is definitely going to be a learning experience. Irma, where do the men eat?''

''Everyone eats in the dining room, 'cept for me. I prefer the kitchen. Makes the men more comfortable, too...not having a woman at the table, you know.'' Realizing what she'd just said, Irma clapped a hand over her mouth. She looked regretful when she dropped her hand and said, ''That was a terrible thing to say to you. Really, honey, the men will be honored to have such a pretty girl eating with them.''

Melanie smiled to show Irma that she hadn't been offended, and mostly it was true. She hadn't been offended by Irma's remark, but she had seen the demise of another of her fantasies—the one of her and Garrett sitting at the dinner table and talking for hours—and that saddened her.

''Oh, goodness, look at the time,'' Irma exclaimed. ''Fifteen minutes till supper. I'm going to have to get busy.''

''In that case, I'll get out of your hair, but can we talk again some other time?''

Irma patted Melanie's hand. "Of course we can. And don't let what I said about eating with the men bother you. Sometimes I talk without thinking."

"Everyone does, Irma. See you later." After leaving the homey but well-equipped kitchen with its good smells and warmth, Melanie headed for the stairs to the second floor.

All her things had been unpacked and put away, and she had washed up and freshened her makeup to look nice for dinner with her brother and grandfather. But that whole concept had flown out the window. She was going to be eating dinner with Eli Forrester! The other men didn't matter. There could be two or twenty of them, and she would, of course, be polite to them. But Eli was the one she would be aware of. She would know when he looked at her; she would know when he didn't.

Melanie recognized that such a strong and immediate attraction to a man was a brand-new experience for her and she wished with all her heart that it hadn't happened. Wishing did no good, however; she could not rid herself of the aftereffects of meeting Eli Forrester. In all honesty, she felt like a giddy high school girl with a crush on the football team's star quarterback. Considering the rather lackluster quality of her love life—past and present—her internal chaos over a man she'd seen for perhaps four minutes was startling indeed.

And yet there it was, gripping her vitals and giving her excellent cause to question her usual good sense. To further prove that she'd undergone a monumental alteration in personality and sense of self while looking into a man's incredible blue eyes, Melanie quickly plucked a dress from the closet and changed clothes.

She walked down the stairs to the first floor just as Irma rang the dinner bell.

* * *

An hour later, seated in rocking chairs on the front porch, the three Kincaids conversed. Melanie could have hugged her brother when he asked, "Granddad, how come Eli missed supper?"

There had been one empty chair at the dining-room table and no Eli. She herself had wanted to ask Garrett about him, but she felt that question coming from her would raise eyebrows. So she'd said nothing at all about the absent foreman, eaten Irma's delicious dinner and endured furtive looks from the other men. She had also wished—ardently—that she hadn't put on a pretty dress and fluffed her long, curly blond hair around her face. Looking her best was ridiculous and maybe even a little stupid with a bunch of strange men.

She'd been glad to see the end of the meal, and elated when Garrett invited her and Collin to join him on the front porch. And now, maybe, she would hear why Eli had not joined them. Expectantly, she leaned forward.

"He went into town," Garrett told his grandson.

Collin chuckled. "Probably had a date."

"Why is that funny?" Melanie asked, speaking a bit more sharply than she'd intended. She should have known a guy that looked like Eli would have women friends, probably dozens of them. Eli probably had so many women chasing him he couldn't keep track of them. Melanie's lips pursed tightly because she could easily picture a horde of beautiful cowgirls hot on Eli's trail.

"It's funny to Collin," Garrett said dryly, "because Eli rarely leaves the ranch, and if he does have a lady friend, no one knows who she is."

"But—" Melanie drew a suddenly nervous breath. "—he likes women, doesn't he?"

"Well, he sure doesn't like men," Collin quipped, then laughed at his own wit.

"Eli is a man who minds his own business," Garrett said, looking directly at his grandson. "The rest of us should take a page from his book."

"Aw, heck, Granddad, you know I was just kidding around."

"I'm sure you were, but what Eli does in his free time is none of your affair." Garrett turned to Melanie. "How do you feel about Eli?"

The question caught her so off guard she felt a wave of heat suffuse her body. "Uh…he, uh, seems nice enough," she stammered. "Why? Does my opinion of your foreman carry any weight?"

Garrett smiled. "I asked you that for a reason, honey. Tomorrow, Collin and I have to drive to Elk Springs for a meeting, and I was thinking of having Eli show you around the ranch while we're gone."

An immediate battle began in Melanie's mind. Spend time alone with Eli? Maybe go riding with him? *Yes!* But what if she became even more attracted to him than she already was, and he was all tied up with another woman and thought Melanie a pest or just another chore requiring his attention?

"Really, Granddad, I can show myself around. Please don't bother, uh, anyone else. I'm sure everyone has work to do, and—"

Garrett broke in. "Melanie, after you're here for a while, I won't worry about your wandering around alone. Please indulge an old man and accept an escort, at least until you get your bearings. I trust Eli's good sense implicitly, and he won't talk your ear off with pointless chatter."

"Yeah, he hardly talks at all," Collin added wryly.

"He hardly talks? Isn't that rather odd?" Melanie asked. "What do you know about him? He ignored me when I asked where he came from. Was that because he hardly talks or does he have something to hide?''

"He's from back east somewhere," Garrett said. "And from his tax information, I gather he's not married or supporting children. Melanie, Eli has worked for me for four years. I made him my foreman a year ago. He's an intelligent man who thinks before he leaps. He works hard and is as steady as they come. Like I said to Collin a few days ago, Eli's the best foreman I've ever had."

"Well, I shouldn't be infringing on his work schedule."

"Nonsense. I'm sure he'd enjoy showing you some of the ranch tomorrow." Garrett pushed himself up from the rocking chair. "It's my bedtime." Leaning over, he kissed Melanie's cheek. "Good night, honey. I'm sorry about tomorrow, but after that, you and I will spend some time together. I promise."

Melanie smiled. "That's fine, Granddad. Sleep well."

"You, too. Good night, Collin."

"G'night, Granddad. See you in the morning." Relaxed and laid-back, Collin stretched his legs out in front of his chair. "It's really great having you here, Mel. How long can you stay?"

"Three weeks...if everyone can stand me that long."

"Granddad and I would like it if you stayed all summer."

"Can't do that. Not if I want to keep my job." Melanie cocked her head. "Listen."

"To what?"

"To nothing. That's my point. I've never heard so much silence before."

Collin laughed quietly. "You're not missing the city already, are you?"

"No way. This place is...magical."

"Yeah, it sort of is. Gets in your blood, Mel. I couldn't

live in a city, or even a town the size of Elk Springs to save my soul. I'd like to live my life out right here on this ranch, and from things Granddad has said in the past, I feel pretty certain I'll be able to do exactly that. One thing I do know for sure is that he wants me to run the ranch when he's no longer able to do it.''

''Is…is he going to leave it to you?''

''Don't know about that, sis. I'm not his only heir. You're as entitled to inherit as I am, and don't forget our cousin Lyle. Even though he's a total jerk and I'd *like* to forget him,'' Collin added disgustedly. ''Are you planning to see Aunt Alice while you're here?''

''Probably,'' Melanie murmured absently, her mind on something else. ''Collin, discussing Granddad's estate while he's alive and thriving seems terribly callous, but since it's come up, have you considered that any one of our newly discovered half brothers could lay claim to anything Granddad leaves to the rest of us? And please don't think I'm worried about receiving a share of this ranch or anything else Granddad might own. But this has been your home for a long time, and you just said you'd like to live out your life here. What if everything Granddad owns— including the ranch—has to be split nine ways?''

Collin looked shell-shocked and for a long moment stared at his sister in mute astonishment. ''My God, why didn't I think of that?'' he finally said in a hoarse, unnatural voice.

Melanie felt like kicking herself. She certainly had never counted on or even thought of inheriting from her grandfather, but Collin had, and now she'd given him cause to worry about the security of the home he loved so much.

She tried to undo the damage. ''I'm sorry I brought it up, Collin. If those boys, or men, or whatever they are, haven't made contact with the family by now, they probably never will. And there's always the chance that they know nothing of their father's background.''

''That's really beside the point, isn't it?'' Rising, Collin went to the porch railing and stared out into the night. Finally, he turned back to his sister. ''The thing is, Melanie, they're entitled.''

''Our half brothers?''

''They're Dad's kids, same as us, and Granddad's grandchildren, just like you, me and Lyle. They're Kincaids.''

''And they didn't ask to be born, did they?'' Melanie said quietly. ''Collin, this could turn into an awful mess. I hope you know that.''

''I do now.'' Collin left the rail and stopped by Melanie's chair to squeeze her shoulder. ''I'm going to bed, Mel. Are you okay out here alone? It's quiet and dark, but there's really nothing to be afraid of.''

''I'm not a bit afraid, Collin. I'll sit out here a little longer, then go to bed, too. Good night.''

''G'night, sis.''

Being entirely alone on the porch did feel a bit eerie to Melanie. The big trees cast enormous, impenetrable black shadows across the front lawn, but dim lamplight spilled from several windows of the house, so Melanie wasn't in complete darkness. It was the quiet that felt so foreign to her. Somewhere in the invisible distance, a dog barked, and if she listened really hard, she could hear the faint rustling of leaves from a high breeze.

The night air was damp and chilly, and Melanie hugged the sweater she'd brought outside with her closer around her shoulders. Her thoughts drifted from one thing to another.

Six half brothers, my Lord! Dad couldn't seem to remember that he had a daughter. He was no father at all, to be perfectly honest—and yet he kept making babies. Poor

Collin. He might have lived close to Dad, but he really didn't know him, either.

Eli Forrester, why are you so secretive? Melanie wondered. When people don't talk about themselves, doesn't that make them secretive? Yes, I think it does. Collin thinks so, too, but Granddad believes everyone is entitled to privacy...which they are, of course. But Eli has worked and lived on the ranch for four years. Any normal person would have gotten friendly enough with someone to tell their life story a dozen times in four years. I can only conclude, Mr. Forrester, that you are hiding something. And where are you tonight? With your lady love?

Melanie heaved a sigh. Was Eli talking, dancing, making love? How could she have been so smitten by him when clearly he'd barely noticed her? The electricity of their handshake had apparently gone only one way—up her arm and straight to her heart.

Oh, don't be so ridiculously melodramatic, Melanie chided herself. Nothing touched your heart when you shook hands with Eli. What you felt was sexual attraction and not one thing more. And whatever you do, when he "escorts" you around the ranch tomorrow, keep your foolish head on straight!

Melanie was still thinking about the handsome foreman when she saw headlights on the long driveway between the ranch and highway. "Eli," she whispered, thrilled in spite of her commonsense advice to herself that he'd returned so early.

Maybe he hadn't visited a lady friend after all!

Chapter Four

Melanie had a restless night, and when she finally did fall asleep toward morning, it was as though she'd been knocked unconscious. She slept through Garrett's and Collin's early rising, through breakfast, through Garrett's talk with Eli, and through all the normal sounds and noises of a ranch coming to life for another day of work.

Finally stirring, she blew her hair out of still-drowsy eyes and yawned. The bed that had felt so strange last night felt exquisitely soft this morning. Sunlight streamed through the room's two windows. Melanie turned lazily onto her back and looked at the brittle old paper on the walls with its pattern of faded pink roses on a background that had probably once been cream-colored but now appeared tan and even darker in some places.

Had her grandmother put up this paper? Decorated this bedroom? The furniture was a matched bedroom suite, constructed of very heavy-looking, darkly stained wood. Melanie thought of the light colors and textures in her apartment.

"So different," she murmured. "So very different." Everything was different here, and it occurred to her that Collin had become a genuine cowboy. He even looked like their grandfather. A much younger version, of course, but at seventy-plus, Garrett was still a handsome man. And whom did she resemble? Sue Ellen in some ways, but did she also look a little like the Kincaid men?

Still not fully awake, Melanie's glance fell on the bedside clock. Her mouth dropped open. She'd slept until almost eleven? Impossible!

Lying back and staring at the ceiling, she heaved a sigh and accepted the impossible. Goodness, the day was half over. If her granddad had asked his foreman to give her a tour of the ranch, Eli had probably long given up on her even showing her face outside.

"Oh, well," she murmured with another sigh, then decided that as long as she'd already frittered away half the day and Eli had undoubtedly gone about his own business by now, she might as well enjoy the uncommon leisure of having absolutely no demands on her time.

She took a long shower and washed her hair. Things that she usually did in seconds, such as shaving her legs, were done at an unhurried pace. She even dried off slowly, applied moisturizer to her damp skin, then fussed with her hair for thirty minutes.

Finally, she got dressed, applied makeup, made the bed, tidied the bathroom, and after almost two hours, she casually strolled from her bedroom and went downstairs.

"Good afternoon, Irma," she said with a laugh as she walked into the kitchen.

"Gracious, you must have been done in!"

"I couldn't get to sleep last night, so I guess I made up for it this morning."

"You know, I have the same trouble in a strange bedroom. You'll probably do better tonight. What would you like to eat, breakfast or lunch?"

"Hmm, lunch, I think. But I can fix it. You've got enough to do without waiting on me."

"Well, help yourself, then. There're all kinds of sandwich fixin's in the fridge. And if you liked that cream of potato soup we had for dinner last night, there's a little of that left you could warm up."

"Thanks, Irma." Melanie crossed over to the refrigerator, opened the door and studied the laden shelves. She took out a bowl. "Is this spaghetti okay to eat?"

"Sure is, but there's not much in that bowl. Will it be enough?"

"More than enough, Irma."

"Just put the bowl in the microwave and set the timer for two minutes. Oh, if you'd like coffee, there's still some in the pot."

"Thanks, but I'm not much of a coffee drinker. I'll have a glass of orange juice instead."

While Melanie was in the process of heating the bowl of spaghetti, Irma looked out the window and exclaimed, "I swear! That Eli's walked back and forth out there most of the morning. Looks fit to be tied, too. Wonder what's bothering him."

Melanie's heart sank. "I...I think he's waiting for me."

Irma turned around. "For you?"

"Granddad said last night that he was going to ask Eli to show me around 'cause he and Collin had to attend a meeting. When I woke up so late, though, I thought for sure that Eli would have given up waiting for me and gone about some other task."

Irma shook her head. "Not Eli, honey. He's a hard man to know, and I can't really say that I do know him, but some of his traits are obvious. I'm certain that he's one of those people who take responsibility very seriously, and I'm sure that his word is his bond. So, no, Melanie, if Eli told Garrett that he would show you around, then he'll either do it or wear himself out trying."

The microwave dinged and went off. Melanie took out the bowl, found a fork in the cutlery drawer and sat at the kitchen table. Irma brought her a glass of orange juice and Melanie began eating. But she couldn't stop thinking of Eli pacing the yard because of her tardiness and she finished quickly and brought her dirty dishes to the sink.

"Just leave 'em, honey," Irma said. "You probably should go out there and talk to Eli. And don't forget to wear a hat. The sun is bright today."

Melanie raced upstairs to her room for a hat. She also grabbed her sunglasses and put them on. It wasn't that she was afraid of facing Eli, but her stomach was in a knot for some reason, and she always felt a little bit invisible wearing sunglasses, which was ridiculous, of course, but still a longtime habit. Lastly, she tucked a pair of leather riding gloves into the back pocket of her jeans just in case.

Then she ran back downstairs and through the house, pausing briefly in the mudroom to catch her breath before stepping outside.

Eli saw her come through the door, and all the harsh words he'd been thinking—*spoiled rotten...inconsiderate...selfish...a princess*—softened considerably. She was stunning in faded blue jeans, a periwinkle-blue T-shirt, brown leather vest, belt and boots, dark sunglasses and a wide-brimmed straw hat. And the way she walked—purposefully, confidently and very, very sensually—further diminished his annoyance and, in fact, telegraphed Melanie Kincaid's beauty and magnetism clear to the center of his bones.

He strode out to meet her and politely touched the brim of his hat. "Hello."

"Hello, Eli. I must apologize. Granddad said something last night about asking you to show me around today, but I overslept, and when I finally did wake up it never occurred to me that you might be keeping an eye out for me. I'm very sorry."

He couldn't see her eyes through her glasses, but she sounded sincerely contrite, and besides, how could a man stay resentful over something as trivial as a six-hour wait? Garrett had talked to him shortly after breakfast, and Eli had watched for Melanie in between chores and discussions with the men. He'd gotten impatient enough to punch something a few times that morning, but he was fine now.

"Apology accepted," he said. "Now, what would you like to see?"

Melanie was amazed that he could speak without any inflection whatsoever. If he was irritated with her, he didn't show it. If he *wasn't,* he didn't show that, either. In fact, she could read nothing in his voice or in the emotionless expression on his face.

But was that a flicker of admiration in his fabulous blue eyes? The kind of admiration a man felt for a woman he found attractive? A thrill of response colored her cheeks a bit, but she managed to keep her demeanor unruffled.

Then, coolly adjusting her sunglasses, Melanie said, "I'd like to see the fillies Granddad recently purchased if it's not too much trouble."

"No trouble at all. This way."

At the fence around the horse pasture, Eli talked about the horses and thought about the woman at his side. Her knowledge about horses was as startling as her looks. She seemed to know a lot about bog spavin, bone spavin and other equine leg problems.

When Eli pointed out the new fillies, Melanie took off her sunglasses for a clearer view and studied the young mares quite thoroughly before saying, "They look promising. Do you know Granddad's plans for them?"

"Broodmares, I believe, but don't quote me on that."

"Well, mated with the right stallion, they could produce some outstanding foals. Especially that little gray out there."

"She's sort of a favorite of mine. I call her Sassy."

Forgetting that her sunglasses were in her hand instead of covering her eyes, Melanie turned toward Eli. "Is she sassy?"

Eli looked into her eyes and said softly, "Very."

Melanie looked into his eyes and said huskily, "You must like sassy females."

A sudden impulse to take her in his arms and kiss her senseless was almost more than Eli could control. He tore his gaze from hers and looked off across the field of horses, forcing restraint upon himself.

Melanie's heart skipped a beat; Eli Forrester liked her! The chemistry she felt around him *wasn't* only one-sided. He was as affected by her as she was by him. How very incredible that something like this should happen on her grandfather's ranch. Heaven knew that she hadn't come to Montana looking for romance. She'd hoped for and envisioned long, heartfelt conversations with Garrett and spending as much time with Collin as he could spare. But on her first whole day here, they had gone off—on business—and left her in Eli's care.

So instead of becoming closer to her family, she was feeling feverish and sexually challenged by a stranger—

who, oddly enough, didn't seem like a stranger at all, even though she knew so little about him.

Putting on her sunglasses once again, she began a slow stroll along the fence of the horse pasture. As she was certain would happen, Eli fell into step beside her. Melanie's entire body throbbed with awareness of the man walking with her, and she wondered if he was enduring the same bittersweet agony because of her.

She had to find out more about him, so she said boldly, "Collin said you never talk about yourself. Why is that?"

"I can see you're not shy about saying what's on your mind," Eli said wryly.

"It's one of my positive traits," Melanie drawled.

"Nosiness is a positive trait? Since when?"

"I hardly think evasion and secretiveness are more positive traits than curiosity."

"Curiosity is just a nicer word for nosiness."

"And you are cleverly turning the tables on me to avoid answering a simple question."

"I have the feeling that very little about you is simple, Miss Kincaid."

"Isn't that strange? I have the same feeling about you, Mr. Forrester. I can go a step further, in fact. You would like everyone to think you're just a good old country boy, but you're not. You went to a good college—"

"As you did," Eli cut in.

Melanie sent him a glance and continued. "You went to a good college...I would guess a school back east, possibly an Ivy League school. I doubt if Granddad or Collin have met many Ivy Leaguers, but I've known some, and underneath that rough, tough cowboy persona you try so hard to project is a polished, sophisticated man. I would bet anything that you grew up in a city."

They were passing behind one of the equipment sheds,

and everything fled Eli's mind but her impudent and much too accurate summation of his life. She was utterly bewitching, and he completely forgot who she was and his decision to keep his hands off her. Moving quickly, he took her by the arms and pinned her up against the windowless back wall of the shed with his own body.

"You'd bet anything?" he challenged. "Are you so sure of that?"

Melanie's heart started beating at a furious pace. He was much bigger than she was, and his body was hard against hers. She wasn't afraid of him. Quite the contrary. Nothing in her life had ever caused the overwhelming excitement she felt with Eli Forrester pressed against her. Instead of wriggling away from him—or even trying to—she leaned into him and seductively moved her breasts against his chest. She saw something flare in his eyes—a light, a flame—and she knew at that moment that she would go as far with Eli as he wanted to take her.

"Yes," she whispered throatily. "I would bet anything. Would you?"

"What would you want from me if you won?" His lips were but a breath away from hers, and his voice had grown hoarse.

"What would you want from me if *you* won?"

"What do you think?" He ran one hand down her side to her hip, then up again to her breast. "You are too damned beautiful," he muttered, and covered her mouth with his in a hungry, devouring kiss.

She threw her arms around his neck and kissed him back in the same impassioned way, opening her mouth for his tongue, rubbing herself against him, letting the hot tide of desire sweep through her as never before. Her hat got in the way and Eli flicked it away. His own hat got in the way and Melanie pushed it from his head and ran her fingers through his hair.

He pulled the hem of her T-shirt from her jeans and went up under it to caress bare skin. Gasping for air, they finally broke the succession of kisses and looked into each other's eyes.

"Where can we finish this?" Eli asked thickly.

"You know the ranch better than I do," Melanie whispered.

"Are you saying yes?"

"I would lie down right here if it wasn't broad daylight and someone could come along and see us." She searched the seemingly endless depths of his eyes. "You don't believe me, do you?"

"I'm just surprised."

"Why? Don't women usually respond to you?"

"Don't even mention other women while I'm holding you." After a second, he added softly, "I've never met one who compares to you." After another short pause, he said almost angrily, "But this is crazy." Suddenly, he stopped touching her and backed away.

Astonished that he would stop when she'd given him the green light, she asked, "Why is it crazy?"

"You know why as well as I do. Fix your shirt."

Tucking it back into her jeans, Melanie realized she was getting angry, too. "Because you work for my grandfather? That's ridiculous, and besides, I got the impression from Granddad himself that he holds you in very high esteem."

"His esteem would take a major drop if he thought I was fooling around with his granddaughter," he said. "Look, I'm hot for you, you're hot for me. That could make a pretty dangerous blaze, lady, and I don't intend to risk my job for a roll in the hay."

With an ache in her heart the size of the Grand Canyon,

Melanie bent over and picked up her hat. Settling it on her head and pushing her sunglasses back in place, she said coldly, "Just don't you forget who started this...this circus!"

"Maybe you're the one who shouldn't forget."

"Are you insinuating that *I* started it?"

"I'm not insinuating anything. I'm saying it straight out!" Settling his own hat, Eli added, "And the best medicine for us is to stay away from each other. You won't be here long and—"

"Three weeks." She relished saying it and then watching his reaction.

"Three weeks!" Muttering a curse, Eli spun on his heel and strode away.

"You jerk!" she shouted, then leaned weakly against the wall of the shed. "I did not start it," she whispered as tears began leaking down her face. Removing her sunglasses, she wiped her eyes with the back of her hand. She was not going to cry over this, but if Eli thought he had gotten the better of her today, he had better think again!

John Wheaton, attorney-at-law, had read and studied every item Garrett had found in Larry's safety-deposit box. Not only studied them but organized them into separate piles, one for each birth certificate and related photos, letters, canceled checks and such, and a seventh pile for items that were not quite so clear-cut.

"So, what do you think, John?" Garrett asked.

"Garrett, before today I would have sworn that I had already seen everything. Let me ask you this. Are you doubting the authenticity of any of these things?"

After a moment of thought, Garrett answered slowly, "I haven't been. Do you think I should?"

"Off the top of my head, I'd have to say no. I didn't

know Larry as well as you, of course, but I certainly can't see him putting a bunch of phony documents and letters in a safety-deposit box to pull a fast one on his family. No, I believe these six stacks represent six men who also happen to be your grandsons, Garrett. The question is, are you planning to do anything about them?''

Garrett stared out the window for a few moments, then brought his troubled gaze back to John. "I should do something, don't you agree?''

"Don't ask me that, Garrett. Whether or not you attempt to make contact with these men has to be entirely your decision. I will not influence it with an opinion, nor should anyone else.'' John turned to Collin, who hadn't spoken in quite a spell. "Perhaps your opinion is the exception, Collin. What do you think of suddenly discovering that you have six half brothers?''

Collin looked at the lawyer over his tented fingers. "I haven't been dancing any jigs over it, John, but as time goes by, I blame my half brothers less and less and Dad more and more.''

John nodded. "As you should. If you want someone to blame, that is. Would you like to meet these men?''

Collin blinked, lowered his hands to the arms of his chair and sat up straighter. "Meet them?'' He sent Garrett a somewhat nervous glance. "I don't know. Granddad, would you like to meet them?''

Garrett took a long breath before answering sadly, "I feel obligated to do something, Collin.''

"You shouldn't! It wasn't you out screwing around having illegitimate kids. It was Dad!''

"Collin, some members of the Kincaid family were able to turn their backs on family. I don't have to tell you the old stories again. I'm sure you remember them very well. And what have I recently been worried about and tried to amend? I neglected your sister and I can only hope that Melanie has a forgiving nature. You see, I don't even know that about her. Collin, I don't want to wonder for the rest of my life if those men know of their paternity."

"You're going to try to find them, aren't you?" Collin said with some bitterness.

"Do you really disapprove?"

After a long, tension-filled moment, Collin's expression softened and he said, "No. Do whatever you have to, Granddad."

"Thank you, Collin. John, what would I run into legally if I managed to find these men and introduced myself?"

"There shouldn't be any problems while you're alive, Garrett, but upon your death they could make a claim on your estate. You should seriously consider altering your will to include a phrase or paragraph recognizing Larry's illegitimate sons, however many there may be. Whether or not you actually leave them anything of value is up to you, but you should not omit them from your will…even if you don't locate them, now that I think about it. Would you like me to rewrite the will?"

"It sounds like that should be done even if I do nothing else," Garrett said. "But give me a few days to think on that before you get started, John. I might want more changes than just a paragraph recognizing Larry's illegitimate sons."

During the drive back to the ranch, Garrett said, "I've not talked about this with anyone before, but now it seems necessary and prudent. My current will leaves the ranch first to your father, then you, Collin. Alice will get my life insurance—a goodly sum—which she may pass on to Lyle if she wishes, and Melanie is to receive the stocks and bonds I've acquired through the years. Now, with six more grandsons to consider, I'm not sure that the present division of assets as listed in the will is fair.''

Collin felt his gut tighten, but he said nothing and drove with his eyes glued to the highway.

"I know you love the ranch more than your father ever did. Your feelings for the land are much like my own, Collin. I still want you to have it when I'm gone, but what do I do about those other boys? Dear God, what did I ever do to deserve such a dilemma? If only Larry had talked to me about his other children.''

"Yeah, if only he'd talked to any of us about his other kids,'' Collin mumbled. "I wonder if Melanie phoned Mom and told her. Maybe she did it today. I hope so. They get along really well, and it would probably be easier for Mom to hear it from Melanie than from anyone else.''

"It's not easy for anyone to hear,'' Garrett said quietly. "It's even harder to accept, but we really don't have a choice, do we?''

Collin sighed. "No, Granddad, I guess we don't.''

After about fifteen minutes of pulling herself together, Melanie followed the fence line back to the compound. It didn't surprise her to see Eli over near a corral, and neither did it daunt her. Holding her head high, she marched right up to him.

"Granddad asked me to break and train those new fillies. I'm sure I could stumble around and find the field or corral or whatever is the preferred training ground in these parts, but perhaps you wouldn't mind telling me where it is and also where any available equipment is kept.''

"Garrett never said a word to me about you or anyone else doing one thing with those fillies, and for your information, I've already started breaking them.''

Melanie was so taken aback that she nearly lost her cool.

"In that case, when Granddad gets back and asks if I've made any headway with the fillies, I'll tell him you refused to believe I had a right to go near them. Thanks for your time...and for calling me a liar."

Frowning, Eli watched her march off toward the house. Had Garrett really asked her to work with those fillies? Something told him *yes*. And now Melanie was going to tell her grandfather that Eli had called her a liar?

"Damnation!" Muttering obscenities under his breath, he ran to catch up with Melanie. "Wait a second, will you?" he growled when he finally reached her.

She stopped and looked at him. "I do believe you're out of breath. Now, what could be so urgent that you actually ran to catch up with me? Oh, I know. You thought of another insult to lay on me. Well, say your piece and get it over with so I can go in."

"The only insults between you and me are in your own mind. I never called you a liar."

"Oh, really? Sounded to me like you did. Not in those exact words, of course, but it was what you meant."

"Did Garrett really ask you to break and train those fillies?"

"Yes, he did."

"Why did he let me get started with them, then?"

Beginning to lose patience, Melanie raised her voice. "How on earth would I know why anyone does anything on this ranch? On *any* ranch?"

"You don't have to get mad."

"But anger is the universal language! It's something even bullheaded, arrogant men understand!" Whirling, Melanie strode off.

"Hey, wait a sec!" Eli caught up again and stopped her by taking her arm.

"What now, change your mind about a roll in the hay?" she demanded in frosty tones.

Eli's jaw dropped in shock and he glanced around to see if anyone was close enough to have heard. "What's the matter with you? Don't you have any inhibitions?"

"Neither of us did for a few minutes behind that shed, sport, but isn't it amazing that anything a man does or says is perfectly acceptable because he's a he, and if a woman says what she's really thinking, she's a tramp?"

Eli groaned. "Where do you get all those crazy ideas? I never thought of you as a tramp and I sure as hell didn't intimate any such thing. I just don't think you should be shouting for all the world to hear that you and I nearly...almost—"

"Oh, for crying out loud, you can't even say it! Eli, I would suggest that you grow up and get a life!" Shaking off his hand, Melanie flounced off, heading once again for the house.

Stunned because she seemed to understand him as no one else he'd met in Montana ever had—even Garrett—Eli stared at her sexy, long-legged, loose-jointed stride. *That's what's so different about her. She* isn't *bogged down with inhibitions! Even her walk announces her free spirit.*

And she was going to be here for three weeks? Eli shuddered. Three weeks of constant temptation was sure to be a living hell. How in God's name would he survive it?

They were only a few miles from the ranch when Garrett spoke after a long spell of silence. "I've been thinking about what Wayne told me on the phone the other night."

"What was that, Granddad?"

"They're planning to sell the Kincaid ranch near Whitehorn."

"They are? How come?"

"The people who adopted Jenny, the little girl who owns the ranch, believe she'd be better off without it. The few Kincaids left on that side of the family have to live with an awful lot of bad memories connected to that ranch, Collin."

"Yes, I suppose they do."

"Do you remember when Larry, you and I went to White-horn and Wayne showed us all around the ranch?"

"Yeah, I remember. Why?"

"Well, those six young men wouldn't be bothered by old events they know nothing about, would they?"

"Not unless that old curse you told me Bart Kincaid's Cheyenne mother put on the place is still hanging over it. Wasn't it something about death and destruction to anyone seeking wealth from that land?"

"I don't put much trust in curses, Collin."

"But you can't deny that some pretty awful things happened to that branch of the family."

"No, I can't deny that, but I doubt it was because of a curse. Anyhow, getting back to what Wayne told me about selling the Whitehorn ranch, what if I bought it and gave it to your, uh, half brothers?"

If Collin hadn't been driving, he would have shown his surprise more. But with his hands on the steering wheel, all he could do was send his grandfather a look of utter astonishment.

"I honestly don't know what to say," he finally got out.

"It would take something away from everyone else's inheritance," Garrett said quietly. "I'm sure Wayne and the other trustees are asking a pretty penny for the ranch, as well they should, for it's one of the best operations I've seen. But if I could take care of those boys with that ranch and leave this one intact for you, Collin, I believe I would be very much relieved."

"Granddad, I realize now how much this has been bothering you, but how are you going to even find those guys to give them anything?"

"I haven't figured that out yet, but I'd like to contact Wayne and make arrangements for you and me to take another look at the Whitehorn ranch. What do you say, Collin? Will you come with me?"

"You know I will, but what about Melanie? She's here to spend time with each of us, so maybe you should ask her to come along, too."

Garrett thought a moment, then shook his head. "I'd rather she didn't. I'd like to ride every foot of that ranch and inspect it thoroughly, which probably means camping out a few nights. No, I'd rather Melanie stayed behind. I'll explain the situation to her and I'm sure she'll understand."

"Will she?" Collin muttered in an undertone.

"What was that?"

"Nothing, Granddad. Nothing at all."

Chapter Five

Melanie positively glowed when Garrett asked her to join him on the front porch that evening after supper was over. They sat in side-by-side rockers and for a while enjoyed a sense of camaraderie in contented silence.

Even contented, though, Melanie could maintain silence for only so long. "I wonder what Collin is doing," she murmured. "I'm surprised he's not out here with us."

"I told him I wanted to talk to you alone."

There was something off-key in Garrett's voice, and Melanie's marvelously mellow mood slipped a bit. "Is something wrong, Granddad?" she asked, then forced a little laugh. "Just listen to me, would you? I've been waiting for a chance to be alone with you. There are so many things I'd like to ask you about, and tonight I have the opportunity, and—"

"I'm sorry, Melanie, but we'll have to save that conversation for another day. What I need to talk to you about this evening is of grave concern to me and possibly to you, as well. Today, Collin and I met with John Wheaton, my lawyer and friend, to discuss the items we found in your father's safety-deposit box. You see, even though Larry had very little in the way of either assets or liabilities—or so I believed—an unexpected death always leaves loose ends that must be tied up by someone. I accepted the task of settling my son's estate in good faith, never dreaming that he had secrets of such magnitude.

"Melanie, those men are your halfbrothers. Does that mean anything to you?"

Melanie looked out across the lawn to the darkening horizon. "I don't know them, Granddad, any more than I knew Dad. I think you would like me to say that yes, they mean something to me, but they don't. If you decide to look for them and actually find them, then I meet them and get to know them, I'm sure I'll feel differently, but as of this moment they are merely six more strangers in a world full of strangers. I'm sorry, but I can't lie about it."

"I wouldn't want you to lie, child, and I'm glad you spoke truthfully. But can you see why I might feel differently than you do about those young men?"

"I would think you'd be so angry with Dad that you would simply wash your hands of the whole awful affair." Melanie gave a brief, brittle laugh. "Oh, I mean the *six* awful affairs."

"You're very angry at your father, aren't you?" Garrett said sadly.

Melanie got up and moved to the porch rail. "I'm more hurt than angry. How could he have forgotten me so completely? All those sons and one daughter. I would think that each time one of his illegitimate sons was born, he would have remembered his only daughter."

Turning around, she leaned her hips against the rail and

looked at her grandfather. "But he never remembered me. And he wouldn't have remembered Collin, either, if Collin hadn't come here to live. I'm sure he treated his other sons the same way, and it's totally beyond me why he even kept mementos of them. But I'd bet you one thing, Granddad. If and when you do find those long-lost grandsons, I bet that not a one of them ever got so much as a birthday card from Dad."

"I wouldn't bet against you on that, honey," Garrett said quietly. "No one knew my son better than me, with the possible exception of your mother. Larry pulled the wool over Sue Ellen's eyes for only so long, though, and when she finally saw through his charm and blarney, she took you kids and left. But whatever he did, Melanie, he was my son and I loved him. Can you understand that?"

"Yes, of course. It's the way Mom loves me."

"Exactly. And you know, child, I'm as guilty as your dad was about never remembering you. I didn't send any birthday cards, either, and I got to thinking about that after Larry died so suddenly. Nothing like a visit from the grim reaper to make a man start adjusting his priorities. Anyway, you're probably the main reason I feel as though I should hunt up those six young men. I don't want any of them saying someday, 'I had a grandfather who knew about me, but he never did anything about it. The old buzzard probably didn't want a thing to do with me.'"

As serious as their conversation had been, Melanie couldn't help laughing. "You're not an old buzzard, for goodness' sake."

Garrett grinned. "Sure, I am...sort of."

Wayne was elated when Garrett called and asked if he and Collin could take another look at the Whitehorn ranch. "I've got a lot on my plate right now, Wayne, what with discovering six new grandsons and wondering where they're living and what kind of men they grew up to be, but I've given some thought to maybe buying Jenny's ranch and giving it to those boys.''

''Garrett, you couldn't have phoned with better news. I've been worried sick about that ranch ending up with strangers.''

''Well, don't get your hopes up too high, Wayne. I'm still a long way from a final decision, but it just sort of struck me as a pretty good idea.''

''Darned good, Garrett. When would you and Collin like to come?''

''Would Thursday through Saturday night be all right? I'm planning on inspecting every detail of the ranch, Wayne, and if we got there early enough, that would give us Thursday afternoon and all day Friday and Saturday. We would leave for home on Sunday morning. Now if our showing up that way would inconvenience you in any way, I'd like you to say so.''

''Garrett, I couldn't be more pleased. Believe me, your visit will not inconvenience anyone. And I don't mind telling you right now that I hope you decide to buy the place. Even if the new owners would be men I haven't yet met, they'd still be Kincaids.''

''They're Kincaids all right. Course, you understand I still have to find 'em, and that could take some doing.''

''Yes, it could,'' Wayne agreed.

It hadn't escaped Melanie that neither her grandfather nor her brother had asked how she'd gotten along with Eli the day they'd gone to Elk Springs and left her in the foreman's hands. It was okay that they hadn't, of course. She wasn't a child after all, and both of them had a lot on their minds. Since they obviously deemed Eli honest, reliable and totally trustworthy, it undoubtedly never occurred to them that he might have made a pass at her.

Not that Melanie harbored any ill will toward Eli because he'd kissed her. Quite the opposite, actually. She'd never thrown herself at a man as she'd done with Eli and his rejection still smarted. He'd called what they'd been doing behind that shed "crazy," and she couldn't quite forget that. She herself saw nothing at all crazy or even inappropriate in two consenting adults being so physically drawn to each other.

But she told herself that if Eli ever lowered his guard and behaved like a human being with her again, *she* would do the rejecting and see how he liked it. In the meantime, she would act as though nothing more than a little impersonal conversation had passed between them. However, Melanie soon found out that was easier said than done.

The day after her talk on the front porch with her grandfather, Eli practically tripped over his feet in showing her where the training equipment and supplies were kept, even escorting her to the training field.

She couldn't help rubbing his nose in it, just a little. "Changed your mind, did you?" she said sweetly.

Granite-faced, he said, "Yes, I changed my mind. Sorry I didn't believe you yesterday."

"We all make mistakes," she said nonchalantly. "Oh, if you wouldn't mind one more imposition, would you please cut Sassy from the herd and bring her out here to me?"

"Don't you know how to rope a horse?"

"Don't you know she should be wearing a bridle?"

"I don't put a bridle on a horse until it's ready for the saddle."

"Big mistake. *Huge* mistake."

"I suppose you're an expert? Look, you could talk to a

dozen people and get a dozen different responses about the best way to break and train a horse.''

''No kidding,'' she said in a deliberately bored tone. ''If Sassy was wearing a bridle, I could walk out in that pasture and get her myself.''

''I wouldn't recommend it.''

''Well, of course not, you...you dolt! None of those horses are wearing bridles, and I'm only talking about the headstall, or head collar, not the full bridle with bit and reins, which I'm sure you know.''

Eli's skin flushed darker at the word *dolt*. ''I think we can differ on methods of training horses without resorting to name-calling, don't you?''

Shooting him a dirty look, Melanie walked off. ''Speak for yourself, Forrester,'' she said over her shoulder.

Melanie's technique with unbroken horses was primarily based on patience and consistency. Once Sassy was wearing a head collar, Melanie attached a lead rope—always approaching the young filly on her left side—and then walked her. Around and around the training field, staying well within its perimeter, Melanie walked Sassy and spoke softly to her.

''There's a good girl. Isn't this nice, you and I becoming friends?'' Mostly the one-sided conversation was nonsensical, but Melanie knew it wouldn't be long before Sassy became accustomed to her presence and voice, which was the first major step in training a young horse.

Melanie noticed Eli watching her and Sassy several times in the next few days, but other than mealtimes, when they sat at the same long table with everyone else, he stayed away from her.

''Big, strong, frightened little boy,'' Melanie mumbled

disgustedly during one sighting. "Who needs you anyhow?"

On Wednesday evening, Garrett announced at the supper table that he and Collin would be leaving in the morning on business. "We'll be back on Sunday. Everyone will, of course, take their orders from Eli."

Not me! Melanie thought. I'm not taking any orders from Eli Forrester and I just wish he'd try to give me one so I could lambaste the hell out of him!

Then Melanie forgot Eli and looked from her grandfather to her brother. They were forever busy, and she'd spent precious little time with either of them. Now they were going to be gone for four days? Doggone it, what about her?

Leaving the dining room afterward, Melanie caught hold of Collin's shirtsleeve. "Where are you and Granddad going?"

"To the Kincaid ranch near the town of Whitehorn, Montana," Collin readily replied. Since Garrett had asked him not to say anything about the possibility of his purchasing the ranch until he'd made up his mind on the matter, Collin merely added, "It's just another business trip, Mel."

"I wouldn't mind seeing more of Montana," Melanie said, hinting shamelessly that she'd like to go along.

"Well, when we get back, I promise to take some time off and show you the whole darned state, if that's what you want."

Melanie smiled weakly. "Be warned, brother. I'm going to hold you to that promise." Spotting Garrett following Eli, she let go of Collin's sleeve, murmuring, "Talk to you later," and returned to the now empty dining room to peek out a window. "Don't do it, Granddad," she whispered as she watched the two men talking not far from the house, fearing that Garrett was again asking Eli to entertain her while he was away.

Irma came in to clear the table, saw Melanie near the window and asked, "What's so interesting?" Then she walked up behind Melanie to peer around her. "Hmm, nothing out there interests me. What're you looking at?"

"Nothing, really." Melanie left the window, stepped over to the table and began stacking dirty dishes.

"You don't have to do that," Irma said.

"I need something to do." Melanie swept from the dining room to the kitchen with a large stack of dinner plates. She was hurt, angry and felt like a fifth wheel. If Garrett had so little time to give her, why had he bothered to invite her to come for a visit? Collin was no better. Darn it, how could they go off for four days and expect Eli to keep her company?

Feeling melancholy the next morning, Melanie phoned her mother. When Sue Ellen answered, Melanie breathed a sigh of relief. "Thank goodness you're home," she said. "How are you, Mom?"

"I'm fine, but you don't sound as though you are. What's wrong?"

"Oh, I'm just being silly. Granddad and Collin went to Whitehorn for four days and the place feels deserted, which is utterly ridiculous because Irma's in the house and a dozen men are outside."

"Why on earth did they go to Whitehorn? The two branches of the Kincaid family never got along."

"That's what I thought. Do you suppose they kissed and made up?"

"I suppose it's possible. If memory serves, Garrett tried to mend old wounds with his cousin Jeremiah years ago and got nowhere. Maybe Garrett's done better with the younger generation.''

''Jeremiah's children?''

''Do you know that I don't recall the names of those kids? Or even if there were any, to be honest. No, wait a minute. A few years back, Collin sent some newspaper clippings about that family. Someone was murdering everyone, or something equally as horrendous. Do you remember if I gave those clippings to you to read?''

''I seem to remember them, yes. Mom, when I called before to let you know I'd arrived safely, I deliberately didn't tell you something because I thought it might upset you. But I've thought more about it, and it's practically all Granddad and Collin *do* think about, so I'm going to tell you now.''

''Oh, goodness,'' Sue Ellen said worriedly. ''This sounds serious.''

''It's getting more serious by the day if I've been reading Granddad and Collin correctly. It's about Dad.''

''About Larry? Melanie, it's not like you to let stale old gossip bother you.''

Melanie sighed. ''It's not gossip, Mom. It's fact. Six facts, to be exact. When Granddad and Collin opened Dad's safety-deposit box, they found proof that Dad had fathered six illegitimate sons.''

''*What?*''

''You're upset. I shouldn't have told you.''

''Of course I'm upset! Six sons? All with the same woman?''

''Apparently not.''

''Not with six *different* women?''

''I...I believe so. I haven't actually seen the birth certificates, so I suppose it's possible that more than one man has the same mother. But your guess is as good as mine on that score."

"Are these sons still children or are some of them older?"

"They're, uh, they're all grown men, Mom. A couple of them are older than Collin, and one is the same age as he is. That really bothered Collin."

Sue Ellen started crying. "Of course it bothered Collin. Dammit, why can Larry still hurt me from the grave? Melanie, I'll call you back. I need some time to pull myself together."

"Mom...I'm so sorry!"

But Sue Ellen had hung up and didn't hear her daughter's anguished apology.

Melanie finally pulled *herself* together and decided that moping around the house and feeling ignored because Garrett and Collin were so close and did everything together, while she was really nothing but an outsider no matter how much anyone tried to sugarcoat the truth, was just too infantile even for a person who had every right to wallow in self-pity.

Plopping her straw hat on her head and donning her dark glasses, she stuck her riding gloves into her back pocket and left the house. For a few seconds she stopped and just breathed in the sweet smell of spring, but then she walked directly to the main horse pasture to pick a horse to ride. It didn't seem possible that this was her fifth day on the ranch and she still hadn't gone riding. Obviously, she'd let too many other things distract her, but it was an easily remedied oversight.

At the fence, she whistled softly through her teeth, and as she'd hoped would happen, several horses perked up their ears and ambled over to meet her. She petted their noses, then decided that the roan gelding was the friendliest. The gate was nearby as were some ropes, looped over posts. Going for a rope, she let herself through the gate, then walked over to the roan, who was still very friendly.

"You're a sweetheart, aren't you?" she crooned while looping the rope around his neck. As docile as a lamb, he let her lead him through the gate. She tied him to a post and went to get a saddle and the other necessary trappings for horseback riding. Removing her sunglasses in the tack room and tucking them into her shirt pocket, she started checking the available saddles for one that would fit her and she'd be able to lift.

"What're you doing?"

She jumped a foot and whirled on Eli. "Do you always sneak up on people? Good grief, you scared me half to death!"

"You look pretty healthy for someone who's half-dead," Eli drawled wryly. "I asked what you were doing."

"Is it really any of your affair?"

"You might not like it, I might not like it, but yes, it's my affair."

Melanie rolled her eyes and heaved a put-upon sigh. "Granddad asked you to entertain me again."

"I wouldn't exactly describe it that way. What he said was to keep an eye on you and especially not to let you go riding by yourself."

"He did not! He knows I'm an experienced rider, and he wouldn't—"

Wearing a no-nonsense expression on his handsome features, Eli clasped her arm. "Simmer down. He would and he did. So you can't go riding right now because I'm busy with something else. Later on—probably in an hour or so— I'll be free to go with you."

Melanie drew herself up to her full height and glared at

Eli. "Number one, I'm not waiting an hour for you or any-one else. Number two, I'm a grown woman and I do not need a bodyguard. Number three, *I do not want you going with me!*" She shrieked that last part, then immediately regretted sounding like a banshee.

And the worst part of this little scene was that if Eli had asked her to go riding with him—sort of like a date—she probably would've been thrilled. Being ordered around just naturally went against the grain, though, and however hand-some he was, and however weak in the knees she felt be-cause they were alone and physically connected through his hand holding her arm, she was not going to let him tell her when she could or could not go riding.

"Spoiled rotten," Eli said grimly. "I knew it all the time. You're going riding no matter what I say, aren't you?"

"Bet the ranch on it, Forrester!" She yanked her arm free. "Now, why don't you trot on out of here and leave me be?"

Eli wondered how he could be so attracted to a woman with her mouth and sense of independence when he'd al-ways preferred the quiet type who didn't argue over every damn thing a man said or did. But there was no questioning Melanie Kincaid's appeal; he felt it in every cell of his body. Would she lie down here with him if he kissed and caressed her, as she'd said she would have done behind the shed that day? Had any woman ever said anything more exciting to him?

Her offer was constantly on his mind; that was the trou-ble. He got hot just thinking about that one sentence. *I would lie down right here if it wasn't broad daylight and someone could come along and see us.* And he, damned fool that he was, had gotten all noble and practically told her they were both crazy. Or something like that. He remembered saying something was crazy anyway, and from the haughty way Melanie had been talking to him ever since, he'd probably said *she* was crazy and she wasn't, dammit! She was beautiful and sensual and he wanted her more than any woman he'd ever known.

Still, she could be nicer about his trying to follow her own grandfather's orders.

"I don't think you realize the dangers you could run into in this neck of the woods," he said flatly while watching her check the weight of a pretty, pale leather saddle. "Wandering across this ranch isn't like riding some protected trail in San Diego, you know."

Melanie couldn't help laughing. "You do come up with some gems, Eli." Turning her head, she sent him a glance. "Do you really think I'm unaware of the many differences between southern California and Montana?" She laid a folded blanket on the saddle, then a bit and its accompanying paraphernalia, and said, "This one will do just fine." Picking everything up, she started for the door.

"Dammit, why won't you listen to reason?" Eli demanded, stepping in her path and blocking her exit.

"Why are you so determined to make me angry?" She stared right at him, not backing down an inch.

He finally threw up his hands. "Okay, fine, you win. I'll go get my horse."

She moved around him to reach the door. "Don't hurry on my account," she tossed back behind her as she walked out.

Muttering about overbearing, bossy women, Eli followed her out, then went in another direction to get his horse, which was in a corral and unsaddled. "Could you possibly bring yourself to wait a few minutes while I saddle up?" he shouted at her retreating backside.

"Nope, not one second! When I'm ready, I'm gone."

Suddenly, it was a game, and giggling under her breath, Melanie rushed to saddle the roan in record time. If he hadn't been such a gentle, well-mannered horse, it would have taken longer than it did, but in a very few minutes, she was on his back in the saddle. And she waited only until she got the feel of the horse beneath her and learned how he responded to commands before she urged him into a gallop, then a run. Laughing merrily, she looked back and saw neither hide nor hair of Eli.

Maybe he would never catch up to her! What fun!

Eli kept his horse at a walk. Melanie and the roan were far ahead of him, but just seeing her was enough for Eli. He was "keeping an eye" on his boss's granddaughter as Garrett had asked him to do, and she wasn't close enough to bedevil him or tempt him into doing something that he knew he would later regret. No matter how much he wanted to sink himself into Melanie's lush female body, instinct told him that he would be better off walking into a lion's den than making love to Melanie Kincaid.

And so he rode and thought, rode and thought, and once in a while he'd remember the job he'd left undone so he could plod along behind a spoiled city woman. She probably thought it was cute and clever of her to stay far ahead of him although he knew his horse was much faster than the roan she was riding and he could catch up with her anytime he felt like it.

God, if ever a woman needed a lesson in good sportsmanship, or even needed to be taken down a peg or two, it was Melanie Kincaid. And wouldn't he just love to be the man to tame that little wildcat? Even if he did regret it for the rest of his days?

Groaning out loud over his own ambivalence, Eli pulled his hat lower on his forehead. Then he noticed that Melanie had taken a new direction and was heading for the sandy, dangerous cliffs overlooking Dove Lake.

"No!" he shouted, but he could tell she hadn't heard him. "Damn!" he cried, and kicked his horse in the ribs. In seconds, it was running hard, eating up the ground and quickly closing the gap between him and Melanie.

Melanie happened to look back, and when she saw Eli running his horse, she laughed and urged the roan into a run, too.

"Melanie, no!" Eli yelled. "Stop! Stop your horse or turn around! There's a cliff ahead of you!"

Giggling, she leaned toward the roan's head. "Faster, sweetheart, run faster!" she urged. "We can't let him catch us!"

But he did catch them, and Melanie stopped laughing when Eli's horse was running parallel to hers and Eli reached out and yanked the reins out of her hands.

"What in hell do you think you're doing?" she yelled.

"Stopping you from killing yourself and your horse." Eli reined in both animals, and the horses' sides heaved from running so fast. "Get down," he demanded.

"I will not!"

"The hell you won't!" Leaping to the ground, Eli put his hands on Melanie's waist and hauled her off her mount. She came down kicking, screeching and slapping, and he grabbed her flailing hands and held them. "I'm going to show you something, and if it's possible for you to stop screaming and keep your mouth shut for five seconds, I'd appreciate it because you happen to be destroying my eardrums."

"Oh, drop dead, you holier-than-thou jerk! What's the big idea, dragging me around like a sack of potatoes? Let go of my wrists!"

"Not until you calm down."

"I have no intention of calming down!"

"Fine. Then we'll take our little walk with me hanging on to your wrists!" Eli said as he started walking and pulling her along with him.

"You insufferable bastard! Let go of me!" she shrieked.

"After you see what's ahead."

"Well, let me walk!"

Eli stopped and looked at her. "Will you?"

"No, I'd rather be dragged in the dirt," she said sweetly.

Eli finally let go of her wrists. However, he was ready to grab her again if she tried to get away, and she knew he could do it, too.

Brushing off her clothes, she said icily, "Okay, what's this all about?"

"Come on and I'll show you. Take my hand and don't get ahead of me."

"I'm not taking your hand."

Eli shook his head. "Fine, *don't* take my hand, but do not get ahead of me. Will you at least agree to that?"

"Yes," she said in that haughty, frosty tone he'd started to expect from her.

They walked about five more steps, then Eli put his arm in front of her to stop her. "Take one more very small step and look over the edge," he told her.

"Look over the edge of what?" True, the terrain seemed to take a dip right in front of them, but so what?

"Just do it," Eli said wearily.

She took that tiny step and gasped. They were at the very edge of a steep cliff that appeared to her to be a good fifty feet higher than a small body of water. "What is this place?"

"That's Dove Lake, and if I hadn't stopped you, you'd be swimming in it right now."

"Or worse," Melanie said quietly. Moving next to him,

she reached out and took his hand. "I'm sorry I called you names. Sometimes my temper gets the better of me."

"Yeah, I sort of noticed that."

Melanie looked down at the little lake for a long moment. "Is that water warm or cold?"

Eli shrugged. "I have no idea."

"You don't come here and swim in warm weather?"

"No, I don't."

"Why not? Don't you like to swim?"

"I don't like water, period."

"Well, I do! And I see a way down this cliff, too!" Releasing his hand, Melanie dashed away.

"Melanie, dammit, what're you doing now?"

"What do you think I'm doing? I'm going to go skinny-dipping, Eli!"

Chapter Six

Eli stared transfixed as Melanie undressed. She did it quickly, shedding boots and socks, shirt and jeans, appearing childlike in her unabashed delight over swimming in such a pristine lake.

"The beaches are usually crowded at home," she said. "Anywhere you go—the ocean, a lake or river—there are always people. Look at this." She waved her hand at the scenic splendor all around them. "No one. Not one single soul." Smiling impishly, she sent Eli a glance. "Except for you and me. Are you really not going to swim with me?"

Trying to shake the sense of unreality that had held him immobile while she removed her clothes, he cleared his throat. "No, and I wish you wouldn't go in that water, either." As she stood there in her panties and bra, she no longer resembled a child and Eli's thoughts were far from being pure.

"Why ever not?" she said playfully, and advanced to

the water's edge to test its temperature with a toe. "Oh, it's wonderful. Cool but not cold. Perfect." She looked back at Eli again and said teasingly, "You didn't really think I would take everything off, did you?" Laughing merrily, she waded out a few feet and then launched herself into the water.

Eli felt himself go pale. His hands clenched at his sides as his heart clubbed his rib cage. What would he do if she got a cramp—or needed assistance for some other reason? He hated and feared water. Ever since his brother's death in that canoeing accident, he had suffered nightmares about water—horrible dreams that would frighten him awake and then never really go away. Even though the details were half-remembered or even lost, the feeling of terror never decreased, his dread of any body of water seeming to grow even greater.

He couldn't stand it, knowing Melanie was underwater and waiting for her to surface. It seemed an eternity, and sweat broke out on his forehead. She came up laughing, again very much like a child, and he called, "I'm going to see to the horses. Be careful." Walking back up the slope to the top of the cliff, he felt queasy. "You deserve to be sick, you damn coward," he muttered. It was how he thought of himself now—as a coward—even though these panic attacks only occurred around water. It was easy enough to avoid Montana's lakes and rivers on his own, but then, unexpectedly, an incident like today would happen and he'd have to relive the whole awful episode of Carson's death and recall how irrevocably it had changed his life. It was times like this that he became heartsick and wondered if his parents were even still alive.

Emotionally overburdened, Eli gathered the reins of the two grazing horses and tethered the animals to a sturdy bush so they wouldn't wander too far. Then he forced himself to approach the edge of the cliff and look down, scared to death that he'd see nothing but the smooth, unblemished surface of the lake.

But Melanie was floating on her back and she spotted him and waved. "This is incredible! Come on in and cool off!"

"No, thanks," he called back, and moved out of sight. He sat on a boulder and thought of the picture she made on her back in that water. Wet, her pink bra and panties concealed nothing. Her nipples were upright, and the feminine arch between her thighs was most pronounced.

Groaning, he covered his face with his hands. Why hadn't he thrown caution to the wind and made love to her that day behind the shed? She'd said in plain language that she wanted him, and like a total moron he'd let what probably would have been the sexual highlight of his life slip away.

Yes, he'd gone to town that night, telling himself all during the drive that he'd relieve the torment in his groin with another woman. But he hadn't even tried. Unable to get Melanie out of his mind, he'd eaten at the Dairy Queen. Then he'd driven around aimlessly until it was time to return to the ranch. He didn't want some other woman, dammit, not then and not now.

Rising to his feet, he took another peek over the bluff and heaved a sigh of relief. Melanie was getting dressed, pulling on her clothes over her wet underwear. He hurried away, going down the slope to help her back up. When he reached her, she was freeing her hair from its confinement at her nape.

"You should have gone in with me," she said. "It was wonderful."

"Yeah, well, I'm not all that fond of swimming."

Melanie wrung the water from her long hair, then leaned

her head to one side to fluff it with her fingers. That was when Eli saw that the water from her wet bra was bleeding through the fabric of her blouse; her nipples were almost as visible as they'd been when she'd been floating on her back in the lake.

Because his gaze was so intense, she looked down to see what was attracting his attention. "Oops," she said with a little chuckle. "By any chance, are these two little bumps bothering you, Eli?"

His expression became resentful and stormy. "You know damned well they are. They'd bother any man who wasn't numb from the ears down."

"I wonder why," she said, deliberately turning thoughtful. "I guess I've always wondered why men are so fascinated by breasts. Every woman has them, so it's not like they're any kind of rarity. What do you think? Got any ideas on that subject?"

Eli nearly choked. "You just love shocking me, don't you?"

She gave her head a disdainful toss. "For heaven's sake, if the word *breast* shocks you, you'd probably faint dead away if I said... No, I better not chance it. I'd never be able to get you on your horse by myself, and if I left you out here unconscious, wolves would probably have you for their supper."

"Very funny," Eli said dryly. "It's time we started back."

Melanie glanced up at the huge, bright sun, which was almost directly overhead. "It's only noon. I was planning on a much longer ride. But you can go back anytime you want. I'm not a bit afraid of lions, tigers and bears. Oh, and wolves!"

"You're just a riot."

"Yes, I can see you're busting your seams from suppressed laughter.'' Pulling her hair to the back of her head again, she secured it with a clasp and reached down to the grass to pick up her hat and gloves. She walked past Eli toward the sloping ground leading to the bluff and said, ''You really should learn how to relax and enjoy yourself, Eli. If you don't have a full-blown ulcer yet, I'm sure one is well on its way.''

Eli followed her and tried not to watch the shape of her behind in those jeans. He failed, and it irked the hell out of him that he had so little self-control around Melanie Kincaid. But her rounded buttocks were just the right size. So were her breasts. Everything about her, from her glorious hair to her long legs and small waistline, was perfection itself.

''I do not have an ulcer,'' he said through gritted teeth, and the words were barely out of his mouth when Melanie tripped on a rock and fell backward. She landed against him, hard, and he fell backward. Hanging on to her, hoping to save her from injury, they slid all the way to the bottom of the slope, him on his back, her on top of him.

''Well,'' Melanie said breathlessly, ''that was quite a ride.'' Turning over but remaining on top of Eli, she looked into his face and saw that his eyes were closed. ''Are you okay? You're not unconscious, are you?''

''I wish I were because I'm in utter agony,'' he muttered without opening his eyes.

''Oh, no! Where are you hurt?'' She took his face in her hands. ''Open your eyes and let me see them.''

He didn't open his eyes at all. Instead, he laid his hands on the back of her head and brought it down so their lips could meet. It was a passionate kiss from the start, and she never tried to stop it for a second. He was a wonderful kisser. His lips were perfect, just soft enough, just firm enough, and his tongue in her mouth, touching her tongue and daring her to be as bold as him, made her head spin.

He kept holding her head down with one hand, but the other began moving over her back and hips. She heard his heavy breathing and her own wild heartbeat. This time, she knew, he was not going to stop as he'd done behind the shed. He was not going to call either of them crazy or even mention the word. The onus was on her shoulders. She could say no and it would end, of that she had no doubt.

But she didn't want to say no. Every cell of her body wanted what he did, and it didn't matter that they were in the open, with the sunshine warming the earth and the two of them—and also any wolves that might be skulking about—because there was no one else for miles and miles.

Melanie had never before experienced such a profound sense of freedom, and if she hadn't been in love with Montana before this, she was now. She'd lost her hat in the fall and the sunglasses in her shirt pocket had probably gotten crushed, but she didn't care. With a haste born of desire so strong and powerful that it was almost painful, she tore at his shirt buttons, wanting him naked or at least naked enough. He did the same with her buttons, and kissing and catching breaths when they could, they managed to undress each other and themselves, and then Eli was the one on top.

In the middle of a long, dizzying kiss, she spread her legs for him, and when he entered her, she moaned and hugged him harder. In moments he was moving in and out of her and watching her face. She looked into his eyes and saw the dark swirls of passion he was feeling. Was this special for him? Was *she* special to him?

He was special to her, she thought. Maybe too special because she didn't have a clue about his feelings for her. Beyond the obvious, that was. She'd known all along that he was physically attracted to her, or she'd suspected it, at least. And heaven knew she'd been attracted to him from the first. But was it all physical between them? Could there possibly be more?

Her questions faded away as she felt the beginning of the end. Striving for it, reaching for it, she arched into him, and he placed his hands in the hollow of her back to help support her for the final ride. She began crying out, at first softly, making little whimpering sounds in her throat, but then it became so intense that she wrapped her legs around his hips, dug her fingertips into his back and hoarsely called his name.

"Eli...Eli!"

"I'm here, baby. Go with it. Let it happen."

It hadn't occurred to her to do anything else, and something way back in a little crevice of her mind wished that he had said something else, something like, "Oh, Melanie, my darling, you're positively incredible. I'm so swept away I can't see straight."

It was, of course, what she was feeling, swept into another world that was all magic and a dozen beautiful colors.

Then he collapsed on her and she realized that he had *not* called her name. It was almost as though he had reached the pinnacle without her or maybe lost sight of what woman was beneath him. If she had been alone right then, she would have wept, but she would not cry in front of Eli to save her soul.

She pushed at his dead weight pressing her into the grass. "Get off me!"

Eli raised his head with a startled expression. "You sound angry."

"Who gives a damn? Just move so I can get up."

He frowned. "You *are* angry. Why? Didn't you...I mean, did I...you know, move things along too fast? I was, uh, sure you were ready, but… Well, it's hard to tell sometimes.''

"If you dare to compare me with other women right now, I swear I'll brain you! Now, move!''

Completely dismayed, he rolled to the grass and stared up at the vivid blue sky. Melanie got up and ran down to the lake, and when Eli realized that she was back in the water, his heart nearly stopped and he got up quickly and started yanking on his clothes.

"Come on," he called gruffly. "I've got work to do, and you're going back with me if I have to tie you to your horse.''

Melanie treaded water and thought about what he'd threatened. He wouldn't dare! But she was ready to go back even though she would prefer riding by herself. Still, was it worth fighting about? God, how could she have been such an idiot? Why hadn't she left Eli alone? She had teased him unmercifully in a dozen different ways—especially when she'd undressed down to her skimpy underwear in front of him—and known in her heart that he was reaching the breaking point.

Well, he'd reached it, she'd gotten what she'd been asking for, and now she had to live with it, whatever "it" might be.

"Melanie, get the hell out of that lake!''

"Why don't you come and get me?'' she taunted.

"I will if I have to.'' It was most definitely a lie, an idle threat, but she didn't know it, he told himself.

He was dressed and standing with his feet apart and his hands on his hips, looking larger than life and all man. Seeing him like that, Melanie relived every moment on the grass with him on top of her. With both of them naked and him inside her.

"God help me," she groaned when waves of heat made

her feel feverish even in the cool water. "I'm coming out," she said with all the righteous indignation she could muster. "So take yourself somewhere else and let me get dressed in peace."

"Good Lord," Eli muttered, "I've just seen and touched every inch of your naked body," he yelled, "and now you're pulling the blushing-virgin act on me?"

"Call it any damn thing you want, but leave me alone!"

"Fine. I'll be up here with the horses. And be careful when you make your way up."

"I hate and despise you, you egotistical, self-absorbed jerk," she mumbled.

"What'd you say?"

"I said I'd be careful. What do you think I said?"

Just as Eli had suspected would be the case if he made love to Melanie, he was almost numb from regret. It surprised him, however, that she also seemed remorseful. Not only remorseful, but angry. Surely she wasn't putting all the blame for what they'd done on him, was she?

Finally, after the two of them had ridden in stony silence for several miles, he could no longer pretend it didn't bother him. "What's your problem?" he asked brusquely.

Her answer was swift and direct. "You are."

"Is that a fact?" he drawled sardonically. "Well, maybe this will cheer you up. You're sort of a problem for me, too."

"Only because you'll have a harder time acting so pure and moral around Granddad with my presence reminding you that underneath that butter-wouldn't-melt-in-your-mouth exterior, you're really nothing but a cad, a rake and a heel."

Her nasty attitude angered him. "If I'm all those things just because we made love, what does it make you?"

"We didn't make love. We had sex!" She kicked her horse, and when it took off running, she yelled back at Eli, "And what that makes me is stupid!"

Again Eli found himself far behind her, but he was honestly afraid that if he got close enough to her he might paddle her behind. Had any woman ever infuriated him the way Melanie could?

And he had to put up with her smart mouth until Sunday, which maybe he could tolerate with a little more patience if he also didn't get almost crazed with desire every time he looked at her. Or thought of her. Or dreamed of her.

"Dammit!" he shouted at the sky, extending both arms outward as though beseeching the gods to ease his misery.

Melanie ate dinner with the men, ignored Eli as if he weren't sitting only a few chairs down from her, then helped Irma clear the table, fill the dishwasher and scrub pots and pans. Irma chatted about this and that while they worked, and the minute the last counter was washed down and dried, she said, "Well, it's off to bed for me."

"You retire this early?"

"Honey, I'm up at four in the morning. What I'll do now is take a bath, read or watch TV for about an hour— which always relaxes me—then go to sleep. Good night, dear. See you tomorrow. And thank you again for your help."

"You're welcome, Irma. Sleep well."

Alone, Melanie wandered around the first floor. It was still light outside. The house felt big and lonely without Garrett and Collin, and finally she went outside and sat on the front porch.

One of the yard dogs trotted around the house, and Melanie encouraged him to come to her. Warily, he approached and sniffed her hand, then lay down next to her rocker.

Putting her head back, she let her thoughts wander. Was Eli an unusually good lover, or did her hormones simply respond to his more acutely than to other men's? Could sex possibly be better for anyone than it had been for her today? Had it been as incredible for Eli?

Such overwhelming sexual attraction could be danger-
ous, you know.

Dangerous, how?

What if you fall in love with him?

Nonsense!

Is it? Think about it. You're only going to be here for three weeks, and one of those weeks is almost over.

I am not going to fall in love! Good heavens, other than great sex, Eli Forrester and I have not one thing in com-
mon. I don't even know who he really is, and I still believe he's hiding something.

"Melanie?"

Raising her head and seeing Eli with one foot on the bottom step of the porch, she sat up straighter and said coolly, "Eli."

"You didn't hear me walk up. Were you dozing?"

"No, I was thinking," she said flatly.

"May I join you for a minute?"

Looking at him in the fading sunlight, Melanie felt his sexual attraction again. She was already too involved with him, and in her heart she knew that what had occurred between them today could happen again. But she couldn't say no and send him away. Apparently, he had something to say to her, and even though she might not like it, she wanted to hear what it was.

Shrugging nonchalantly, as though he didn't affect her an iota, she said, "Suit yourself." Eli took the remaining steps and sat in the rocker next to hers. The dog got up and went to lie next to him, and Melanie muttered, "Traitor. You liked me just fine when I was the only one out here.''

Eli scratched the dog's ears. ''He knows me better. He's a good old guy, aren't you, Bo?'' Melanie sat quietly, waiting for Eli to say what was on his mind, and finally he did. ''You wouldn't even look at me during dinner.''

''Why would I?'' she asked.

''After today—''

''That subject is off-limits.''

''Oh, I see. You intend to pretend it didn't happen. Well, that's fine, but I'd still like to say something,'' Eli said.

''I'm waiting with bated breath.''

''Do you always fall back on sarcasm when you're uncomfortable?''

''Good Lord, I'm not uncomfortable! If you have something to say, say it!''

''Okay, I will. I've been thinking of what you said about my pretending to be so moral with Garrett, and I need to ask if you really believe that or if you were merely lashing out because you were angry.''

''Oh, for pity's sake! If that's your biggest worry, you're a lot more fortunate than most.''

''Melanie, I value Garrett's respect, and…and…'' He couldn't do it. He couldn't ask her not to say something to her grandfather about their lustful encounter at the lake. In truth, sitting next to her was stirring and heating his blood again. She always put on something pretty for dinner, and tonight she was stunning in a pink skirt and blouse. No matter how pretty the clothes, though, he'd rather have her without any, as she'd been at Dove Lake. Naked and in his arms. Breathing normally had suddenly become difficult, and he got to his feet. ''Sorry, but I guess I didn't have much to say after all. Good night.''

Startled by his abrupt departure, Melanie watched from

her chair until he disappeared around the side of the house. Then she got up, went to the rail and watched him walk off toward the bunkhouse.

No one she'd ever known looked that good in jeans.

Chapter Seven

On Friday morning, Melanie loitered upstairs until the men were through eating, then she went downstairs and ate her own breakfast in the kitchen.

Irma chattered like a magpie. "I can't tell you how good it is to have a woman in the house. Men don't talk. Oh, they say 'hello' and 'how are you' and that sort of stuff, but they never really talk."

"But they talk to each other, I bet. Good old boys' club and all that macho malarkey. It's probably even worse in Montana where men are really men than it is in San Diego."

"Aren't men really men in San Diego?" Irma, who'd never lived anywhere but Montana, asked with a surprised look.

"Of course they are. I didn't mean that the way it sounded. But the men I know at home…" *Some of them are very athletic and buff, but does even one of them mea-*

sure up to Eli's virility and rugged good looks? "They're
as masculine as the men here, Irma. They're just different."
One guy she dated occasionally came to mind. He was a
great tennis player and quite handsome, but he always tied
an expensive tennis sweater around his neck after a match.
Everyone else she played with used a towel, and that
sweater had always seemed to her like a silly affectation.
She couldn't see Eli ever putting on airs like that just to
make himself more noticeable.

"Probably more of them are educated," Irma said.

"That's possible, I suppose. Almost anything is, Irma."
Pausing a moment, Melanie added casually, "Eli's educated, isn't he?"

"Everyone thinks so. Have you noticed his accent? Not
that he and I have indulged in any long conversations,"
Irma said with a sniff. "Your grandfather's the only man
on the ranch who seems to understand that I'm not a robot
chained to the kitchen stove and good for only one
thing...filling the crew's bellies three times a day."

"Oh, surely the others aren't that callous!"

Irma sighed. "No, of course not. I just get lonesome to
talk to a woman sometimes." Her countenance brightened.
"Which is the reason I'm taking this Sunday off and driving to Elk Springs to attend church and visit some old
friends. Don't worry. When I leave for a day, I make sure
there's a big pot of soup or stew on the stove to warm up
and a huge tray of sandwiches in the fridge. Besides, most
of the men take Sunday off, too. They stay on the ranch
all week, then spend Saturday, Sunday or both with their
families. A lot of these fellows are married, you know."

"No, I didn't know," Melanie murmured, uneasily wondering if Eli would leave for the weekend. But did she
honestly care? She'd been planning on avoiding him anyway, so what difference should it make if he was there or

somewhere else? Rising, she brought her dishes to the sink.
"Well, let's hope they take the time to talk to their wives,
right?" she said to Irma.

The older woman grinned and nodded her head. "Right
you are."

Eli spotted Melanie working with Sassy at the training
field, but he never went near her. She hadn't eaten breakfast
with the men, and he found out at noon that neither was
she eating lunch with the crew.

It worried him. She wasn't avoiding the ranch hands. She
was avoiding him! Probably until Garrett got back and she
could tell him that his trusted foreman wasn't trustworthy
at all, but just another horny guy who'd seduced her when
she wasn't looking. It would be a lie, of course. Melanie
was the hottest little number he'd ever run into and she'd
teased and taunted him from the moment they'd met.

But what man would appreciate hearing that sort of information about his granddaughter? Truth was, even if she
took half the responsibility for what they'd done together—
and make no mistake, they had *definitely* done it together—
Garrett wasn't apt to slap him on the back and call him
friend. What would more than likely happen was his getting
fired by a stern-faced, disappointed Garrett, and even Eli
wouldn't be able to blame his employer for letting go a
man who couldn't be trusted to keep an eye on a woman
for a few days without behaving like a sex-starved animal.

Well, that description might be a bit harsh; he really
hadn't behaved like an animal. All he had done, in fact,
was respond to Melanie's siren call, her come-hither looks
and teasing challenges. And, pray tell, what man would not
have responded? Lord above, when she'd undressed down
to her underthings at Dove Lake, he'd nearly come unglued,
and then after her swim, when she'd come out of the water

and might as well have been naked for all the cover her wet bra and panties had provided, he'd almost lost it again.

Actually, he'd shown remarkable restraint, all things considered. When she'd fallen backward on him, though, his restraint went flying. *Yeah, it went flying right along with your common sense!*

And so Eli stewed all of Friday, especially when Melanie didn't show up for the evening meal, either. He ate quickly and left the house.

Saturday was worse. As far as Eli could tell, Melanie never even went outdoors. It appeared to him that she was hibernating until Garrett got back. With a very heavy heart, Eli wondered where he would go after Garrett fired him.

However, Melanie wasn't hibernating at all—she was cleaning the house. With a scarf over her hair and wearing a pair of cutoffs and a sleeveless T-shirt, she dusted and vacuumed every room, even the upstairs bedrooms. She scoured the bathrooms and the laundry and mudroom, and by late afternoon the furniture gleamed and the entire house smelled as clean as it looked.

"So," she said to Irma, "what do you think?"

"The place looks absolutely wonderful. My goodness, you're a whirlwind of energy. I couldn't have accomplished what you did today in a week."

"Maybe not, but you can cook," Melanie said with a laugh.

"I'm sure you can cook, too."

"Not the way you do. Do you think Granddad will notice?"

Irma thought for a moment. "Couldn't say. He probably would for sure if he didn't have so much on his mind. Your grandfather told me in confidence about the six grandsons just popping up out of nowhere. Such a shock. It's a good thing your grandfather has a strong heart, I can tell you.''

"Irma, you knew Dad. Did you like him?"

"Couldn't help liking him, honey. He enjoyed talking to me, or he seemed to. He'd come in the kitchen and peek into pots on the stove and say things like, 'Irma, you're the best darned cook west of the Mississippi. Maybe in the whole country. A good-looking woman, too. I bet you've got a dozen boyfriends in Elk Springs.' And I'd tell him that he was a smooth-talking rogue and to save his soft soap for someone dense enough to believe it. He'd grab a piece of pie or a handful of cookies and leave the kitchen laughing. Oh, yes, I couldn't help liking your dad, Melanie. You would have liked him, too, 'cause most everyone did.''

Melanie felt tears of heartfelt sorrow stinging her eyes. Turning away, she murmured, "I'm sure you're right. Well, it's off to the shower for me. See you later, Irma.''

"Okay, honey. And thanks for polishing up the old place. I know it really needed a good cleaning.''

That night, Melanie went to bed early and fell asleep almost at once. Her bedroom windows were open, and she woke up in the middle of the night, shivering. Pulling all the blankets on the bed over herself—she'd shoved them aside earlier because it had been warm when she retired—she realized that not only was it a whole lot cooler, it was also raining.

She jumped out of bed and hurriedly shut the windows, then raced back to burrow under the covers. She was positive that she could hear each individual drop of rain that fell on the roof—and what a marvelous sound it was. Snuggling into her blankets, she listened to the almost melodic pattering of the rain until sleep took her again.

At seven, she came wide awake and instantly remembered that Irma had told her she would be leaving around seven so she could have breakfast with friends before church. Melanie sighed heavily, suddenly feeling as gloomy as her room looked. She would be all alone in the house until Garrett and Collin got back from Whitehorn—which could be very late in the day—and it was still raining.

If only the weather hadn't changed, she thought. If it wasn't raining, she could pass the lonely hours ahead working with Sassy or she could have taken a nice long ride. On the other hand, it certainly wouldn't kill her to get rained on. And who knew? Maybe the rain would stop and the sun would come out before she finished showering. Inspired by that hope, Melanie hopped out of bed.

But it was still raining when she was through with her morning routine. In fact, it was no longer the pleasant, lazy drizzle of before; it was pouring!

Chewing on a piece of toast, Melanie peered through the window over the kitchen sink. It was going to be a dreary day, and she was getting darned tired of Collin and their grandfather going off without her. Why couldn't she have gone to Whitehorn with them? Good grief, her grandfather wasn't so old-fashioned as to believe that a woman's place was in the home, was he? Did he think she knew nothing about business? Why, some of the things she had to do in her job—along with dealing with all kinds of people with all kinds of personalities—would make running a ranch look like child's play.

Well, there had to be more to running a ranch this size than what she'd seen with her own eyes, so she really shouldn't be comparing her job with her grandfather's. But what, really, did Collin do? Eli obviously directed the men, but who directed Eli? Did Garrett pass his wishes and orders down to Collin, who in turn passed them on to Eli?

"Oh, who cares?" she mumbled. She was bored stiff, and if things didn't change, if her granddad and Collin continued to traipse around Montana and leave her behind, she was going to cut her vacation short and go home.

It would take very little effort for you to return to San Diego and never set eyes on Eli Forrester again, you know.

Melanie bit down on her bottom lip and frowned. Was that what she wanted—never to see Eli again, to go on with her life as it had been before meeting him and try to put him out of her mind for all time?

It was very disconcerting not to have an immediate and definitive answer to that question, and for several hours Melanie tried to bury it by reading, watching television and phoning people in California who weren't at home to take the calls. Visualizing her friends on a tennis court or swimming in a gorgeous aquamarine, sun-speckled pool or just getting together for a barbecue further lowered Melanie's spirits.

She was almost ready to throw something when she heard someone come into the house through the mudroom door. A voice! A face! Someone to talk to! She didn't care who it was. He wasn't getting away without a little conversation. She hurried from the living room to the kitchen.

But when she saw who had come in, she came to an abrupt halt at the kitchen doorway. Eli took his head out of the refrigerator and saw her. His legs turned to jelly. She was dressed in a plainly styled, longish, sage-green skirt and matching top—appropriate for a rainy day in the house—and her hair had so much curl it was almost frizzy, but it was around her face the way he liked it, and she was wearing makeup, and he'd never seen anyone so beautiful.

"Want some lunch?" he asked quietly.

"Uh…is anyone else coming in for lunch?"

"Everyone's gone."

"Every single man? How come?"

"Because it's Sunday and it's raining and there was no reason for them to hang around the bunkhouse."

"Are you saying that you...and I...are the only people on this ranch?"

"That appears to be the case, yes."

Because she was so startled, Melanie resorted to flippancy. "Should I be worried about that? I mean, would I be safer if I locked myself in my bedroom?"

Folding his arms across his chest, Eli leaned against the refrigerator. "I guess that depends on how safe you want to be."

"Okay, forget that," she said, rolling her eyes. "Let me ask why you're happy to hang around the bunkhouse on a rainy Sunday when none of the other men are."

"Did you hear me say I was happy about it? About anything, for that matter? If you'd care to remember, I promised Garrett to keep an eye on you. I'm sure he'll fire my butt for seducing his granddaughter, but till then—"

Melanie held up her hand. "Whoa there, sport. Are you going to tell him?"

"*Me* tell him? Do you think I'm nuts?"

"Well...yes." The I-don't-believe-you-said-that expression on his face caused a giggle to well in Melanie's throat, but before she let it out, she added with a sassy lifting of her eyebrow and a direct stare, "In a way."

Her bawdy sense of humor and infectious giggle made Eli grin. "Let me tell you something, cutie. If I'm crazy, it's your fault. Before you came along, I was a sane and sensible man."

"Oh, so you think I'm cute?"

Eli's grin vanished completely. "What I think is that you're the sexiest, most beautiful woman I've ever known. And even though I know that you're trouble with a capital

T and that I should never lay a hand on you again, I can't stop thinking about making love with you on the grass at Dove Lake.''

A wave of feverish longing flared in the pit of Melanie's stomach and radiated from there to every cell of her body. It was a lovemaking sort of day—rainy outside, cozy inside. At least it felt cozy now that she wasn't alone. Melanie took a few steps in Eli's direction.

''It's been a long and lonely morning,'' she said breathlessly. ''I bet we could think of something to do to liven it up a bit.''

Eli was suddenly scared spitless. Letting his hands drop to his sides, he stepped away from the refrigerator as though he'd figured out her plan to trap him there. Whatever her plan, though, he knew in his soul that falling for Melanie Kincaid would be a grave mistake. As sexy as she was, she wasn't a woman to dillydally around with and then forget about. She was his boss's granddaughter, and his job was the most important thing he had. He would never return to Baltimore and his family, but neither did he want to go anywhere else. He had come to love Montana and was contented living on the Kincaid ranch. Or he had been until Melanie's arrival.

''Uh, I'm sure we could,'' he said. ''How about a nice lunch together and then a game of cards? Do you play cribbage? Or gin rummy?''

Melanie's jaw dropped. She'd just offered him her body and he wanted to play cards? And hadn't he said but a minute ago that he never stopped thinking about their lovemaking by the lake? What was wrong with him?

And then she knew. He was afraid of getting in too deep with her. The wretched man probably thought she was trying to lure him into marriage! As if!

Smiling sweetly—boy, was he going to pay for that insult!—she said that his plans sounded simply marvelous. Then, making sure she got close enough to him for her skirt to float against his legs and the subtle scent of her perfume to invade his next breath, she dodged around him and opened the refrigerator. "Now, what's the most tempting tidbit in this kitchen?" she said, deliberately sounding as though she was talking to herself. She glanced at Eli, who appeared to be a man in great pain, and smiled again. "How hungry are you, Eli?"

He swallowed awkwardly and mumbled, "Starved."

While the Elk Springs area enjoyed a normal spring rainfall, the Whitehorn area was under siege by rain so dense it wasn't safe to drive. Garrett had decided to delay their departure until it let up some, and he and Collin waited for a break in the weather in the Whitehorn ranch's main house, where they had stayed the past few days while touring the ranch.

They were alone because last night Garrett had told both Wayne and Rand Harding, the ranch foreman, that he and Collin would be leaving early in the morning. "Tomorrow's Sunday, and you should be home with your families."

And so Garrett and Collin paced the old mansion like two caged lions, peering out windows and grimacing at the ongoing storm.

"Maybe I should give Melanie a call," Collin suggested. "She's probably expecting us back soon, and we could be stuck here for hours yet."

"Good idea, Collin," Garrett agreed. "Tell your sister we'll be home as soon as possible and ask her if it's raining there. We don't need a deluge like this one, but we could use some rain, that's certain."

But when Collin picked up the phone to place the call,

there was no dial tone. "The phone's dead," he told Garrett. "Must be the storm."

"Then we can't even call Wayne," Garrett said with a rather disgruntled frown. "Well, we might as well look around the house again while we're waiting."

"We've already seen it all."

"If you're not interested, just stay put and keep an eye on the storm. I'm going to do a little wandering." Garrett left the large parlor and headed for the staircase and the second floor. He'd seen something in what had once been Jeremiah's room that he'd like a closer look at. It was a photo album, one that pages had been added to until it was about eight inches thick, and Garrett suspected it contained family pictures.

He sat in a chair by the window—and still needed to turn on a lamp—with the huge album on his lap and began turning pages. The first section contained very old black-and-white photos without names or titles, and Garrett recognized no one. But instinct told him he was looking at pictures of his own ancestors. He knew what family history had been passed down through the generations—he and Wayne had discussed everything each had been told quite thoroughly—and he wished he could pick out certain people.

Caleb Kincaid, Garrett's grandfather, for instance, and his sons and heirs to one of the richest spreads in Blue River County, Zeke, Garrett's uncle, and Barton, his father. In the mid-1920s, when Montana was little more than a rough western territory, Zeke and Barton had started feuding. Zeke had been fair-haired and blue-eyed like his father and generations of Kincaids before him; Bart's hair had been black and straight, and he'd had dark brown eyes and skin. Zeke had believed that his younger brother was the product of his father's philandering with a Cheyenne woman and therefore not a true Kincaid.

Bart was not yet eighteen when their father died, Zeke being eight years older. That was when the trouble really began. Eventually, Zeke drove his brother away and they had never seen each other again.

Sitting in that chair, looking at those old photos and thinking of the past, Garrett felt a sense of pride swell in his breast. He recalled his father Bart's dark good looks and gentle personality, and if he had truly inherited those attributes from a Cheyenne mother, a woman named Ruth Whitefeather, then God bless her.

And could he doubt the veracity of the story? Garrett's hair was white now, but it had once been as black as his father's. He wasn't ashamed of his Native American blood, either. On the contrary, he was proud of it, proud of his father and proud of his birth mother, who had given Bart to his father, Caleb, to raise as an Anglo.

The old stories included some of Ruth Whitefeather's fate after that. As she had agreed with Caleb, she had no contact with Barton but watched from a distance as he grew into a privileged young man. She had suffered shame and humiliation for having an Anglo child out of wedlock, but she'd felt that her son's comfortable upbringing and eventual riches would make up for anything she went through.

But then she'd learned that her son had been cheated out of his inheritance by his own brother, and with a mother's rage she had drawn upon strong Cheyenne magic. The Kincaid ranch had been cursed, destined to bring unhappiness, death and destruction to any who sought wealth there.

Garrett stopped to ponder that curse. Was it the reason so much tragedy had occurred on this beautiful ranch? He had never been a superstitious man, but even so, he couldn't deny that there were many unexplainable things between heaven and earth.

Sighing, he turned another page in the album.

Ostensibly searching for a deck of cards, Melanie pushed three boxes to the back of a drawer, smiled at Eli, who was waiting for her to locate some, and opened another drawer. She threw up her hands.

"Eli, I've looked everywhere and there just aren't any cards in this house."

"I guess I could go get some from the bunkhouse."

Melanie's heart skipped a beat. "I suppose you could, but it's pouring rain and you'd get soaked, and—"

"My slicker is hanging in the mudroom."

"Oh. Well, do what you want," she said with very little enthusiasm. "But let me warn you that I know nothing at all about cribbage and I've only played gin rummy a few times."

They were so alone, Eli realized. Alone in the house, alone on the ranch. The word *rarity* would be an understatement. Someone was *always* there, and of course, he could consider that there was someone there today, as well. Only it wasn't just him and one of the men, it was him and the most exquisitely sensual woman ever created. What's more, she had unabashedly let him know—again—that she found him outrageously attractive, the same as he felt for her.

And Garrett could only fire him once.

"Well," he said softly, "maybe we can find something a little more exciting than a game of cards to pass the time."

Melanie's system went on full alert. "I believe I voiced that very opinion before we ate lunch."

"I believe you did." Eli took her hand and led her to

the living room. "How about a little music? That radio looks pretty old, but it might still work."

"Let's find out." Melanie looked at the old-fashioned knobs and figured out which ones did what. Turning on the radio, she fiddled with the tuning knob until she found a static-free station. It was playing beautiful, dreamy, semi-classical music. "Well, it ain't Garth or Willie," she drawled, "but I like it."

"So do I. Come here and dance with me." Eli held up his arms.

"Dance? Now there's a surprise." Surprised or not, Melanie walked straight into Eli's arms.

The second she was up against him she knew he was sexually aroused. She didn't make any attempt whatsoever to put space between them. Instead, she wound her arms around his neck and pressed her body even closer to his.

They barely moved their feet. Looking into each other's eyes, they held nothing back and wantonly rubbed against each other. Eli lowered his head and feathered kisses to her face, and she closed her eyes and savored every moment.

"You're very sexy," she whispered huskily. "I think we—you and I—have some kind of unusual chemical imbalance. I mean, your chemistry overpowers mine...or something like that."

"You're the one with the overpowering chemistry. I don't even know who I am when I'm holding you like this."

"I feel the same with you." Rising on tiptoe, she put her lips a mere breath from his and whispered, "Kiss me for real."

He did, kissing her hungrily, throwing caution to the winds, doing everything he'd been aching to do since their first intimate encounter at Dove Lake. Working up her skirt, he caressed her thighs and hips. It wasn't enough.

"Baby…sweetheart…Melanie…I want you naked," he said raggedly.

"Me, too. Oh, me, too!"

They moved apart and began tearing at their own clothes, watching the other undress while getting naked themselves. Then they rushed to each other again, both gasping at the delight of bare skin against bare skin. Their kisses had them panting for air and groping each other's feverishly hot body in seconds.

"This is even better than the first time," Eli whispered thickly in her ear.

"I know…I know," she moaned. "The sofa! Let me lie on the sofa and you—"

"I know what to do. Don't worry about that."

She lay on her back and Eli followed her down, sliding into her velvety depths at the same time. Totally lost in the magic of flawless sex, Melanie was only vaguely aware of the music coming from the radio, and yet it was part of the moment. As was the rain and the gloomy, pewterlike quality of the room. She could sense that final glorious bolt of lightning getting closer, and she clung to her lover as though she would never set him free.

"Oh, Eli…Eli," she cried. "I'm almost there. Don't stop…please don't stop." Then she froze. Someone had slammed a door. Someone was in the house! "Stop…stop," she whispered, and pushed against Eli's shoulders.

"Wha-what's wrong?"

"Didn't you hear? Someone came in. Oh, my God, it's Collin and Granddad. I can hear them talking in the kitchen."

"Melanie!"

"That's Granddad! He's looking for me. Oh, Lord! Eli, hurry and get dressed."

Eli jumped up and began scrambling for his clothes. Melanie rushed over to her skirt and picked it up off the floor. And then, in the very next moment, Garrett was standing in the doorway with an expression of utter disbelief.

Melanie jerked the skirt up in front of her, and Eli yanked on his jeans. A glance around the room horrified her. There was her bra in plain sight, her panties, Eli's briefs. There was no use pretending that this was anything but what it was—the most humiliating experience of her life. She couldn't even speak, couldn't say she was sorry, because nothing she could ever say would erase this scene from Garrett's memory.

Or from her own. Sick at heart, she watched the disbelief on her grandfather's face become something else, something unreadable but frightening.

"Get dressed, both of you," he said in a hard, distant voice that brooked no argument. Turning then, he walked away and left them alone.

"What do you think he's going to do to us?" Melanie whispered while she hurriedly threw on her clothes.

"He probably won't do anything to you, but I'm sure my job is history."

"Oh, no! He wouldn't really fire you, would he?"

"Damn right he would." He shot Melanie a disgusted look. "And I knew that would be the outcome if he found out about us. That's the worst part of it. So why in hell didn't I keep my pants on? Out by the lake was bad enough, but we both knew he was coming back today. Instead of using my head and getting the hell out of here after grabbing something to eat, I asked you to dance. And I knew where it would lead because that was what I wanted to happen!"

"Well, so did I," Melanie hissed. "It's not all your fault."

"I doubt if that's going to be much comfort when I'm out on my butt and looking for another job."

"I'll beg him not to fire you. I will, Eli. It wouldn't be fair for you to receive all the punishment."

Eli's lips twisted cynically. "Actually, baby doll, it wouldn't be fair for me to receive *any* of the punishment. This whole mess is your fault, and you know it, too, don't you?"

Melanie flushed. "I believe it takes two to tango!"

"Yeah, but there weren't two until you came along. And don't tell me you didn't shake that pretty butt of yours in my face every chance you got, because I know better."

"You know? You know? As far as I'm concerned, you don't know your ear from a hole in the ground, you big jerk!" Fully dressed by then, Melanie flounced out of the room. She stopped dead in her tracks when she saw Garrett leaning against the wall near the door of his office.

He beckoned her with his hand and said gruffly, "Bring Eli with you. I'll be at my desk."

Melanie's heart sank clear to her toes. Eli came up behind her. "What'd he say?"

"To bring you with me to his office."

"This is it, then," Eli said grimly.

She caught Eli's sleeve as he tried to get around her. "Eli, I…I'm scared."

"Don't worry, he's not going to do anything to you. You're a grown woman and you can leave anytime you want. Besides, he's blaming me, which I'd probably be doing, too, if I were in his shoes. Let go," he said with a glance at her hand clutching his sleeve. "I'd just as soon get this over with."

"I'm going with you."

"Suit yourself." Eli began walking toward the office

door, striding like a man who was unafraid of anything, even of Garrett Kincaid's justified wrath. Admiring Eli's courage but quaking in her own shoes, Melanie followed at a slower pace.

Chapter Eight

Wishing she had never set foot in Montana and fighting desperately to maintain some semblance of dignity, Melanie entered the office about five seconds behind Eli. As promised, Garrett was seated at his desk. His brow was furrowed, aging him, reminding Melanie that her only living grandparent was past seventy.

She wanted to cry. The urge was a lump in her throat and an ache in her heart. Tears stung the backs of her eyes, but she absolutely would not let them escape and embarrass herself in front of Eli. For some reason, she didn't want Eli to see that she was no stronger than the weakest woman alive when it came to family controversy, and she stood stiffly until Garrett said, "Sit down. Both of you."

Eli waited until Melanie had sat before he did. Melanie expected to hear a lecture about how strongly her grandfather disapproved of loose morals, especially in a woman, *especially* in his granddaughter, especially in his own house. She knew Eli was expecting to get fired, and so they sat, the two of them, guilty as sin itself but willing to hear Garrett out without sass or argument because of their respect and affection for the older man.

Thus Garrett's first words surprised Melanie. "Eli, are you an honorable man?"

Eli sent Melanie a quizzical glance. "Yes, sir, I've always believed so."

"Fine. Then you'll have no objections. Melanie, are you an honorable woman?"

"Uh...I...I guess so." *What on earth is that kind of question leading up to?*

"You're not positive?"

Melanie squared her shoulders. "I've never thought of myself as dishonorable."

"In that case, you will not object to my plan."

Melanie and Eli exchanged nervous glances. This was not going as they'd supposed. Where were the lectures, the anger?

Garrett rose to his feet. "We're driving to Missoula. Collin is coming with us. I just talked to my friend, Judge Joseph Briggs. After hearing the shocking facts behind my request, he agreed to marry you tonight. He will have the license ready and waiting at his home."

Melanie found her voice first. "Marry us! Granddad—"

"Please don't tell me you made love with Eli under this roof without being *in* love with him, Melanie. Marriage is the only acceptable solution for people so much in love that they don't even seek privacy for their more, uh, shall we call them elemental urges?"

Melanie was speechless. Unless Eli could think of a way out of this, they were going to be married!

Clearing his throat, Eli rose from his chair. "Garrett, I accept full responsibility for—"

"As you should."

"Well…I do…and, uh, I don't think Melanie wants to, uh, get married."

"Nonsense." Garrett started for the door. "Come along. We'll take the car so we can all ride together."

Melanie was so stupefied by what was happening that it never occurred to her to fix her hair and makeup, and she followed her grandfather out to the car like a mindless windup toy. It was still raining, but she barely noticed.

Eli felt dazed, too, but he wasn't nearly as overcome as Melanie seemed to be. He wished she would say something to him and he sidled up next to her just before they reached the car. "Melanie, is this what you want?" he asked in an undertone.

Collin ran up before she could even register the question, let alone answer it. "You two are getting married? Pretty fast work, Eli," he teased with a friendly grin.

"Everyone get in the car," Garrett said forcefully. "Collin, you please do the driving. Melanie, you and Eli sit in back."

Eli was relieved by the seating arrangement. It would give him a chance to speak quietly to Melanie, find out if she was in favor of this hasty, shotgun marriage. But she sat so close to the door, almost hugging it, that there were several feet of space between them. Garrett kept looking back at them while Collin curiously checked them out in the rearview mirror. To Eli's frustration, it was impossible for him to say anything that wouldn't be heard by the other two men.

Finally, he inched his hand along the seat and touched her arm. She jumped as though burned and turned her face to the rain-covered side window. "Melanie," he whispered. She ignored him so completely that he wondered if she'd heard him say her name. "Melanie," he whispered again, "look at me."

Without turning around, she shook her head. Frowning, Eli drew his hand back and tried to make sense of this whole thing. Did Melanie *want* to get married? She couldn't possibly be in love with him, any more than he was in love with her. Love simply didn't happen that fast.

But if she was having those kinds of thoughts, why not share them with him? Now, in his case, marrying into the Kincaid family wasn't that bad of an idea. Not to get his hands on any of Garrett's wealth, for heaven's sake. If money was important, he could go back to Baltimore and claim his own. It was being related to Garrett that made this marriage palatable, and, of course, he and Melanie did have one thing in common. Eli suppressed a smile over that rather lusty thought, because there was an emotional tension in the car that made even a smile seem sacrilegious.

Melanie felt the tension, too, but her mind wasn't working nearly as well as Eli's. In fact, it was difficult for her to think beyond the disappointment she'd seen on her grandfather's face when he'd stood in the living-room doorway and realized what she'd been doing during his absence.

What in God's name had gotten into her in Montana? She'd always enjoyed a good laugh with a man, but she had never been promiscuous before, and *promiscuous* was the perfect word for her behavior with Eli. Still, even though she might deserve a dressing-down for behaving so wantonly, wasn't a hurry-up, forced marriage going too far? Why couldn't she find the gumption to stand up to her grandfather and say that she was *not* marrying a man just because she'd had sex with him?

And then, in the next heartbeat, her brain *did* start functioning. A marriage with no preliminaries whatsoever might not be completely legal. Didn't one have to be a resident of a state to get married without some sort of waiting period? Perhaps not in Montana, she thought with a sigh, but there had to be something wrong with such a hasty ceremony in a judge's personal residence yet. But don't forget Granddad saying that Judge Joseph Briggs was a longtime friend. Maybe Judge Joseph is such a good friend that he would bend the law just a little for his old pal.

I'll have it annulled, that's what I'll do. I'll go through the ceremony to appease Granddad, but when I get back to San Diego, I'll see a lawyer about an annulment. Which means, of course, that Eli and I cannot consummate the marriage.

Well, I can handle that. He's not so irresistible that I can't say no if he should try something, and when I explain my plan, he'll probably be eager to cooperate. After all, why on earth would he want to stay married to me?

The rain was only a fine drizzle in Missoula though the clouds over the city looked low enough to touch. A dreary, gloomy day—my wedding day, Melanie thought cynically.

Collin had obviously been to the judge's home before because he drove the streets of Missoula without instructions from Garrett. In fact, Melanie realized, her grandfather had hardly said a word since they'd left the ranch.

But then, no one had. So what was Garrett thinking about? How differently young people behaved today from when he was a young man? Or that his granddaughter was a lot more like her father than he could have guessed?

Melanie stiffened at that thought. *Was* she like her dad? A person completely without morals or scruples? A person who could make babies and then forget they'd ever been born?

That wasn't totally the case with Larry, however. The contents of his safety-deposit box were proof that he had *some* conscience. And so did she, dammit! She could never abandon a child, never!

Collin pulled into the driveway of a large, imposing brick house. Turning off the engine, he said quietly, ''We're here.''

Garrett drew a deep breath. ''So we are. Well, let's not dawdle. Joe's waiting for us.''

Melanie's mouth went dry. She should say now, ''No, Granddad, I am not doing this.'' Why couldn't she? Her heart was pounding with trepidation. She'd always thought of marriage as a monumental step in a person's life, and here she was letting someone else make that decision for her. But for the life of her she could not defy her grandfather. Meekly, she got out of the car when he opened her door. Eli and Collin got out on the other side, and it was Garrett's hand on her arm that steadied her during the short walk between driveway and house.

Collin and Eli lagged behind, a slowing of steps because of Collin's hand on Eli's arm and the plea in Collin's eyes. ''Eli, what in hell is going on? You and Melanie sure aren't acting like a couple who's dying to tie the knot.''

''Garrett didn't tell you?''

''All he said was that we were driving you and Mel to Missoula to get married. What brought this on so suddenly?''

Eli shook his head. ''You'd do better to question Garrett, Collin. Sorry.'' He felt badly about leaving Collin in the dark, but he couldn't tell Melanie's brother about the uncontrollable passion between Melanie and himself. It was just too personal, too private, and obviously Garrett thought so, too, or he would've already told Collin what he'd seen in the living room.

What an awful scene for a grandfather to stumble upon. Eli's arousal had to have been visible even though he'd managed to pull up his jeans. Then there was Melanie, hiding her nudity behind her skirt and looking as though she wished the earth would open up and swallow them both. And the personally painful part of it for Eli was that he'd just been on the verge of an explosive orgasm when Melanie had stopped everything by announcing that someone was in the house. Eli would be willing to bet that she'd been right there with him, too, and wondered if she was also feeling the aftereffects of stopping too soon.

The front door of the house opened before they could ring the doorbell, and a stern-faced man of Garrett's vintage told them to come in. He introduced his wife, Mrs. Briggs, who, Melanie saw, had merry eyes with a devilish twinkle in spite of the gravity conveyed by the rest of her expression. Melanie gave her a small, rather shaky smile.

The judge whisked them all to his den, told everyone where to stand and got right to it. In three minutes flat, he said, "By the authority vested in me by the State of Montana, I now pronounce you husband and wife. Eli, you may kiss your bride."

Melanie turned her head and Eli's kiss landed on her cheek. She stepped back from him immediately and took another peek at the ring on her finger. Garrett had produced it, announcing rather formally, "This is the ring I put on your grandmother's finger almost fifty years ago. I hope it brings you and Eli the happiness it brought to Laura and me."

And then it was over. Goodbyes were said, and Mrs. Briggs took Melanie's hands in her own and wished her well. "Ah, to be your age again for just one night."

Melanie surprised herself by blushing, for it was perfectly obvious to what Mrs. Briggs was referring. A night of wedded bliss. A long night of lovemaking, of a husband and wife adoring each other's body and of saying all the beautiful, wonderful things that a couple in love said to each other.

Sorry, Mrs. Briggs, you're a kind, sweet lady, but what you're thinking is simply not going to happen.

Settled in the car again—the same seating arrangement— Melanie huddled on her side of the seat and maintained as much distance from Eli as was physically possible. Staring out the window, she turned the gold ring around and around on her finger. Her grandmother's ring; she had not foreseen her grandfather's parting with something so dear to his heart.

But how could she foresee anything Granddad might do? She still hardly knew him. He'd spent precious little time with her—instead running here and there with Collin to conduct business—so why had he gone out of his way to phone her long distance and invite her to the ranch?

Garrett glanced back at the happy couple and was stunned that they weren't at least holding hands. Surely they cared for one another. Had he made a dreadful mistake by arranging their wedding?

But neither had said a word against it, which was really all it would have taken. Perhaps he'd inhibited them with his stern reaction, even though what he'd walked in on in his own living room was hardly conducive to smiles and jocularity. Truth was, he was so weary of licentious, careless behavior. Larry's gambling had been bad enough, but his womanizing had been downright scandalous.

And now *he* had to make some very serious decisions about Larry's illegitimate sons. Larry hadn't expected to die at age fifty-four, but why hadn't he done something about those boys before it was too late? If he *hadn't* planned to do something about those six sons, why had he kept the evidence?

"Thunderation," Garrett muttered under his breath. He'd

made mistakes with Larry—for one, permitting him far too much freedom by giving him a steady paycheck that he hadn't deserved—and now, this very night, he'd forced a wedding that perhaps should not have taken place.

"What'd you say?" Collin asked.

"Nothing. I was just thinking out loud," Garrett responded.

"You sound tired, Granddad."

"I'm exhausted, Collin. It's been a long day."

In the back seat, Melanie furtively wiped away a tear. It had to have been the most awful wedding any woman had ever suffered through.

When they finally got back to the ranch, the sky was clear, promising a bright, rainless tomorrow. The second Melanie was out of the car, she headed for the house. Collin ran to catch up with her. "Mel, you've got to tell me what's going on. I asked Eli, and he said to ask Granddad. But you'll tell me, won't you?"

"Yes, I'll tell you," she said flatly, without emotion. "When you and Granddad got home today, he caught Eli and me in the living room, literally with our pants down."

"You're kidding! You knew we were coming home today. Doggone it, Mel, why'd you take that kind of chance?"

"Because I'm a stupid, brainless idiot who obviously thinks with her hormones."

"You are not! You must be in love, right?"

Melanie sent her brother a sympathetic look. "Thank you for that, but no, I'm not in love. Neither is Eli."

"Then why—I mean—how come you let Granddad force you to get married?"

"Because along with suffering a lack of brain cells, I'm also a spineless wimp. Please, Collin, no more questions tonight. I'm heading straight for a hot shower and bed. Good night.''

Garrett had stopped Eli by the car. ''You and Melanie are married now, so it's only fitting that you share the same bedroom. Bring your things in from the bunkhouse. Her room is the last one on the south end of the second floor. You'll find it just fine, I'm sure.'' He offered his hand, which Eli shook. ''And God bless you, son. Welcome to the family. I think Melanie made a fine choice.''

''Thank you,'' Eli managed to croak. Melanie made a fine choice? Melanie hadn't made a choice at all, other than the lustful decision to sleep with him. Or rather, to badger and tease him into sleeping with her.

Eli started walking toward the bunkhouse and in a few seconds caught himself whistling softly. It amazed him that he felt pretty darn good about the day. Actually, he felt pretty darn good about being married. In fact, he chuckled a bit because now, tonight, he and Melanie could finish what they'd started in the living room. And they could make love now whenever the mood struck—in the middle of the night, in the morning when they first woke up, any damned time they felt like it.

Melanie entered her bedroom, shut the door and heaved a sigh of relief because she was finally alone. *I just might stay in this room until I go home!* That notion gave her pause. Should she leave right away? Her reasons for coming to Montana hadn't changed. She hadn't yet spent any quality time with her grandfather, and maybe she should be angry and resentful over what he'd done today, but she still loved him and wanted him to love her, too. If she left now and he died…?

Shuddering over that depressing thought, Melanie undressed, threw every garment into the laundry hamper and walked into the bathroom stark naked. Positive that she had never needed a shower and shampoo more than she did at that moment, she turned on the water full blast. After setting the temperature, she stepped into the shower stall.

Eli had already cleaned up when he quietly rapped on Melanie's door. He'd taken a quick shower in the bunkhouse and put on fresh clothes. He had his shaving gear and toothbrush with him, but he would bring his other things to the house in the morning. He was about to knock again when he heard water running. "Of course," he murmured, and tried the knob. The door wasn't locked, so he opened it and walked in. Just as he'd thought, Melanie was in the bathroom taking a shower, and it pleased him that she'd left the bathroom door ajar.

Setting his small leather case of personal items on a bureau, he undressed and crawled into bed. Locking his hands behind his head, he stared into space and thought about being married. It was a different feeling, no doubt about it. He was now connected to just one woman. To a very beautiful, very sensuous woman. It didn't matter that they weren't crazy in love with each other. In truth, he wasn't sure what "crazy in love" even meant. If it meant that a man got breathless and sexually aroused around a woman, then maybe he was in love.

Hearing the shower go off, Eli shut his eyes and pictured Melanie standing there naked and wet. "Ahh," he sighed, recalling the delectable curves of her remarkable body.

Melanie toweled her hair dry, then patted the rest of herself with a fresh towel. As she stood before the mirror, the flash of gold on her finger was a constant reminder of the farce of her marriage, and when she couldn't stand it a second longer, she slid off the ring and put it in her cosmetic case.

Then she applied moisturizer to her entire body, poked at the curls in her still-damp hair, eventually gave it a final fluffing and, switching off the bathroom light, walked into her bedroom.

Eli nearly choked when he saw her come in wearing nothing, not even a towel. She didn't immediately look at him, and he wondered if she was going to tease him a little by pretending not to know he was there. She was, after all, an accomplished tease, an incredibly beautiful temptress, and she must have some idea of the impact she had on him.

She opened the bureau drawer and took out a nightgown, which she started to put on.

"Hey," Eli said softly, "you don't need that, sweetheart."

Melanie gasped, whirled around and gaped at him openmouthed, but only for a moment. Recovering quickly, she yanked on her nightgown, flashed daggers at him through fury-laden eyes and said with enough frost in her voice to destroy Florida's entire citrus crop, "What in hell are you doing in my bed?"

Confused by such a vicious attack, Eli propped himself up on his elbow. "We're married. Where else should I sleep?"

"Sleep in the barn! Sleep in...in the horse trough! Do I give a damn where you sleep? What's wrong with your usual bed? Just get your fanny out of mine!"

"Garrett told me to move my things into your room."

"Well, *I'm* telling you to move them back to the bunkhouse!" Melanie looked around. "Where are they?" She marched to the closet. "Did you dare to hang your clothes next to mine? I swear I'll throw every damn thing you own out the window!" Her gaze fell on the neatly folded clothes he'd laid on a chair.

Eli's mellow mood vanished more quickly than a snowball in July. "Don't even think it," he warned. "Other than what I wore over here, I didn't bring any clothes. I'll do that in the morning,'' he said, speaking every bit as icily as she had.

"You most certainly will not!"

Pulling the covers up to his shoulders, Eli turned on his side, showing her his back. "If you're planning to scream all night, please go to another room. I'd like to get some sleep."

"Go to another room! This is *my* room, you arrogant jackass!"

"Just shut the hell up," Eli muttered.

Melanie's fury suddenly disintegrated. He intended to stay right where he was, no matter what she said. This wasn't happening to her. It wasn't!

"What are you trying to do, make Granddad think you and I are a match made in heaven?" she asked scornfully.

"Fat chance of convincing anyone of that with you screeching all night."

"I am not screeching."

"Not at the moment, but I doubt that you're through yet."

"Just answer me one thing. If you're sleeping in that bed, where am I supposed to sleep?"

"This is a big bed. Crawl in and don't worry. Believe me, any foolish ideas I might have had when I climbed those stairs out there are completely gone."

"Seems as though my options are limited. I either sleep in that bed with you or on the floor."

"Don't tell me your troubles." Eli yawned. "Just land somewhere and turn off the damn lights, would you?"

"Oh, go to hell," she retorted irritably. Still, she switched off the ceiling light and gingerly approached the opposite side of the bed from Eli. Sliding back the sheet and blanket, she turned off the bedside lamp and lay down.

Her heart was thumping hard, mostly because she could hear Eli's steady, even breathing.

Why, he was already sleeping, the wretch! And she probably wouldn't sleep a wink all night!

The next morning when Eli and the ranch hands were seated around the table for breakfast, Garrett signaled for silence.

"I have an announcement," he said with a yard-wide grin. "Eli and my granddaughter, Melanie, were married last night."

Eli had just taken a swallow of coffee and he coughed and choked on it. The guy next to him pounded him on the back until Eli shot him a dirty look and mumbled, "Knock it off, Wilson." Eli felt Collin's eyes on him and picked up sympathy and understanding from Melanie's brother. Had she told him the truth of yesterday's fiasco?

Some of the men stood up and offered to shake hands with Eli. After congratulations, everyone began eating. While he ate, Eli thought about last night. He had about as much understanding of his wife—His *wife!* Good Lord—as he did of nuclear science. Why had she married him if she didn't want him in her bed? She wasn't some wet-behind-the-ears kid, for Pete's sake. She was a sexually experienced, independent adult, and everything that had happened between them since the day they met was her doing. He never would have made a move on her if she hadn't let him know so clearly that she was hot to trot. Now when they no longer had to sneak around, she didn't want him touching her. Did he have to put up with treatment like that? She should at least talk to him and tell him what was at the bottom of the anger she'd hurled at him last night.

By damn, he was going to *make* her talk about it. Eli got

up and said for all to hear, "Garrett, I'm going to move the rest of my things from the bunkhouse."

"You go right ahead," Garrett told him with a man-to-man smile. Silly grins appeared on some of the other men's faces—they always got a kick out of any reference to sex, be it vague or blatant. Garrett rose, too, and followed him from the dining room. He put his hand on Eli's shoulder. "I didn't want to say this in front of them, but don't think you have to rush to work this morning. Take your time...if you get my drift."

Eli nodded. "Thanks, but I'm sure I won't be long."

"Never rush love, son," Garrett said gently, sincerely.

How about the argument from hell? Should I rush that? "Thank you, Garrett. I know that's good advice."

"It really is, Eli. Women don't respond to haste."

Eli managed a weak smile and then hurried out of the house, grabbing his hat from a hook in the mudroom as he passed through it. In the bunkhouse, he stuffed his clothes into a pillowcase because the duffel bag he'd arrived with four years ago had long since disappeared. He'd seen no reason to replace it when he hardly ever left the ranch and, in fact, hadn't been away from it overnight since the day Garrett had hired him.

Toting the crammed pillowcase on his shoulder, Eli returned to the house. He avoided the dining room by cutting through the kitchen, where Irma accosted him. "Did I hear right? Are you and Melanie married?" she asked.

"Yes."

"Oh, it must have been love at first sight! How wonderful." The housekeeper looked ecstatic. "Are you going off by yourselves for a honeymoon?"

"Uh, I don't think so." He shifted the bulging pillowcase to his other shoulder. "This is getting heavy. Talk to you later, Mrs. Clary."

"Eli Forrester, it's time you started calling me Irma. You're part of the family now."

"Yes, ma'am…I mean, Irma." Eli made his escape and hurried through the house. He began slowing down near the top of the staircase because he was beginning to feel uneasy about confronting Melanie. She had a mind of her own and a temper, and she'd said in no uncertain terms last night that if he brought his clothes to her room, she'd throw them out the window.

She wouldn't really, would she? "No telling what that woman might do," Eli muttered as he reached the second floor. If his things were strewn all over the yard, he was going to be mighty embarrassed. The men would never let him forget it, and he'd have to laugh and pretend their jokes didn't bother him. Could he do it? He sure wasn't known for his sense of humor to begin with, and to be laughed at by rough, tough men who were true sons of the West would be damned hard to take.

Eli stopped at the door to Melanie's room. His room, too, he told himself, but he knew she wouldn't agree to that. Or she wouldn't have last night anyhow. Was she in a better mood this morning? What if she was? What if, when he opened the door, she sat up in bed and gave him one of her incredible smiles? What if she held out her arms, said something sexy and funny and invited him to get back into bed with her? He got hot just thinking about it. If all she did was hint that she'd welcome intimacy between them, he'd undress and hop into that bed so fast his head would spin.

Groaning at the immediate ache in his groin, Eli put his forehead against the door frame and told himself to cool down. Then, moving slowly, cautiously and nervously, he put his free hand on the doorknob and turned it.

Chapter Nine

Melanie had been awake for about fifteen minutes. She had gotten up with every intention of staying up, but after she'd brushed her teeth, depression had set in and she'd crawled back under the covers. Eli's side of the bed was mussed and empty. Obviously, he'd awakened at his usual early hour, dressed silently and tiptoed out. It unnerved her to remember how positive she'd been last night about not sleeping a wink and then conking out so soundly that she'd not once been aware of a man in her bed. And he wasn't just any man; he was her *husband!*

"Oh, Lordy," she whispered, shaken to her soul. She had let humiliation at being caught with Eli in such a debasing situation overwhelm her good sense and certainly her courage. If it had been anyone else but Garrett who'd walked in on them, she knew that she would not have come so unhinged. But her grandfather had seen her with nothing but a skirt held up in front of her, while the rest of her clothes were scattered all over the living-room floor. She could close her eyes still and see Eli's briefs next to her panties. Discovering Melanie in such a compromising situation must have completely shattered Garrett's trust in her and destroyed any pride he might have felt in his one and only granddaughter.

Now she was married and so she must get herself *unmarried!* Preferably without telling her mother anything about the mess she'd gotten herself into. Sue Ellen would go ballistic if she found out her daughter had been married without her. And without the long white gown and veil, the attendants, formal church ceremony and huge reception she'd planned for Melanie ever since her daughter had been old enough to know what a wedding was all about.

Sick at heart, Melanie moaned and turned on her side. Maybe she'd stay in bed all day. Maybe she'd stay there until she went back to San Diego! She would leave today if she didn't have to come up with a plausible explanation for her mother about why she'd cut her visit so short.

Her back was to the door, and when it opened and Eli came in, she never moved a muscle even though her heart was pumping in double time. Even with her eyes shut, Melanie sensed his stare and wondered how long she could lie still and pretend to be asleep. The hardest part of her act was to breathe shallowly; she simply wasn't getting enough air and she had to take a big breath.

Since it was a dead giveaway, she stopped all pretense, opened her eyes and asked coldly, "Why on earth are you gawking at me?"

"Any man would gawk at you. You're incredibly beautiful," Eli said quietly from the chair he was sitting in. "You know it, too, don't you? You also know how to make a man do any damned thing you want. A tilt of an eyebrow, a hint of a smile, a toss of your hair, the subtlest twitch of your hips. Oh, yes, you know all the tricks.''

''I didn't *want* a loveless marriage,'' she said sarcastically, then flopped onto her back to glare at the ceiling.

''No, you just wanted some fun and games while you were in Montana. What did you do when you got here? Rank all the men and decide that I'd be the easiest one to manipulate?''

''Don't be absurd! Every other man on this ranch who isn't a relative is old, dense as a door or just plain unattractive.''

''Meaning I'm not?''

''You know darned well you're not.''

''Really.'' Eli moved from the chair to the bed, sat down and leaned over her. ''What am I, then?''

''Don't…don't sit there. Go…back to the chair,'' she stammered.

''But I like it here. *You* like me here, too, don't you?''

''If I liked you in or on my bed, I would have done more than sleep last night,'' she retorted.

''Let's not confuse last night with this morning,'' Eli said softly, his face drawing even closer to hers. He drank in the sight of her. ''How come you look so beautiful in the morning?''

''I don't! Eli, don't do this, please. Look, there's something we have to talk about.'' He slipped his hand under the covers, and she got panicky because it felt so right holding her breast. Pushing back the blankets, she lifted his hand from her body and put it on his own thigh. ''I mean it, Eli. You have to listen to me.''

He put his lips against her ear and whispered, ''You're my wife, and I want to make love to you.''

''No, Eli,'' she moaned. ''I can't.''

''But you want to. I can see it in your eyes.''

She shut her eyes against his penetrating gaze and said in an agonized whisper, "If we made love now, our marriage would be consummated. I intend to get an annulment and I'd like to be truthful when I tell my lawyer that we never, uh, slept together after the ceremony."

"We *slept* together last night."

Her eyes flashed open. "You know very well I'm not talking about sleeping!"

He studied her face. "Do you actually believe that you and I can get in the same bed night after night and do nothing but sleep?"

Eli wondered if she would stick to her schedule and leave when her vacation time was up. It was a surprisingly unnerving prospect and he wasn't quite sure why. Was it because he now knew she intended to nullify yesterday's ceremony or because once she left he'd probably never see her again?

His mood changed and he suddenly didn't feel so kindly toward her. She'd used him to service her sexual needs, nothing more. Not one thing that had occurred between them meant a damn to her.

"I can," Melanie said. "It's you I'm worried about."

"Oh, I see. You've completely curtailed *your* sex drive."

The hard note in his voice hadn't been there before and it made Melanie wary. "I have it under control, yes," she said slowly.

"Which, of course, is the reason your nipple got hard the second I touched it."

"I think you know that's an involuntary reaction."

"Sort of like this one?" Taking her hand, he brought it to his fly.

She jerked her hand back. "That's quite enough of that! Are you going to cooperate with my annulment plan or not?"

Eli got off the bed and then stood next to it, looking at her. "Nope."

Startled, Melanie sat up. "Why not? You certainly don't want to *stay* married, do you?"

"Were you against our getting married yesterday?"

"Well, of course I was! Why didn't you stop it?" she asked.

"Why didn't you?"

Groaning in frustration, Melanie plopped down and pulled the pillow over her head. "Go away. You're making me crazy."

"We do seem to affect each other that way, don't we? Okay, I'm leaving now. I'll see you at dinner if not before. Oh, by the way, if you should happen to lose some of that remarkable self-control you seem to have suddenly developed, give me a yell. Remember that I'm your man if you get hot, sweetheart." Eli started for the door, then stopped to say, "One thing more. My clothes are in that pillowcase over there. If you should start feeling wifely, it would be a real nice gesture to hang my shirts and pants in the closet and put my underwear and socks in one of the dressers in here."

He was almost to the door when she hit him in the back with a pillow. She was a darned good shot.

He left with the strangest ache in his gut. *Just try to remember yours isn't a real marriage, old sport, and that your dear wife isn't going to be your dear wife for very long!*

Garrett saddled his favorite horse for a ride that day. He did his best thinking on horseback—always had—and God knew Garrett Kincaid had a lot on his mind. Leaving the compound, he felt Collin's inquisitive gaze on his back.

More often than not, they rode together, but today he needed to be completely alone.

Melanie and Eli's marriage gnawed at him. He'd behaved like a small-minded, old-fashioned tyrant yesterday, when what he should've done was ignore what he'd seen until he'd thought it through. After all, young people were much different today than when he'd been Melanie's age.

But *are* the generations really so different? Garrett wondered. *My beloved Laura was pregnant when we married over fifty years ago, and I was no more than a randy young sapling—younger than Melanie, for a fact. What if I forced a marriage yesterday that should not have taken place? Who am I to make such a major decision for someone else?*

But Melanie is such a lovely young woman, and she should not be giving herself to a man she doesn't love and maybe doesn't love her. At least Laura and I loved each other. Every day of our marriage we loved each other. Sometimes I still miss her so much I can't bear it.

It's strange, Garrett thought, *that neither Melanie nor Eli made the slightest objection to getting married. It's all very confusing.*

And my mind is also vague on what to do about Larry's other sons. Or should I do anything at all? Do any of those young men know who their father is? Isn't it odd that not a one of them ever came looking for Larry? How will they react to inheriting a share of the Kincaid family's Whitehorn ranch?

I must make a decision about that. Wayne agreed to let me know if a serious buyer should materialize, but it wouldn't be fair to leave my cousin hanging indefinitely.

Walking his horse over his own land, Garrett wondered if Collin and Melanie were worried now about the future of their inheritances. And he hadn't yet told Alice about Larry's six sons. Actually, he hadn't told his daughter because he had a pretty good idea how she'd react to the news. It had to be done, of course, and maybe this afternoon he'd drive to Elk Springs and drop in on her.

Or maybe he'd do that tomorrow.

Sighing heavily, Garrett brooded about the swift passage of time and the fact that each year seemed to go by faster than the one before. And he thought of the mistakes people made with the ones they loved most, the hurts they caused each other, and he wondered again if he'd done the right thing for Melanie yesterday.

Melanie finally dragged herself out of bed and into the shower. Dressed in jeans, plaid cotton blouse and her riding boots, she headed downstairs. She had just reached the first-floor landing when the telephone started ringing.

"I'll get it, Irma," she called. "I'm right next to Granddad's office." Sitting in the desk chair, she picked up the receiver. "Kincaid ranch."

"Melanie, it's me."

"Mom! Uh, hi. How are you?" Melanie was beside herself. She wasn't emotionally prepared to talk to her mother today. All it would take was a tiny slip of the tongue for Sue Ellen to catch on that something was awry in Montana.

"Melanie, I've done a lot of thinking about what you told me. About your father's six illegitimate sons, you know? I've tried not to worry about you and Collin. I mean, please don't think I'm greedy or selfish because I want my children to receive their rightful inheritance. You must never think that I'm hoping for any financial gain for myself, but you and Collin are Garrett's legitimate heirs and it concerns me that Garrett might do something foolish with his estate."

"Such as splitting it nine ways?"

"Nine?"

"Aunt Alice, Mom."

"Oh, yes, Alice. Have you seen her?"

"Not yet. Everyone's so busy, and I'd like Collin to go with me."

"Has Collin been too busy to spend time with you?"

"Everyone's busy here, Mom."

"Well, heavens, what do you do all day?"

Well…yesterday I got married, Mom. Melanie winced. "Let's see. I've been training a pretty gray filly, and I've gone riding and swimming. Did you ever swim in Dove Lake when you lived here?"

"Oh, my, I haven't thought of Dove Lake in years. Yes, your father and I went swimming there in good weather."

There was a giddiness in Sue Ellen's voice that made Melanie smile and think, *And what else did you and Dad do at Dove Lake, Mom?* But then she remembered what *she'd* done at Dove Lake, and her own face colored and she steered the conversation in another direction.

"And there's Irma to talk to, and Saturday I cleaned the house. Believe me, Mom, there's something to do every minute of the day. I'm not bored, believe me."

Melanie winced again because she'd said "believe me" twice in the space of two seconds. She was trying too hard to sound happy with her visit, wanting to convince her mother that everything was great. On the other hand, she realized that she hadn't really lied. She definitely was not bored, nor had she been bored for one moment since she'd arrived. For a quiet, out-of-the-way place, a lot sure went on here.

"Melanie, getting back to the reason I called, has Garrett indicated in any way if he intends contacting those, uh, men?"

"Dad's other sons? Not to me, he hasn't. He seems troubled, though, and I have a strong hunch that he's giving the situation a great deal of thought.''

''Hmm, no telling how this could end up.''

''At this point, I'd have to agree.''

''If anything changes, would you please call and tell me about it?''

''Mom, I really don't want to conspire behind Grand-dad's back.''

''Gracious, I'm not asking you to do anything criminal. You know I'm not that sort of person, Melanie. But as your and Collin's mother, I feel that I must look out for your best interests. I'm not sure that either of you will do that even though you're right there under your grandfather's nose. When you have children of your own, you'll understand my concern.''

Melanie had heard similar remarks before. *Only when you have children of your own will you truly understand the joys of motherhood…or the worry…or what a parent goes through or gives up for his child. And it's for life, Melanie. A loving mother doesn't stop worrying about her child just because he or she has grown up.*

''Yes, Mom,'' she said with a soft sigh.

''May I count on you, then?''

''If something of consequence takes place, yes, I'll phone you,'' Melanie conceded.

''Thank you, dear.''

Melanie put down the phone feeling like an awful liar.

Irma stuck her head in the door, and Melanie noticed that the housekeeper did not appear to be her usual upbeat, chipper self.

''Do I offer congratulations or what?'' Irma said.

''You know?'' Melanie got up and walked around the desk. ''Who told you?''

"No one told me. I overheard Garrett's announcement at breakfast."

Melanie's jaw dropped. "He told *everyone?* At the breakfast table?"

"You seem so shocked. Was it supposed to be kept a secret?"

"Uh, no, I suppose not," Melanie mumbled. "I just didn't expect..."

Irma moved close enough to take Melanie's hands in hers. "Child, did you know Eli before you came here?"

"No," Melanie admitted reluctantly.

"Oh, Melanie, you don't know him any better than the rest of us do. Unless he's told you things he hasn't told anyone else. Has he? Has he talked about his past? His family? Where he hails from? Maybe even the reason why he's so unusually closemouthed?"

Melanie drew a deep breath. "No, he hasn't."

"Oh, mercy," Irma said worriedly. "Melanie, far be it from me to rain on someone else's parade, but I can't for the life of me figure out why your grandfather permitted you to marry a man you've known little more than a week. Even if you and Eli believe with all of your hearts that you can't live without each other. I know that love can be a powerful force, but you're so young, honey, and a little time doesn't destroy love if it's the real thing."

Melanie felt like the lowest form of life at that moment. Irma's personal ethics were obviously of the highest standard. Never would she understand a young woman's having sex with a man just to satisfy normal biological needs. In Irma's day, good girls kept themselves chaste until their wedding night. And Melanie realized, sadly, regretfully, that dear Irma thought of her as a good girl.

The most confusing part of this conversation was that Melanie had always thought of herself as a good and decent woman. Having sex with a man didn't make a woman a bad person. Some women went too far, of course, and had a different man in their beds almost every night. But there were men who did the same, and Melanie went out of her way to avoid that sort of man just as, she was sure, a lot of men avoided women with tarnished reputations.

But she could explain none of that to Irma, no more than she could ever explain it to her grandfather. There were some areas of life where the generations would never see eye to eye. Sex was one of them.

"Thank you for your concern," Melanie said gently as she was truly moved by Irma's caring nature. "But you mustn't worry about me, Irma. Eli, either. Everything is going to be fine, I promise you." *Oh, yes, just as soon as I get that annulment, everything will be back to normal and just fine. But why in heaven's name did Granddad have to make that announcement at breakfast? It's hardly anyone else's business, is it?*

Irma looked at Melanie, and after a long moment, she sighed. "I do wish you the best, Melanie. Please don't misunderstand."

"I know you do." Melanie smiled. "Now, I'm close to perishing from hunger. I have got to eat something."

Irma looked appalled. "Of course you do! And here I am keeping you talking when I should be feeding you. Let's go to the kitchen and see what we can scare up."

As hungry as Melanie had thought she was, when she sat down to eat she could hardly put a bite in her mouth. Her stomach had turned queasy and nothing tasted good. *It's my nerves, she decided. They're shot all to hell today, and why wouldn't they be? I'm married! I'm really married and my husband wants his conjugal rights, and I lied when I told him that I had my libido under control, because Eli and I might have nothing else in common, but there's no denying the chemistry between us. He's right. How are we going to share the same bed night after night and do nothing but sleep?*

Finally, with such nerve-racking questions gnawing at her, Melanie could not pretend to be enjoying her food a second longer. "I'm sorry, Irma. I guess I wasn't nearly as hungry as I thought." She got up and brought her plate to the sink. "I think what I really need is some fresh air."

Irma patted her hand. "It's only natural for you to be a bit jittery today. Melanie, if you, uh, have any questions…I mean…about, uh, men and women…or rather a husband and wife…and, er, what he expects to happen at night…"

"You're a dear, Irma, but my mother explained everything to me some time ago." Since she couldn't shock Irma to death by telling her that she knew through firsthand experience not only what a man expected from a woman but also what a woman expected from a man, Melanie figured that was the best way to allay Irma's well-meant concern.

"Oh, that's good," Irma said, obviously relieved. "Well, shoo, then. Go outside and get some fresh air."

Melanie was working with Sassy when she spotted someone at the fence out of the corner of her eye. Her heart skipped a beat, but when she turned to look, it was Collin she saw, not Eli. Leaving Sassy alone for a few minutes, Melanie walked over to the fence.

"Hi," she said quietly, noticing the worry in her brother's eyes. First Irma, now Collin, she thought unhappily.

"Mel, are you all right today?"

"Collin, I don't want you worrying about me so much," Melanie said.

"How can I help worrying? I don't know what got into Granddad yesterday. He's just not himself these days. I think he's so upset over Dad's shenanigans that he isn't thinking straight, but still, making you marry Eli…'' Dolefully, Collin shook his head.

Melanie laid her hand on her brother's arm. "Collin, it's going to turn out okay, but you can't tell Mom about it. You haven't talked to her already today, have you?"

"No, but why don't you want her to know? Mel, you can't hide something like this. You're married!"

"I know the situation, Collin, far better than you, and…" It occurred to Melanie that her annulment plan would proceed much more smoothly if no one but her and Eli knew about it. "You simply have to trust me on this, Collin. You're not as close to Mom as I am, and I'm afraid of what it would do to her if she was told on the phone that I got married in a civil ceremony. You see, she's always wanted me to have a big wedding with all the trimmings. Whenever she sees a wedding dress in a magazine, she studies it closely, and if she thinks the style might be right for me, she cuts out the picture and adds it to what she calls *her* hope chest."

"Jeez, Mel, I had no idea." Collin looked miserable. "What're you going to do? She's got to be told sooner or later."

"I plan to handle it when the time is right. Just promise me you won't say anything if you talk to her."

"I won't, I swear I won't."

Melanie felt miserable, too. "I'm sorry to involve you in this. You shouldn't have to lie for anyone, least of all your sister."

"I won't lie, Mel. I just won't talk about it."

"Collin, why do you think Granddad told all the men about it this morning at breakfast? Irma overheard the announcement and she was still shook up over it hours later when I came downstairs."

"I'm sure he told the men because of Eli, Mel. I doubt that it really had anything to do with you. But those men work for Eli, and Granddad probably felt they should know why he moved his things from the bunkhouse to the main house."

"Yes, I see what you mean," Melanie murmured. "I didn't think of it that way."

"Mel, if you don't love Eli and he doesn't love you, why are both of you letting so much happen? I mean, now you'll be sleeping together every night. Next thing you know, you'll be pregnant."

Melanie shook her head because she was taking a very reliable birth-control pill. And besides, she was going to do her level best to keep the nights uneventful. She could acknowledge—to herself—the chemistry between her and Eli, but she certainly had enough willpower to keep it under control.

"That's not going to happen. Trust me," she said again.

Eli automatically headed to the bunkhouse for his usual before-dinner shower, then he remembered where his clean clothes were. He felt foolish and changed direction. He entered the Kincaid house quietly, at first feeling like an intruder. But then, in the mudroom, he hung his hat on a hook and told himself that he was now part of the family, welcomed into it by Garrett himself, and that he should relax and make himself at home.

The arrangement was a long way from perfect, however, what with Melanie keeping him at arm's length and talking about an annulment. But she still had almost two weeks on the ranch if she stuck to her original plan, and an awful lot could happen in that period of time. It would be best, of course, if he knew exactly how he wanted the whole thing to turn out and could therefore decide on a definitive course of action.

But other than aching to make love to Melanie and wanting her to want him, as she'd done *before* they'd sworn to love and honor each other for the rest of their lives, he really didn't know how he felt about her.

Truth was, they simply didn't know each other. She'd flirted; he'd responded. He'd made a pass; she'd responded. And he'd never experienced hotter, more exciting sex. Maybe because of that, his mind had remained below his belt since that day at the lake, and he hadn't given himself the chance to know Melanie.

It could be the same with her, he mused as he passed by the kitchen doorway and saw Irma standing at the stove stirring something in a large pot. If she heard him, she didn't let on, and he was glad because he'd rather not talk to her right now. He'd seen enough raised eyebrows and knowing looks for one day. In fact, he was just a little bit grouchy because the men who'd razzed him the most about marrying the boss's granddaughter were the ones he'd always liked the least.

On his way up the stairs, he couldn't help wondering if Melanie was in their bedroom. *Their bedroom.* What an erotic term that was, bringing forth images of sexual delights that would warm the coldest heart, and his was already overheated. Maybe tonight she would let him touch her, hold her, caress her.

"Don't get your hopes up," he muttered just as he pushed the door open.

Melanie was sitting on a chair, dressed for dinner in a pretty floral-patterned skirt and rose-colored blouse. "Can we talk?" she asked flatly.

"I don't know. Can we?" Eli shut the bedroom door and

spotted his clothes, still in the pillowcase, probably wrinkled and crushed beyond redemption.

"I never did feel wifely," Melanie said when she saw the direction of his gaze.

"Should I be surprised?"

"No, you shouldn't. And neither should you sound annoyed or irritated. Even if this was a real marriage, I wouldn't be jumping up and down at your command. You've taken care of your clothes without my assistance for, I expect, a good many years. I'm sure you're quite capable of continuing to do so." Melanie stopped for breath. "Now, let me start by saying that, like it or not, we're in this mess together and we're not going to get out of it unless we agree on a solution."

"An annulment." Scowling, Eli took the loaded pillowcase over to the closet and started hanging up jeans and shirts.

"Do you have a better idea?"

"Sweetheart, I've got all kinds of ideas, and the funny thing is that before we called on Judge Joseph you would have loved every one of them."

Melanie flushed. "You think you know so much about me, and you don't."

"But what I do know would melt the polar ice cap, sweetheart."

Jumping up from the chair, Melanie raised her voice. "Stop calling me sweetheart in that insulting tone of voice! I know I behaved badly with you, and I don't need any reminders!"

Frowning, Eli turned from the closet. "You never behaved badly. Why would you say something like that?"

"Don't patronize me, Eli."

"I'm not! It's just that I admired your free spirit and sense of fun from the first day you got here, and I'd hate to think now that you've chalked up everything you've done to bad behavior.''

''Only because it lets you off the hook,'' she said.

''Then I misbehaved, too?'' Eli began walking slowly toward her.

''Oh, for heaven's sake, we both did! And now we're paying for it, aren't we?'' Noticing how much closer he was to her, she moved away. ''And if we don't do something about it, we're going to keep on paying...and paying...and paying! Don't you get it? Hasn't it sunk in? We're married, and I don't want to be married!''

Eli felt stabbed, and it took a second for the unexpected pain to abate. ''I don't want to be married, either,'' he said gruffly. ''Get the annulment whenever you want. Would you rather I moved back to the bunkhouse?''

''No!'' Melanie's eyes became huge. ''Everything has to stay the same until I go home.''

''For God's sake, why?''

Melanie began pacing back and forth. ''The reason I came to Montana was to get to know Granddad. My father died, and I will forever regret not knowing him, no matter what kind of man he was. If the same should happen with Granddad, I would never forgive myself. Only, just before I arrived, he found out about Dad's other children and he's been too busy to spend any one-on-one time with me. I will not have any more vacation time coming for another year, and besides, if I went home early I'd have to lie to my mother. And she's a very bright lady who seems to have a sixth sense about lies.'' Melanie threw up her hands. ''It's just a big fat mess, that's what it is.''

Eli grasped about half of Melanie's frantic explanation. But he said politely, ''It appears to be a lot more complicated for you than I could have guessed. Certainly it's much worse for you than it is for me.''

"You'll help me, then? For sure?"

"Absolutely."

She startled him by flying across the room and throwing her arms around his neck. "Oh, thank you, thank you!"

Then, realizing that an embrace was not the best way for her to thank him, she pulled back. "Sorry, I promise that won't happen again."

"Forget it. It didn't mean a thing to either of us." Eli was clenching a plastic hanger from the closet in his hand so tightly it was a wonder it didn't break. *It didn't mean a thing? You damn liar!*

"You're right, it didn't," Melanie said with a bright cheerfulness that was so phony she nearly gagged on it. Backing away, she added, "Well, I'm going downstairs. The bathroom's all yours."

"Thanks. See you at dinner." Alone in the room, Eli stumbled to a chair and fell into it. Melanie, his gorgeous, sometimes witless, sometimes brilliant wife, was too much woman for a mere man like him to deal with. She'd managed to extract a promise from him that he'd never intended making.

An annulment meant no lovemaking, and he'd agreed! God help him.

Chapter Ten

Melanie was taken aback in the dining room. The men, whom she'd certainly not seen as romantics, had changed the seating arrangement at the table so she and Eli would be eating right next to each other. With a weak little smile, she accepted their congratulations and sat in her new place—on Eli's right. Collin was almost directly across from her now, and his smile wasn't much happier than hers. His eyes conveyed worry, disappointment and disapproval, all but breaking Melanie's heart.

She tried to bolster her spirits by telling herself that he was no more disappointed or disapproving than she was herself, but it was a pretty lame effort when down deep she knew that she was a hundred percent to blame for her dilemma. Eli was an accessory to her crime—if any crime had been committed—but he hadn't been the instigator. She had.

And even though the result of her outrageous flirting was

a marriage she didn't want, she could not admit—even to herself—that she regretted the lovemaking. Actually, neither did she regret her flirtatious teasing with Eli because it had been fun, loads of fun.

No, she thought with a sigh. In all honesty, the only thing she regretted was getting caught, and even that would have been tolerable if it had been anyone but her grandfather who'd walked in on her and Eli.

She sent Garrett a sheepish little glance and saw him eating with his eyes on his plate. It struck her that his expression was sorrowful, and he seemed separate somehow, not one of them tonight. *Oh, what pain his family has brought him! First Dad, then me!*

The table talk was subdued tonight. In deference to the newlyweds? Melanie wondered sadly. Newlyweds who were careful not to touch or smile or even speak to each other. Where were all those flirtatious urges now, the teasing glances, the daring, feminine smiles that said, "I'll get you to unbend yet, Mr. Forrester!"

Suddenly full of tears, Melanie was about to excuse herself so she could bury her face in a pillow in her room and bawl her eyes out. But before she could make her move, Irma came in with a beautifully decorated three-tiered wedding cake.

She smiled at Melanie, but it wasn't a big, happy, jovial smile; it was a sad little movement of her lips that tugged at Melanie's heartstrings.

"Every bride deserves a cake," Irma announced.

"It's lovely," Melanie said huskily because of the tears in her throat.

"Eli, it's also for you," Irma added.

"Thank you." Eli gave her a warm smile.

Irma disappeared for a few seconds and returned with a tray containing small plates, dessert forks and a cake knife

with a pink ribbon tied around its handle. "The bride and
groom should make the first cut in the cake together," Irma
said. "For good luck."

Melanie's mind raced, but she could think of no way out
of this. Everyone had meant well—the men who'd arranged
for her to sit next to her husband, and Irma, who did not
approve of such a hasty wedding but would make the best
of things.

Since she could do no different without making herself
look like a fool, Melanie got up from her chair. Forcing a
laugh, she tugged on Eli's arm. "Come on, Mr. Forrester.
This is one of the *other* things that a husband and wife do
together," she quipped for the benefit of the men, who
guffawed and elbowed each other in the ribs. Only Collin
and Garrett looked bereft; everyone else seemed to be enjoying the impromptu party.

To Melanie's relief, Eli went along with her. "Anything
you say, Mrs. Forrester," he agreed meekly, much like a
henpecked husband, which brought another round of laughter from the men.

Melanie picked up the cake knife and Eli laid his hand
over hers. "You've done this before," she whispered quietly, then wondered about the questions Irma had asked her.
Has he talked about his past? His family? For the first time
since they'd met, Melanie fully grasped how little she knew
about Eli. Perhaps most disturbing was that no one else on
the ranch knew much of anything, either.

"Do you want to discuss that now?" he whispered back.

The table had fallen silent as everyone watched the cake-
cutting ceremony. The cake tasted as delicious as it looked,
but Melanie had a hard time eating it. A wedding cake for
a loveless marriage didn't seem quite right to her, and pretending otherwise put a strain on her acting skills.

When it was finally over, Garrett pushed back his chair

and said, "Eli, could you please come to the office with me?"

"Yes, of course." Eli rose and left the room right behind Garrett. The men filed out, including Collin, and Melanie and Irma looked at each other.

"I shouldn't have made the cake," Irma said dolefully. "I thought it might cheer you up, but it caused just the opposite. I'm sorry, Melanie."

Melanie got up. "You must never apologize for being kind, Irma. The cake was wonderful and everyone loved it. Thank you for going to so much trouble." Melanie began stacking dirty plates, but Irma stopped her with a hand on her arm.

"No, not anymore," Irma said firmly. "You have things to work through, important things, and you are not going to spend your evenings in the kitchen with me. There are three men on this ranch who are all torn up, and you are probably the only person in Montana who can heal their wounds. Go find one of them and play the part of the weaker sex. Put on a sweet smile and let him tell you where it hurts and why. I know all three are older than you, but don't forget that women are the nurturers and probably all those big tough men need is a few minutes of your full attention."

"I can't quite believe it would be that easy," Melanie said with a sigh. "But I'll try." *Not with Eli, because I already know what even just a little "nurturing" would do to him. But Collin and Granddad are miserably unhappy, maybe because of me, maybe because of something else, though I sincerely believe that my name tops their list of problems. How could it not?*

Well, maybe Dad and his secret sons hold the number one spot, but I would certainly have to be a very close second.

Feeling terribly guilty, Melanie started looking for Collin. When she saw that the office door was closed, indicating a private discussion between Eli and her grandfather, her stomach tensed. They weren't shut up in that office to talk about ranch business; they were talking about her!

What if Eli told Garrett about her annulment plans? she wondered. Granddad would probably tell her to pack her things and go home! He'd probably say, "If that's what you're going to do, why put it off?" And he'd never ask her back again. Then he'd die and she'd never know him any better than she knew Dad!

Forgetting all about finding and consoling Collin, Melanie frantically ran up the stairs to her bedroom.

Garrett had begun the discussion with a blunt question. "Do you and Melanie love each other?"

Eli never moved a muscle, but the question penetrated his gut and lay there like a lead weight. He felt trapped between a rock and a hard place. Whatever he said was going to hurt someone—either Garrett or Melanie.

You made a promise to Melanie.

True, but you work for Garrett and you've known him a whole lot longer. Melanie plans to cut all ties with you; Garrett doesn't. Think of yourself, what's best for you.

The problem with that advice was that in trying to foresee his future, Eli saw nothing but a vast wasteland of loneliness. It was a startling insight, but he no longer wanted things the way they were before Melanie had burst upon the scene. He'd lived alone long enough. He liked being part of the Kincaid family, and he liked Garrett and Collin.

Truth was, he *more* than liked Melanie, and another truth was that they were married and he wanted to *stay* married!

Eli cleared his throat. "I can only be honest with you about that, Garrett. My personal belief is that Melanie and

I were in the process of falling in love when you saw us together." *It's not a lie, it isn't! Not when I can't believe that Melanie sleeps with just any man.*

"A most unfortunate incident," Garrett murmured. "I overreacted, of course, for which I apologize."

Eli leaned forward. "Garrett, in your shoes, I would have reacted in exactly the same way."

"Why didn't you object to the marriage?"

Eli sat back again. "Why didn't Melanie? Garrett, there are feelings between Melanie and me that neither of us has admitted or talked about."

"You seem to be admitting them now."

"Maybe facing them is a better term."

"Yes, well, facing and then admitting them to yourself would be a crucial first step, wouldn't it? Do you feel that Melanie is going through the same emotional exercise?"

"I...couldn't say."

"The two of you haven't discussed it?"

"No, sir, we haven't."

"That's right, you said only a moment ago that you and Melanie hadn't admitted or talked about feelings." Garrett tented his fingers and soberly regarded Eli over them. "So that really is the way it's done today? Without one word of affection between a couple, they freely enjoy the physical side of a relationship?"

Eli felt about two inches high. He'd known from the time he started working for Garrett that the ranch owner was a dignified, reserved man of honor. Eli could recall wondering more than once how a man of Garrett Kincaid's nature could ever have produced a son with Larry's irresponsible characteristics.

It hurt terribly for Eli to see the situation as Garrett must. A man he trusted seducing his beloved granddaughter? Defeated without firing a shot, Eli's shoulders slumped. Of course Garrett didn't know what a sensual woman Melanie was, and how could Eli tell him? There was nothing he could say in his own defense. In fact, he might have already said too much with that statement about Melanie and him being in the process of falling in love. Maybe she did sleep with just any guy. It sure wasn't something most women would boast about to their brothers and grandfathers, and Eli couldn't doubt that Melanie was an accomplished flirt.

"All I can do is apologize, Garrett," Eli said quietly.

"No, son, there's a lot more you can do. You can be a good husband to my granddaughter. I didn't do right by that girl. Neither did Larry. I invited her here to try to make amends. So what happened then? As I told you and Irma in confidence, I learned about six grandsons I never dreamed existed. Again I neglected Melanie, and it wasn't fair of me to turn her over to you. I wasn't thinking of her or of you. My mind was full of problems I didn't know how to solve. I'm not at all proud to say that I still don't."

Garrett leaned forward. "Let me ask you something, Eli. If you were one of those young men, one of Larry's illegitimate sons, would you appreciate or resent a grandfather you'd never met—and possibly never knew about—suddenly appearing out of nowhere?"

Eli didn't immediately answer that question. If they were talking about him, he would have to say, "Garrett, I left my family on purpose and I would not appreciate any of them contacting me." But Garrett was speaking of those faceless, unknown young men who might be thrilled to death or deeply angered to meet any relative of a father who'd never been there for them. At least that was the impression Eli had from what he'd been told of Larry's secret sons. "That's the question you've been wrestling with, isn't it?" Eli finally acknowledged.

"It's been bothering me, that's certain."

"Garrett, do you have any reason to think—or perhaps some actual proof—that any of those men know about Larry's family?"

"Eli, I don't have proof that any of them even know about Larry."

"But someone mentioned birth certificates."

"Yes, copies of their birth certificates were in Larry's safety-deposit box, Eli. I left them with my lawyer until I could figure out which end is up."

"Well, I would think they'd have the originals, wouldn't you? Is Larry named as father on them?"

"Yes, he is." Garrett's eyes narrowed slightly. "You're right. If those boys are in possession of their birth certificates, then they'd know the name of their father. But that's even more confusing, Eli, because not a one of them ever came around looking for Larry."

"How do you know? Garrett, it's painfully obvious that Larry didn't tell you everything."

"He sure didn't, Eli, but he wasn't the only one, was he?" Garrett asked.

Eli felt a wave of embarrassment color his neck and face. "No, Garrett, he wasn't."

Garrett swung out his hand. "Go and spend some time with Melanie."

Eli got to his feet. "I'm sorry I wasn't more help."

"Eli, I'm beginning to wonder if anyone can help me with this problem. It's so far out of the ordinary that I've never heard of anything even remotely similar before. I mean, one or maybe two illegitimate grandsons would have been shock enough—but six?" Garrett shook his head and said sadly, "Larry should have told me." When he noticed Eli still standing there—and looking concerned—he said again, "Go on. Spend what's left of the evening with your wife. You're not without problems yourself, you know."

"Yes, sir, I do know." Eli hurried out and shut the door behind him.

The Kincaid family was in turmoil, and while Melanie didn't feel that she was alone in the eye of the storm, neither did she feel united with anyone. Even Collin, sympathetic as he seemed to be with her predicament, was much more unnerved and on edge over the problem of all those half brothers he'd known nothing about.

And it hurt that Garrett, the grandfather she'd wanted so very much to get close to, would rather discuss her and Eli's relationship with Eli rather than her. Why hadn't he asked her to join him in his office after dinner instead of Eli? She hated to think that Garrett might be a die-hard chauvinist with little respect for women's intelligence, but wasn't that the way he'd treated her since her arrival? He'd been acting as though she couldn't possibly understand the business that he and Collin were forever driving off to take care of, so she should be happy staying behind while the big, strong men of the family braved the rigors of complicated business affairs.

Melanie was suddenly disgusted with the whole situation. She probably understood the business world better than Collin ever would. Not that she resented her brother's close ties to their grandfather. In fact, she was glad that Collin had made a good life for himself in Montana. But why leave her out of everything they did together? Dare she go so far as to blame them for her and Eli's present situation? If they had taken her with them instead of putting her in Eli's hands, then maybe nothing would have happened between them and they wouldn't be trapped in this farce of a marriage.

Frowning, Melanie sank to the edge of the bed. Was there any truth in that conjecture? A bit of truth, at least?

Was anyone other than herself to blame? She'd been attracted to Eli when they'd been introduced—outrageously attracted, to be honest. But she'd certainly never thought that a little flirting or even some wildly exciting lovemaking would lead to this.

The bedroom door opened and Melanie turned her head to see Eli walking in. "It wouldn't kill you to knock," she said coldly. "I could have been undressing...or something."

"Turn off the chill, okay? I'm in no mood for another unnecessary argument." Eli went into the bathroom and closed the door.

Melanie waited anxiously until that door opened again. "Did you and Granddad have an argument?"

"Garrett and I have *never* had an argument. I was talking about us—you and me." Eli set his hands on his hips and gave her a long, challenging look. "What I can't figure out is why you were so hot on my tail before Sunday and now you can't keep enough distance between us."

"I think I explained it clearly enough," she retorted.

"The annulment."

"Yes, the annulment. Speaking of which, did you tell Granddad about it?"

"No, but from some of his remarks, I doubt that he'd care if you went to an attorney tomorrow."

Shocked and disbelieving, Melanie jumped up. "What did he say to make you think that?"

"He apologized for overreacting on Sunday."

"He did? And what did you say?"

"I said that in his shoes I probably would have reacted the same way. Then he told me to go and spend the evening with my wife."

Melanie frowned. "That doesn't sound like he wouldn't

mind if I saw a lawyer tomorrow. What did he say to give you that impression?''

Eli realized that he'd already said too much. If he had any chance at all of changing Melanie's mind about that annulment, then *he'd* better change his tune.

''You know something? You're right. I don't know how I got that impression when Garrett said not once but twice that I should spend some time with my wife.''

Melanie's eyes widened. ''He said it twice? My Lord, he's really thinking of us as a married couple.''

''Afraid so,'' Eli said, his gaze downcast. ''But then, why wouldn't he? We went through the ceremony without a single objection, and now we're sleeping together.''

''With *sleeping* being the key word,'' Melanie reminded him sharply.

''You and I know that. No one else does.''

For some reason, Melanie's gaze strayed to the bed. Last night had been easy because they had both fallen asleep so fast, but what about tonight? And tomorrow night and the next and the next?

Her heart sank because she knew herself so well. If she should awaken in the middle of any given night with that feeling, that curling heat in the pit of her stomach, and Eli—a man who wasn't just sexy and gorgeous but also happened to be her husband—was in reach...?

Panic seized her. ''Eli, we have to do something about the, uh, the bed.''

Eli looked at it. ''Is something wrong with it?''

Melanie began walking in a frenzied circle. ''What's wrong with it is that there's only one!''

Eli held back a hoot of laughter. ''Do you know of some way to, er, make it multiply?''

She stopped to glare at him. ''Don't you dare make fun of me! This is a serious problem.''

"Seems to be quite a few of those floating around the ranch these days," Eli drawled.

Melanie startled him by dropping onto a chair, covering her face with her hands and moaning, "I'm so confused. You're right, even if you were trying to be funny. This place is overrun with problems, and I'm one of them!"

Eli read her agony as real and heartfelt and he knelt in front of her to offer consolation. "The situation's a problem. You're not."

Melanie let her hands fall. "For crying out loud, Eli, I *caused* the problem!"

"Not alone, you didn't," Eli said softly. "I was there, too, in case you've forgotten."

Looking into his eyes was like languidly swimming in a warm sea of brilliant blue. "No," she whispered, shaken and unable to hide it. "Don't remind me of anything we did, please."

"Isn't it constantly on your mind the way it's on mine?" Eli laid his forearms along the outside of her thighs. His chest was against her knees, and he leaned forward to bring his face closer to hers. "Are you absolutely, one-hundred-percent certain that you want to forget everything we did? Melanie, *can* you forget?"

"Why are you doing this?" she whispered raggedly. "I *have* to forget, and so do you."

"No, sweetheart, maybe you think you have to forget, but I'm not even going to try."

"Eli, you're not going to talk me into…into—"

"Into bed?" He chuckled softly. "I've already got that, haven't I? The way I see it, Melanie, is that it's just a matter of time. You loved making love with me before, and you can tell yourself to forget it 'til hell freezes over, but no one ever forgets the kind of passion you and I shared."

He was right. She would never forget her vacation fling

with her grandfather's foreman, but that didn't mean she intended to stay married to him. Abruptly pushing her chair back and herself to her feet, she got out of Eli's way while he tried to catch his balance. He nearly fell flat on his face, but she knew better than to laugh or even smile.

Besides, she wasn't in a laughing mood even if his scramble to maintain his dignity was pretty funny. Lifting her chin, she said coolly, "You'll have to sleep on the floor, that's all there is to it."

After practically dumping him on his head, she was now issuing orders? Picking himself off the floor, Eli growled, "In your dreams, babe." He pointed to the bed. "*That's* where I'm sleeping. In fact, I'm going to bed now." He started unbuttoning his shirt.

"Do that in the bathroom!" she demanded. "And wear pajamas."

"I don't even own a pair of pajamas, nor do I intend to own any." Eli sat down to pull off his boots.

"You're just going to undress in front of me?"

He sent her an incredulous look. "It isn't as though I've got something under these clothes you haven't seen before, you know."

"*Which* I don't care to see again."

Eli grinned. "Bet you would."

"Oh, for Pete's sake." Muttering under her breath, Melanie marched into the bathroom. "Call out when you're under the covers. If it's not too much to ask, of course."

"Sarcasm doesn't become you, babe," he called cheerfully.

"Phony good cheer doesn't become you, either," she yelled. "When did you become such a happy camper? You hardly cracked a smile when I first met you."

"Guess it was you who put the smile on my face, Mrs. Forrester."

Melanie leaned weakly against a wall. She figured she'd be able to get through the days, but how in heaven's name was she going to deal with the nights?

She had to insist that her grandfather spend some time with her so they could talk, really talk, about the past, about her dad, about her job and Garrett's life as a rancher. There was so much for them to talk about, and until they at least made the effort, she couldn't go home. She wasn't even sure if it was Garrett's love she needed so badly because she felt now that sharing any part of his heart would help ease the ache in her own.

But home was where she belonged, not here in this bedroom with Eli when he made what he wanted from her so plain that even a dunce would get the message. She was far from being a dunce, but she knew she would never understand why some innocent fun with a sexy guy had boomeranged into a marriage she didn't want. And neither did Eli want it, damn him. What Eli wanted, and *all* Eli wanted, was for her to crawl into that bed and snuggle up to him.

Well, it wasn't going to happen. "Aren't you in bed yet?" she called impatiently.

"Just now. Come on in. I guarantee your delicate sensibilities won't be offended because I am covered from whiskers to toenails."

"Very funny," she said with a derisive expression as she walked into the bedroom. She stopped several feet from the foot of the bed. "I need some of those blankets."

"What for?"

"Well, if you're not gentleman enough to sleep on the floor, then I guess it's up to me."

"Oh, *you're* a gentleman. Sorry, but I didn't notice. Well, sure, mister, just help yourself to whatever blankets you want. Here, you'll need a pillow, too." Eli sat up, picked up the pillow he hadn't been using and tossed it at her.

She fumbled to catch it, then shot him a murderous look. "You're actually going to let me sleep on the floor?"

"Well, hon, I thought you wanted to."

"You...moron!" Melanie threw the pillow back on the bed. "Now you listen to me, Eli Forrester. Do you see that knob at the top of the headboard? If you follow that line straight down to the end of the mattress, it cuts the bed into two equal halves. You are to stay on your half, do you understand? And I mean all of you is to stay on your half. I don't want to feel a toe or a finger or any other part of you creeping over that line in the night. Do you get my meaning?"

"Since you put it so subtly, I might have to think about it for a while. No, on second thought, I do believe I have it." Reaching up, he laid his hand on the center knob, then he moved over a little so he could squint one eye down the invisible line Melanie had described. "Okay, let's make sure I understand completely. You want me to huddle on this half of the bed all night even though I'm twice as wide as you are and you won't take up even a half of your half?"

Her lips thinned. "You are not twice as wide as I am, and yes, I want you to 'huddle' on your half if you have to hang on to the mattress with your fingernails! You slept all right on your side last night, didn't you?"

Eli deliberately put on a guilty look. "I'm pretty sure my foot crossed the line a couple of times."

"You snored all night!" she screeched. "How would you know what your stupid foot did?"

"*You* snored all night. How would *you* know what my stupid foot did?"

She gasped. "I do not snore!"

Eli scratched the side of his neck, appearing remorseful

that he was the one delivering such heartbreaking news. "Sorry, sweetheart, but you do. Hasn't anyone ever told you that before?"

Melanie puffed up with outrage. She turned, walked over to the bureau and took out a pair of pajamas. *At least one of us will have something on! He probably isn't even wearing underwear!*

Chapter Eleven

Unlike the night before—when Melanie had slept so soundly that she hadn't been aware of Eli's presence for even one groggy moment—this night she could not ease the tension she was feeling enough to close her eyes. She tried repeatedly but found it a strain to keep them shut, so she gave up trying to attain the precious oblivion of sleep and stared into the dark.

She could hear Eli's even, quiet breathing—he was obviously not suffering insomnia as she was—and he was as far from her side of the bed as he could get and still be on it.

A tear formed in the corner of her eye and slid down her temple. How had she let her life get so out of hand? Had she left her independence in her San Diego apartment along with her courage and the iron will that made her a strong competitor in everything she did? Why was she a different person around her grandfather than she was with anyone else? When Garrett had talked about Judge Joseph and a wedding, she should have jumped up and said, "Whoa there, Granddad! *I* will decide when and whom I marry." And then she should have turned to Eli and asked, "Where is *your* backbone? Tell him no the way I just did."

Instead, they had both behaved like spineless wimps. True, they'd been terribly embarrassed, but embarrassment would never make the list of the ten best reasons for getting married—if there were ten. Wasn't there really only one truly sound reason for two people to stand before a judge or cleric and say "I do"?

"Love," Melanie whispered. Maybe she was a romantic—though she'd never really thought so before this—but loving a man till it hurt seemed to her to be the only reason she would willingly get married. And, of course, she certainly did not feel that way about Eli.

So what *did* she feel for her...? Oh, Lordy, could she even think the word *husband* tonight, when all she had to do was stretch out her arm a little to touch Eli?

Melanie's mouth was suddenly dry. Her feet felt hot, and she drew them from under the covers to cool them off. In fact, she felt rather feverish all over. Angrily, she pursed her lips though she knew in her heart that nothing she could do would stop the honesty of her thoughts. Nor the resentment that accompanied them.

Okay, dammit, I admit that's how it is. Eli is unutterably sexy and my hormones respond to his. It's a purely clinical reaction, easily explainable, I'm sure, by a biologist or a...a physiologist. Certainly it has nothing to do with the emotional kind of forever love that good marriages are founded on.

But admitting Eli's enormous sex appeal when they were in the same bed was not the smartest thing she could have done, and her feeling of restlessness would not permit her to lie still a moment longer.

She folded back the covers and got up, not really caring if she disturbed Eli. Not that she deliberately jostled the bed or anything like that, but if her quiet movements happened to wake him, then tough, she thought. This was a lot more her bed than his, and why should he be sleeping like a baby when she couldn't even keep her eyes shut?

Going to the open window, she breathed in the cool night air and looked up at the star-laden sky. Her thoughts jumped around, from *Should I leave Montana tomorrow, get the annulment over with and just put everything that's happened here behind me?* to *Granddad is terribly distraught over Dad's other sons. Why does he feel so responsible for* his *son's amoral behavior?* Then, *I'm married. It can't be true, but it is. Mom would keel over if she finds out. She must* never *know!*

"Melanie? Are you all right?"

She jumped a foot but didn't turn away from the window to face Eli. Not that she would be able to see him all that well in the dark. In fact, there was a modicum of comfort in knowing that neither could he see her.

"I'm fine," she said without warmth. "Go back to sleep."

"You're sure you're not ill?"

"A little heartsick, but not ill." The second the words were out of her mouth, she regretted them. "I'm fine," she said again. The last thing she wanted was his sympathy.

Eli laid his head back on the pillow, but he was awake now, and worse, he felt the intimacy of being alone with Melanie in a dark bedroom. He glanced at the lighted clock on the bedstand and saw it was almost midnight. Everyone on the ranch would be asleep. Only he and Melanie were awake, and that simple fact seemed to intensify the sensations tormenting his body.

"Come back to bed," he said softly.

The tone of his voice told Melanie exactly what his thoughts were. "Forget it," she said sharply. "It's not going to happen."

"You could still get the annulment. There are other acceptable reasons you could use."

"Like what?"

"Uh, abandonment? Nonsupport?"

"You're guessing. You don't know any more about it than I do, which isn't much. But I do know that a refusal to, uh, have sexual relations is grounds for an annulment."

"Yeah, but you're the one doing the refusing. Have you thought about that?"

Stunned, Melanie slowly turned around. "Maybe… maybe *you'll* have to get the annulment. Would you? I mean, if we find out that I can't?"

"I'm not sure I believe in annulment."

"But you believe in forced marriages? Good God!"

"Look at it this way, Melanie. If a lawyer asked me to explain why I wanted an annulment and I said because my wife didn't like sex, I'd be lying, wouldn't I? Because you do like sex, sweetheart. You love to make love. At least, you did before we got married. And, of course, that's what I'd have to tell my attorney. I can't imagine what he'd make of that, can you?"

"Why would you tell him so much?" she demanded furiously, just barely managing to keep her voice down. "All you'd have to say is that I refused you your marital rights."

"You don't want to lie to a lawyer, but it's okay for me to omit all sorts of pertinent facts? I don't think so, babe. A lie by omission is still a lie."

"And I'm sure you've never told a lie before," she drawled dryly. "As a matter of fact, everyone on the ranch thinks you're hiding some kind of horrible past because you never talk about yourself. I'd call that a lie by omission, wouldn't you?"

Eli became very still. "No, I'd call it exercising my right to privacy. Good night." He turned his back to her and pulled the covers up to his shoulders.

Melanie was so surprised by his reaction that she was momentarily speechless. *Boy, did I hit a nerve! Okay, Mr. Forrester, what's so terrible you can't talk about it?*

"Are you ignoring me?" she finally asked.

"I'm sleeping. Good night."

"Fine. Good night. Who wants to talk to you anyway?" Melanie moved to the bed and lay down. Hugging the very edge of her half, she covered herself with the blankets and settled her head on the pillow. After a few minutes of lying there, she heaved a woebegone sigh. Five minutes later, she did it again.

"That does it!" Eli exclaimed, and he turned over and slid across the bed so quickly she had no time to get out of his way. His next move was to rise up and pin her to the bed with his body. She gasped and struck out at him, but he caught and held her hands above her head, then brought his mouth down on hers, hard. When he'd kissed her breathless, he raised his head. "Be honest," he said hoarsely. "Tell me you want what I do."

"Does it matter what I want? You're forcing me to—"
Eli rolled away from her and, breathing hard, lay on his back. "Wha-what're you doing now?" she stammered.

"*Not* forcing you."

Melanie couldn't believe it when he scooted to his side of the bed and again showed her his back. Her lips still burned from his sizzling kiss, and the fire he'd ignited in the pit of her stomach didn't feel as though it was going to go out by itself.

But she'd caused her own frustration by talking about force! *You idiot, can't you do anything right anymore? You want him, you don't want him. Would you please make up your pitiful excuse for a mind? You're not only driving him crazy, but you're doing it to yourself!*

And so she lay there for a long time—wide awake, confused and miserable.

Garrett awoke at his usual time, but instead of immediately getting up as was his habit, he lay in his bed and thought of the dreams that had plagued him throughout the night. They were dreams of frustration in which he felt an overwhelming sense of urgency to complete some simple, everyday task but was unable, for various, inexplicable reasons, to accomplish anything.

He hated that kind of dream because the sense of frustration remained long after the dream itself had faded. He could feel it now, nipping at his vitals and chafing raw nerves. Truth was, he hadn't had a peaceful moment since opening Larry's safety-deposit box and he was still haunted by heartrending questions: Should he attempt to contact those boys or leave them alone? What would be best for them?

And those grandsons weren't the only ones he must consider. He had to think of Collin and Melanie, Alice and Lyle, and yes, even the Whitehorn Kincaids. Bringing six strange men into the family could have catastrophic results. What kind of men were they—honest and intelligent or greedy and self-serving?

Garrett heaved a sigh. He should not have this sort of problem at his age.

In the next heartbeat, he snorted and got out of bed,

disgusted with himself for permitting even that one brief moment of self-pity. His age didn't have a darned thing to do with his dilemma. He would have been just as stymied at age fifty as he was at seventy-two.

It was while he was dressing that he thought of Melanie again. The timing of her visit was unfortunate, *most* unfortunate. All his doing, of course. He'd invited her to the ranch after all. But then had come the shock of discovering those six grandsons, and every day since, they had been uppermost in his mind.

Proof positive of that was how heedlessly he'd reacted to walking in on Melanie and Eli. Maybe—as Eli had told him—they'd been in the process of falling in love, but dragging them off to get married before they were ready for such a momentous step had been a terrible thing for him to do. He'd talked to Eli about it; now he really must apologize to his granddaughter.

Yes, he would do that today.

Collin got to Melanie before Garrett did. Spotting her heading for the training field that morning, he called, "Hey, Mel! Wait up!"

She changed direction and walked toward her brother. Her all but sleepless night had caused dark circles under her eyes, and she was wearing sunglasses to avoid questions about her state of health. She wasn't physically ill after all, just down in the dumps over permitting anyone— even the grandfather she adored—to run her life.

"What's happening, bro?" she asked, putting a lilt in her voice she certainly didn't feel.

"I'm taking a truck to town for a load of supplies. Want to come along?"

She didn't need to be asked twice. "Yes! Am I dressed all right?" She was wearing jeans and boots.

"For Elk Springs?" Collin chuckled. "Sis, you're right in style. Come on, the truck's over there. That yellow one."

"Oh, a big truck." They started walking toward it.

"Need the space for the fifty bags of grain I'll be picking up at the feed store." He pulled a piece of paper from his shirt pocket. "I've also got a list of things to buy at the supermarket for Irma."

"I could fill that while you're loading the grain," Melanie offered.

"Yeah, guess you could."

Melanie playfully socked him on the arm. "I'm sure you didn't think of that yourself, did you?"

"Never crossed my mind," Collin said with a teasing grin.

"Yeah, right," she drawled with a grin of her own.

The farther they got from the ranch, the more light-hearted Melanie felt. One could not leave troubles behind that easily, but on the road with her brother, in a rattling truck with the windows down and a warm breeze on her face, she was able to shove them to the back of her mind.

"This is the reason I came to Montana," she told Collin.

"To take a ride in this old truck?"

She laughed. "To spend time with you, silly! And with Granddad, of course."

"I'm sorry it hasn't worked out the way you planned, Mel. It's funny how everything happened at once...your visit...opening that damn box of Dad's. I know Granddad was really happy you were coming, and then we went to the bank and everything changed. Don't get me wrong. I'm sure he was still glad you were coming. It's just that the things we found in that box were such a shock. He's wrestling with it all the time, you know."

"Not all the time," Melanie said a bit dryly. "He put

that worry aside long enough to arrange a wedding, don't forget.''

Collin frowned. "You don't hate him for it, do you?"

"No, I could never hate him. But I bet Mom could." They both thought about Sue Ellen for a few moments, then Melanie sighed and changed the subject. "Collin, why did you and Granddad go to Whitehorn last week?"

"You know about the old Kincaid family feud, don't you?"

"Mom told me about it. Why?" Melanie's eyes widened curiously as she looked at her brother. "Collin, did your trip to Whitehorn have something to do with that old feud?"

"I suppose in a roundabout way it did, but there really isn't a feud anymore. You see, about a year or so ago, Granddad, Dad and I went to Whitehorn to meet our cousin, Wayne Kincaid. Do you know who he is?"

"I have some idea, yes, but please go on."

"Well, Wayne has quite a history. He served in Vietnam and everyone thought he was dead, but he'd really been captured, and while he was gone his brother Dugin and his dad were murdered by Lexine Baxter."

"I know that part. Tell me what happened when the three of you finally met Wayne."

"Guess I really should say that Granddad and I met him. Dad was more interested in the ladies of Whitehorn than he was in getting to know Wayne."

"Oh, Collin," Melanie said sadly. "Was Dad really that bad?"

"Mel, if there was an attractive woman anywhere in the area, he was after her like a dog after a bone." Collin sent his sister a disgusted look. "How else would he have fathered a batch of illegitimate kids? I'll say right now that I think Granddad should forget he ever opened that Pandora's box in the bank.'' Collin made a left turn from the highway and explained, ''I'm going to take the scenic route to town so you can see Elk River.''

''Thank you,'' Melanie murmured. There was the most horrendous ache in her heart because the father she'd longed for all her life hadn't deserved love from any of his children, neither those legitimized by marriage nor the ones born out of wedlock. ''Did...do you hate him?'' she asked tremulously.

''Dad? No, I don't hate him, but even the piddling amount of respect I still had for him when he died vanished after I read those birth certificates, Mel. I know you feel that you missed something by not knowing him, but believe me, the only thing you missed was having to put up with his skirt-chasing, gambling, hard-drinking reputation. Count your blessings, Melanie.''

''You sound so bitter,'' she said, wiping away a tear.

''Did anyone tell you how he died?''

''Wasn't it a heart attack?''

''Our father died at age fifty-four of cardiac arrest while drinking bourbon, smoking a cigar, perusing the *Wall Street Journal* and getting a back massage from one of his current girlfriends.'' Collin angrily slapped the steering wheel. ''He died exactly as he lived, and it was all so damned unnecessary. Yes, I'm bitter, but I'll tell you, Melanie, it was just like Dad to die too young and leave a mess for someone else to clean up. And who's going to do it? Who feels an obligation to do it?''

''Granddad,'' Melanie whispered brokenly. ''How could he have had a son like Dad?''

''I think we're all asking ourselves that question, Mel.''

''Is Wayne like Dad?''

''Heck, no. Wayne's a great guy. He has a wife and kids

and he's devoted to his family, Mel. Dad never knew the meaning of the word *devotion*.''

Melanie heaved an emotional sigh, then changed the direction of their conversation. ''You still didn't explain why you and Granddad went to Whitehorn last week.''

''The Kincaid ranch over there is up for sale. Granddad is thinking of buying it to give to our half brothers.''

''My goodness,'' Melanie said in surprise. ''He really does feel obligated, doesn't he?''

''I wish he didn't,'' Collin said grimly.

Melanie was about to say something else when she realized the road was running parallel to a river. ''Collin, it's a white-water river!'' she exclaimed. ''Oh, look at the raft out there. I've always thought that would be so much fun.''

''The Elk River is good rafting at this time of year, Mel, because it's high from spring runoff. By the end of summer, the water level will be so low that the rocks creating those exciting rapids will be about all you'll see.''

''Really.'' Melanie was practically on the edge of her seat, watching the big orange raft carrying eight people— wearing orange life vests—bob up and down with the swift river currents. ''Collin, have you done that?''

''Lots of times. I used to pal around with a guy who worked as a river guide.''

''And you went rafting with him?''

''Yes. What was really fun was that he had a small raft of his own. It wasn't qualified for commercial use—there are lots of safety restrictions and rules if you're doing it as a business—but we'd pile two or three friends in it and spend the entire day on the river.''

''Isn't he your pal anymore?''

''I'm sure he is, but since Dad died…'' Collin heaved a weighty sigh.

Melanie turned and touched her brother's arm. ''I understand,'' she said softly. ''Nothing's been the same for you and Granddad, has it?''

''I think we were doing okay until that day at the bank. Granddad was sad, of course. I could always tell when he was thinking about Dad, but I believe he was healing.''

''Were you healing, too?''

''Mel, Dad and I had a pretty weird relationship. Granddad was more of a father to me than Dad ever was. When I got old enough, Dad wanted me to go drinking and carousing with him. I really believe he would've liked me better if I'd done it.''

''Collin, did...did he ever talk about me?''

''No,'' Collin said quietly. ''I'm sorry, Mel, but I can't soft-pedal the truth. Try to take heart in the fact that he never would've known I was alive, either, if I hadn't been living under his nose.''

Melanie nodded. ''I know that. I've always known it, I suppose, but isn't it strange that he could so easily forget me, barely notice you, then keep a bunch of mementos of six sons that no one knew he had?''

''Damn strange,'' Collin muttered. ''Sometimes I think it was his way of having the last laugh. I mean, here's all that stuff in the safety-deposit box and then that letter he wrote to Granddad and me. At the end it said something about his not having anything to give those sons, but maybe Granddad or I did.''

''That's terrible! No wonder Granddad feels obligated.''

''Yeah, no wonder,'' Collin said bitterly. ''But you see what I mean about Dad's having the last laugh?''

''Yes, I see,'' Melanie whispered, and had to take off her glasses to wipe her eyes again. ''Why would he be so cruel to Granddad?''

''You got me, Mel. And can you imagine Granddad—a good and decent man like him—blaming himself for Dad's shortcomings? And for Aunt Alice's nasty temperament? He was talking about that not too long ago."

Melanie registered the remark about Alice, but she was more interested in discussing their father. "Then he admits Dad's faults? I've wondered about that."

"I'm sure he always knew the truth, Mel, but did you know that even though Dad rarely did a lick of work on the ranch, Granddad gave him a steady paycheck?"

"For heaven's sake, why? Maybe if Dad had been tossed out on his ear and told to earn his own living, he would've shaped up."

"I don't think Granddad could ever toss anyone out on their ear, especially a family member. The obligation he feels toward our dear half brothers is serious business, Mel."

"Don't be angry at them, Collin," Melanie said gently. "Nothing Dad did is their fault. No one asks to be born, nor does anyone get to choose his parents."

Collin fell silent, but after a few minutes he grinned at his sister. "Let's lighten up, okay? Are you sure you want to take a rafting trip down the river?"

Melanie's face lit up. "Yes! Can you go with me?"

"You bet. We'll make the arrangements in town today."

"Sorry, Collin, but we're booked solid through May," Franny Lester said with a sincerely apologetic expression on her face.

Melanie was terribly disappointed, but she didn't say so because Franny was such a pleasant woman.

"Darn," Collin said, showing his own disappointment. "Franny, if someone should cancel out, would you call the ranch and let me know?"

"Be glad to, Collin."

On their way from the little building housing the Elk

Springs Rafting Company back to the truck, Collin explained, "It's just a small operation, sis. It really couldn't be anything else with the season so short."

"It's all right, Collin. You did your best."

Collin was silent until they were in the truck, then he said, "Wait here a minute. I'm going back inside and ask Franny if Sean is working for them this year."

"Sean is the friend you were telling me about? The one with his own raft?"

"Right. Sean Acton. Sit tight. I'll be right back."

Melanie watched her brother sprint across the street and wondered how the Lesters made their living when the rafting season was over. *The Lesters are none of your business. If you're in a worrying mood, take on one of the many problems nearly crippling the Kincaid family, yourself included.*

"Melanie Forrester," she whispered. "Melanie Kincaid Forrester." Thinking of her married name made her feel a bit dizzy. Then her thoughts jumped to the dozen or so nights she had left of her vacation. She could make it through the days just fine, but in her heart she knew that the nights were going to get tougher and tougher. Last night, Eli had kissed her, and he would have done more if she hadn't used the word *force* on him. It concerned her that one of these nights *she* might be the one to start something. Eli certainly wouldn't object the way she had. Then where would she be, married and legally unable to do anything about it except file for a divorce? *Everyone would know then! I can't let that happen. Mom would be devastated, and so would I.*

Collin got into the truck, startling Melanie. She'd been so entangled in her own thoughts she hadn't seen him returning. "Well?" she said.

"He's working for them again this season, but he's off

today. I'm going to drive by his house.'' Collin started the engine.

''You're thinking of asking Sean to take us rafting with his own equipment?''

''Yeah, I'm hoping he can.''

''Not today, though, right?''

Collin grinned. ''Getting cold feet already?'' He looked at his sister and his grin vanished. ''Mel, we can forget the whole thing, you know. Rafting a white-water river isn't for everyone.''

''I don't want to forget it, Collin, but I rather think a person should be wearing sneakers instead of cowboy boots.''

''You're right about that. Besides, we have to go to the feed store and the supermarket today. We'll just run by Sean's place and see if he's home.''

When they drove into the driveway of a large brick home with a perfectly manicured lawn, Melanie gaped in surprise. ''*This* is Sean's home? Why did I have the impression that he was a…a…fly-by-nighter?''

Collin chuckled. ''He might have been if he hadn't inherited all of his parents' worldly goods. Sean's in a position to work when he feels like it. When the rafting season is over, he does odd jobs around town—mostly volunteer work. He does some writing, too. Quite a few of his articles on Montana wildlife have been published in sportsmen's magazines.''

''Sounds like an interesting character. Is he your age?''

''Sean's a few years older. Oh, there he is now.'' Collin opened his door and got out. ''Sean…hello!''

Melanie watched the tall, lanky guy in cutoffs and sleeveless T-shirt walking toward the truck. He had longish, almost white, blond hair and a fabulous tan. She immediately thought of the surfers on the California beaches. Sean

Acton looked a lot more like them than he did the other men she'd met in Montana.

"Collin, how're you doing?"

The two men shook hands. "Not too bad, considering," Collin replied. "Sean, I'd like you to meet my sister, Melanie."

Melanie slid across the seat to the driver's door and got out. She smiled at Sean Acton and he gave her such a dazzling smile in return that she was flattered.

"Very nice meeting you, Sean," she said.

"The pleasure is all mine, Melanie. Collin, you dog, when you mentioned your sister before, you could have at least hinted that she was movie-star gorgeous."

Melanie flushed a little and Collin laughed. "Just watch it, you silver-tongued devil. This is my baby sister you're coming on to. Sean, we only stopped for a minute. Melanie wants to go rafting while she's here, and the Lesters are booked for the remainder of her visit. Do you still have your equipment?"

"Sure do." Sean smiled at Melanie again. "Would one day next week be all right? I'm pretty tied up this week."

"Next week would be great," Melanie said. "If it's all right with Collin, that is." She looked at her brother. "Collin?"

"Any day next week is fine with me," Collin said. "You name it, Sean."

"Aw, heck," Sean said with a teasing grin. "Are you going along? I thought I was going to have Melanie all to myself. Oh, well, so be it. How about Thursday?"

"Great." Collin held out his hand for another handshake. "Sorry we have to rush off, Sean, but we've got some errands to take care of before heading home. What time should we be here on Thursday morning?"

"Around eight. I'll have everything ready to go."

"Thank you, Sean," Melanie said before climbing back into the truck.

Sean waved them off, calling, "See you next Thursday."

When they were under way, Melanie laughed. "Your pal is quite a flirt."

"Yeah, but he's really a good guy. If he'd known you were married, he never would have said what he did."

Melanie's heart sank. She sure hadn't been feeling married and, in fact, she'd enjoyed Sean Acton's flattery. How odd, though, that the second she thought of Eli she felt a tingle dance up her spine and her breath catch in her throat. As cute as Sean Acton was, she realized he would never affect her the way Eli did. She sighed heavily.

"Anything wrong?" Collin asked.

"A lot," Melanie replied unhappily. "But let's talk about something pleasant, okay?"

"Sure, Mel," Collin said quietly.

Chapter Twelve

The greatest misery of Eli's life was the drowning death of his brother. Not even a close second to that tribulation, but painful nonetheless, had been his parents' grievous anger. Eli had been there, and why had he let it happen? Surely there must have been *something* he could have done to save his brother.

Eli had always known that Carson had been the Forresters' favorite son. He had accepted second place in his parents' affections without resentment because he, too, had adored his fun-loving, charismatic younger brother. From childhood on, Carson had had more friends than he could keep track of. His lively wit, his intelligence and his incredible good looks had been like a flame, attracting people wherever he went.

Never once had it occurred to Eli to envy Carson's popularity. They'd been as close as two brothers could be, and it had nearly killed Eli that anyone would think that he hadn't done everything humanly possible to save Carson. Almost mindless with grief himself, it had taken a while for Eli to grasp the reason for his parents' cold withdrawal, and when it finally dawned on him that they were blaming him for Carson's death, he hadn't even attempted to defend himself. Instead, he'd left Baltimore and headed west.

It was time, he'd figured, to prove himself. He'd never wanted to be an attorney anyway—his father's idea—and he'd known in his soul that he could make it on his own without the cushion of his family's wealth and contacts. He had, for all intents and purposes, left his past—and the accompanying agony it held—behind.

But, he had recently realized, there was more than one kind of agony in this world. Sleeping with a woman he would happily walk barefoot over hot coals for if she would treat him as she had before their marriage was a unique sort of anguish. He had to wonder how Melanie could run so hot and cold. She had teased and flirted with him unmercifully prior to their sad little wedding ceremony, and now that anything they might want to do in their bedroom—or anywhere else, for that matter—was legal and even blessed, she wouldn't let him near her.

The question that Eli kept bumping up against was why he was so hung up on Melanie. Yes, she was a knockout in the looks department, but he'd known beautiful women before and not had the almost constant ache in his gut that he suffered now. Same with intelligence, education and sense of humor. That left Melanie with one thing that was so much more potent than anything he'd felt in any other woman—sex appeal, oodles of sex appeal, *mountains* of sex appeal.

That conclusion wasn't at all comforting, not when he had to sleep in the same bed with her night after night.

Unless, of course, he betrayed her confidence and told

Garrett what was really going on between him and Melanie, then moved his clothes and things back to the bunkhouse. It would give the men a good chuckle, but did he care if anyone laughed at him?

No way, but what if they joked and laughed at Melanie's expense?

Ah, that was a whole other ball game. He could not put Melanie's reputation at risk no matter how agonizing were the nights. He would live through them—somehow.

Garrett's somber demeanor at the dinner table that evening reduced conversation to comments such as ''Pass the salt.''

Melanie ate in silence, as the others were doing, and worried about her grandfather. *This thing with Dad's other sons is getting him down. Maybe Collin is right. Maybe Granddad should forget he ever found out about them. Look at him tonight. He seems to be aging before my eyes. Why should he take on Dad's responsibilities when Dad himself apparently never made a move toward those six kids?*

''Did you take Melanie to Alice's house when you were in Elk Springs today?'' Garrett asked Collin.

''No, sir,'' Collin replied. ''I never even thought of it, to be honest. Did you, Melanie?''

''I'm sorry, Granddad, but no, I'm afraid Aunt Alice never entered my mind. I do intend to see her while I'm here, of course.''

Collin grinned. ''Mel was too excited about rafting the Elk River to think of anything else.''

Eli stared at Collin, feeling as though someone had just stabbed him in the heart with a red-hot poker. ''You...you're not taking her rafting, are you?'' he stammered.

Melanie turned her head to see Eli's face and was startled by the ashen color of his skin. "Is there some reason he shouldn't take me rafting?" she inquired, genuinely curious about Eli's peculiar reaction.

"It...it's dangerous," Eli mumbled without looking at her.

"It can be," Collin agreed, "but Sean knows that river like the back of his hand."

Eli was aghast. "Sean Acton? You're taking Melanie on the river in Acton's little raft?"

Melanie frowned. Eli was acting like a concerned husband and he didn't have the right. "Don't argue with Collin about this," she said in an undertone, hoping Eli was the only one at the table who heard her. "It was all my idea. I'm going rafting, and that's the end of it."

"Like hell it is," Eli muttered.

Melanie was outraged. How dare he try to tell her what she could or could not do? In fact, she was suddenly so angry that she got up, excused herself and left the dining room. At first, she went outside and stood on the front porch, hands on the rail, breathing deeply to calm herself, and looked out across the lawn and the fields beyond. The anger that had flared so quickly in the dining room gradually diminished, but the question of Eli's gall remained. Why on earth would he object to her going rafting, and how did he even have the nerve *to* object?

She mulled the questions over for a while, and could not accept the only conclusion that made any sense—he was taking his role of husband seriously! Why else would he warn her that rafting was dangerous and then act all protective and macho about it?

"Well, we'll just see about that," she fumed to herself. When she and Collin had finally gotten back to the ranch, it had been too late for her to shower and change into a dress before dinner as she'd been doing every day. Since her mood wasn't the best at the moment—she couldn't possibly be good company for anyone—she decided to go up to her room and shower now.

Because she wanted it out of the way before Eli showed his face in "their" bedroom, she showered and shampooed quickly. Wearing a white terry robe and running a comb through her damp curls, she walked into the bedroom to get some clean pajamas from the bureau. She stopped cold when she saw Eli getting up from a chair, but then she ignored him and began looking through her lingerie in the bureau drawer. There were no clean pajamas left, she'd worn them all and hadn't done any laundry. But there were several slinky, silky nightgowns, and pursing her lips in frustration, she slammed the drawer shut and turned around to face Eli.

"You're up here this early for a reason, which I'm sure you're dying to lay on me," she said coldly. "But if it's about my rafting trip, just keep it to yourself."

"It *is* about rafting, and I *can't* keep it to myself. Melanie, at this time of year the river is treacherous. Taking the rapids in one of the Lesters' large commercial rafts would be bad enough, but doing it in Acton's toy raft is pure idiocy. Please don't do it."

"And your advice is based on what? Are you an expert on white-water rafting?"

"No, I'm not, but I've lived here for four years, and there have been some fatal accidents on that river during that time alone. Ask anyone, they'll tell you the same thing. I'm surprised that Collin would let you, his only sister, take such a risk."

"Collin's not a coward, and neither am I."

Eli became very still. "Meaning that I am?"

Melanie looked him in the eye. "How am I supposed to

answer that when I know so little about you? You could be a terrible coward or the bravest man in Montana and I wouldn't know it. I don't understand why you're so against river rafting when it's such a popular sport, and yes, I'm sure there are accidents, but there's danger in everything a person does. You're risking your neck when you get out of bed in the morning, for Pete's sake.''

"Hardly the same thing," Eli muttered darkly. She thought he was a coward and when it came to water she was probably right. But it stung all the same. He should tell her about Carson, but how could he talk to anyone about something that still hurt so much he could barely stand thinking about it?

His thoughts changed abruptly. She was sexy in a shapeless robe that would look like a sack on most women. She was sexy with damp hair, bare feet and a shiny face completely devoid of makeup. What he'd like to do was untie the sash of that robe and make love to her until she swore he was the greatest man who'd ever lived. She wouldn't call him a coward then, by God!

He didn't trust himself *not* to do it, so he turned and headed for the door.

Melanie's eyes widened, but she didn't try to stop him from leaving. When he was gone, she shook her head in dismay because she truly did not understand him. For crying out loud, why would he care if she put herself in danger?

That question led to one that weakened her knees. *Did* he care? Sinking to a chair, she thought of another perturbing question: Did she *want* him to care?

In his office, Garrett was on the phone with Wayne. "Glad you called, Wayne, always glad to hear from you, but I'm having a heck of a time making a decision about buying the Whitehorn ranch. It's because I can't decide what's best for Larry's six sons. One minute I believe those young men should know the truth of their heritage, and the next I worry about the turbulence I might bring into their lives by even locating them, let alone introducing myself as their grandfather and then talking about Kincaid family history.''

"It's a tough one all right," Wayne agreed. "But I told you I'd let you know if a serious buyer came on the scene, and a representative of Beale Corporation has already inspected the ranch twice. I think he's getting ready to present an offer, Garrett.''

"Beale Corporation! Thunderation, that outfit already owns millions of acres of ranch land all over the country! Wayne, it'd break my heart to see Kincaid land swallowed up by a heartless entity like Beale. They run their ranches like assembly lines."

"I know, Garrett, but if they present a good offer, what can I do?"

"You can tell 'em it's already sold to a fellow named Garrett Kincaid, Wayne."

"You're serious, Garrett? What'll you do with the place if you decide against contacting Larry's sons?"

"I'll cross that bridge if and when I come to it. Wayne, Collin and I'll be coming to Whitehorn tomorrow and we'll be staying until the ranch deal is wrapped up nice and legal."

"Sounds like good news to me, Garrett. I'll pass it along."

After Garrett hung up, he went to find Collin, who was outside talking to Eli.

"Sean's never had an accident on the river, Eli, and don't forget that I'll be in the raft with Melanie. Do you think I'd let anything happen to her?''

Eli felt sick to his stomach. *Do you think I'd let anything happen to Carson?* He couldn't remember actually saying those words to anyone, but he'd certainly been as positive as Collin was about keeping his sibling safe from harm. The arrogance of men was incredible. *Nothing will go wrong because* I'll *be there!*

"Collin, neither you nor anyone else can predict—"

"Evening, Eli," Garrett said. "Collin, come and take a little walk with me. I have something to tell you."

"Sure, Granddad. See you later, Eli."

Eli watched them walking off together, then he strode around to the front of the house and sat on the porch. He couldn't convince Melanie. He couldn't convince Collin. They were going to get into that little raft with Sean and something terrible was sure to happen.

Groaning, Eli put his head in his hands. If he lost Melanie…

Slowly, he dropped his hands. How could he lose something he'd never had? Oh, he'd had her briefly. At Dove Lake, for instance, she'd been his completely for a short time. And the day that Garrett had walked in on them, she'd been loving, sexy, playful and hotter than Hades. She'd been all his for about thirty minutes that day, and if they hadn't been interrupted, she might have belonged solely to him for hours and hours.

So what was all this intimate introspection about? Was he falling in love with Melanie?

It was such a startling idea that Eli jumped to his feet. He'd take a walk to cool down his libido before going to bed and he would *stop* thinking such crazy thoughts!

Collin listened to his grandfather talking about buying the Whitehorn ranch without interrupting him, but finally he had to say something. "Then you've decided to contact those men?"

"Those men are your half brothers, Collin."

"Those men probably don't even know we exist."

"Possibly, but I know they exist, and so do you, Collin."

"The whole county probably knows it by now," Collin mumbled.

"Whom are you so angry with, Collin?" Garrett asked gently. "Me? Your dad?"

"I...I wish we'd never had to open that safety-deposit box," Collin blurted.

Garrett surprised him by saying, "So do I, Collin, so do I. But we did open it, and what kind of person could ever forget what it contained?"

"Dad was counting on your feeling that way," Collin said with some rancor. "He turned his own back on six sons, but he knew you would immediately think of them as grandsons. He knew what family meant to you. He used your strong sense of responsibility to get you to do what he had neither the guts nor the money to do himself...find his illegitimate kids and make them a part of the Kincaid family."

"I'd hate to think Larry was that devious," Garrett said sadly. He sighed.

"He was worse," Collin said, this time conveying the breadth of his anger and bitterness in every syllable.

"Collin," Garrett said quietly, "do you really feel I should do nothing?"

Guilt assailed Collin. He loved his grandfather. Garrett had taken him in when he'd been a surly, know-it-all, unlikable teenager and made a man out of him. What if someone had said then, "Don't put yourself out for that kid, Garrett. He's not worth the effort."

"I'm not angry with you, Granddad, and no one has the

right to judge any decision you make about those kids. But I can't help being disgusted with Dad, and yes, I believe he was devious enough to put the mess he'd made of his life squarely on your shoulders.''

''He didn't know he was going to die, Collin. Maybe he had all sorts of plans for those boys.''

''Like he had for Melanie? He never once sent her a birthday card, for God's sake!''

Garrett frowned. ''Melanie, yes. She's not been treated well by the Kincaid men, has she? Except for you, that is. You never forgot your sister, did you?''

''No, I didn't. Granddad, I know the Whitehorn deal is important and I know you want me there, but what about my promise to take Melanie rafting next Thursday?''

''Hmm, you're right. I really don't want to disappoint her again, but I feel that you should go to Whitehorn with me.''

''Maybe Eli would take her,'' Collin suggested thoughtfully. ''He might even feel better about her going rafting if he was with her.''

Garrett looked pleased. ''Eli is worried about her rafting the river? Well, well. Maybe something good will come of that marriage after all.''

Eli quietly turned the knob and opened the door. The bedroom was dark, but a sliver of light coming from the bathroom permitted Eli to enter without crashing into something. It was a kindness he hadn't expected, and he would have thanked Melanie if she'd been awake.

Actually, her back was to the door and most of the room, so Eli could only guess about her being asleep or merely pretending to be. In either case, it was best to leave her be, so he tiptoed into the bathroom to brush his teeth, then snapped off the light and went to his side of the bed. After undressing down to his briefs, he cautiously slid down the covers and sat on the bed. Finally he lay on his side, turning his back to Melanie, and shut his eyes. He was tired and fell asleep within minutes.

Melanie wanted to scream. How could anyone fall asleep that fast? Even when she didn't have a dozen things to worry about, it took her a while to go to sleep. Good grief, the worries she'd acquired in Montana would probably keep her awake for the rest of her life!

And while Eli had no vested interest in Larry Kincaid's horde of illegitimate kids, one would certainly think that a forced marriage would be enough to disturb his slumber just a little. Maybe *she* should disturb his slumber, she thought resentfully. It certainly wouldn't be hard to do. In fact, she could slide over and snuggle up to him with her eyes closed. Act as though she was dead to the world and totally unaware of anything she was doing.

But what if she awakened a lion instead of a lamb? And what if she awoke her own passion, kept so tightly under control since that fateful Sunday?

No, she dared not start anything with Eli, not even in fun. Maybe that was the hardest part of this farce of a marriage, smothering her natural tendency to tease and kid around and make people laugh. Granted, she hadn't only been thinking of laughter when she'd teased Eli. He'd gotten under her skin from the very beginning, and he'd been so darned serious about everything that she hadn't been able to resist the temptation of getting him to unbend.

Yeah, that was really brilliant. Now you're married to him.

"Married," she whispered as fresh shock waves slammed through her. It was a word she would never get used to, and why should she even try to get used to it when the whole awful thing was going to be nullified as soon as she returned to California and the law allowed?

Although she was horribly restless and positive that she would never fall asleep, she was awakened hours later by eerie sounds. Her eyes opened wide and her heart began thudding. After taking a few seconds to get her bearings, she realized that it was Eli making those strange, frightening noises. When he began thrashing around, she knew he was suffering a bad dream.

Without a second's hesitation, she reached across the bed and shook his arm. "Eli...wake up! You're having a nightmare."

He moved his head back and forth on the pillow and shouted, "No...no!"

She tried again, moving closer and leaning over him. "Eli...wake up before you wake everyone in the house! Come on now, pull yourself out of that dream and open your eyes."

Getting so close to him had been a mistake, Melanie realized when his arms began flailing again. She ducked and dodged, but his right hand connected with the left side of her head. It wasn't a love tap, and she fell back against the pillow and actually saw stars.

"Ouch, you big jerk," she moaned.

Eli was suddenly awake and aware of Melanie lying next to him. The nightmare and the blow he'd struck were jumbled in his brain. He hoisted himself to an elbow to peer at her face.

"Tell me I really didn't hit you," he said hoarsely. "Damn, Melanie, I'm really sorry." Without preamble, he stretched over her to switch on the bedside lamp. Then he turned his attention back to her. She was holding her hand just to the left of her eye. "Let me see what I did."

She moved her hand and watched him wince. "What?" she said, alarmed by his reaction.

"I think you're going to have a shiner tomorrow. Aw, hell." Eli fell back against the bed. "How are you going to explain that to Garrett?" he groaned.

"Is there anything wrong with the truth?" she asked.

"I...I was dreaming, Melanie." Dreaming about deep water with treacherous undercurrents, and a capsized canoe, and him swimming and diving like a crazy man to try to find his brother. He hadn't had that horrifying nightmare for some time and supposed it had been triggered by Melanie's determination to go rafting.

"No kidding," she drawled sarcastically. "What was all the thrashing around about? And the weird sounds you were making? You woke me up, you know."

"I...was swimming."

She blinked incredulously at him. "That's all it was? A dream about swimming? Good Lord! What would you do to someone who tried to wake you up during a really awful dream?" She finally caught on to how intently he was looking her up and down, then remembered that she was wearing a nightgown instead of pajamas.

The immediate heat she felt in the pit of her stomach was startling and discomfiting. She didn't dare get carried away with Eli again. He wasn't just any man. He was her husband, and she had to break that bond as soon as possible, not make it stronger with more intimacy between them.

"Move to your own side of the bed," she said, forcing frost into her voice. Quickly switching off the lamp so that everything was dark and her nightgown could no longer be a point of interest for Eli, she sat on the bed. "Did you move over?" she asked warily before lying down herself.

"I'm over," Eli said, and when she had settled down on

her side of the bed, he said, "I have to ask you something. Why did you tease me into making love before?"

"It...didn't mean anything."

"Do you do that all the time?"

Melanie sucked in a shocked breath. "No, I do not!"

"Then why did you do it with me?"

"I...I'm not sure. I mean, I can see why you might have thought that I was, uh, easy pickings, and I do like to kid around a lot, but..." Melanie frowned in the dark, then said in a small, confused voice, "I don't know why I went so far with you."

Eli slid over, and before she could do more than gasp, he had gathered her into his arms. "Don't worry. I just want to hold you."

"I don't believe you. I saw the way you were looking at my nightgown." She sounded breathless to her own ears, but she couldn't help the sudden hard pounding of her heart. And she hadn't objected to his embrace nearly as strenuously as she should have. But his arms around her and his body curved into hers felt so right, so good, and it seemed to fill a void within herself.

"How does your eye feel?" Eli said softly with his face so close to hers that she could feel his breath on her cheek.

"It's...all right."

"You said you didn't know why you came on to me, but I think you do know and you won't let yourself admit it."

"I flirted with you, yes, but I wouldn't call it coming on to you!" she exclaimed indignantly.

"You wanted me right from the start," he whispered in her ear. "If, as you said, you don't act that way with other men, then I must be special." He slid his hand across her waist. "Am I special, Melanie?"

A good thirty seconds passed before she whispered, ''I guess you are.''

''You guess?''

She was getting very aroused and very nervous about it. If he moved his hand up or down her body just a few inches, he would be caressing either her aching breasts or the stressful yearning she felt between her legs.

''Eli,'' she said breathlessly, ''you had better return to your side of the bed.''

''I'm only holding you.''

''You're doing a lot more than that. You're touching me, your body is pressed against mine, your skin is hot and…and…''

''And I'm hard and you can feel it.''

''I'd have to be numb not to feel it!''

''And we both know you're not the least bit numb, don't we, sweetheart?''

His bedroom voice had become sensually persuasive. Melanie's own senses had started betraying her. She wanted so much to be kissed and caressed, and then when she reached the point where nothing was enough anymore, she wanted him inside her. Him, Eli, her husband, no one else, no other man.

''Oh, no,'' she moaned in a husky cry of defeat. She wouldn't be able to honestly tell a lawyer that she had not made love with Eli. But, dear heaven, she wanted him so.

She turned toward him and put her arms around his neck. He responded instantly by kissing her passionately, hungrily, then rolling them both over so that she was on her back and he was on top of her. She whimpered a little as his body pressed hers into the mattress. She could feel every manly inch of him and ignored the voice in her head that said, *You can't do this, Melanie Kincaid Forrester, you can't!*

But her body was no longer listening to her brain, and when Eli's mouth sought hers again, she parted her lips and her legs at just about the same moment. It was all so simple to accomplish because their every movement was in tandem. Together they got rid of his briefs and her nightgown and then, naked and feverish, they kissed each other almost savagely.

Neither said anything intelligible, but the communication between lovers wild for each other didn't require words, and Eli knew when something he did pleasured her, and she knew that *everything* she did increased his desire.

When he finally entered her, their unbridled ride to completion was so hot and intense that Melanie could not hold back her cries. Eli heard her, but right at that moment he didn't care if everyone in the house heard both of them. They were adults in an adult household, and they were married. No matter how much noise they made, no one would be tactless enough to mention it.

"My love," he whispered, then roared her name as he reached the crest of the wave.

Under him, Melanie was moaning softly. He moved to the bed to take his weight off her, and she whispered huskily, "I've just seen the other side of the moon." Then turning onto her side, she curved her backside against his belly and fell asleep.

Chapter Thirteen

Melanie awoke with a smile on her face. She stretched lazily, as a cat does after a nap in the sun. The peace within her was astounding.

But even afloat in her sea of tranquillity, she knew it couldn't last. All she was feeling was the aftermath of profoundly satisfying lovemaking. Eli was an incredible lover, and they fit together so perfectly it was as though they were two halves of something.

"Two halves of a peach," Melanie said under her breath. "Or a pecan?" Laughing softly, she stretched again. Then a new thought erased her smile. *You could very easily become addicted to Eli's brand of lovemaking. Then where would you be? Certainly not in San Diego hoping for that job promotion!* "You are such a fool," she muttered, and threw back the covers, winced at her nudity, then ran for the bathroom.

* * *

Eli had heard the term "walking on air" before, but he'd merely attributed it to some overly romantic female's imagination and let it go at that. He'd certainly never heard any of his male friends use the phrase and he grinned rather foolishly when it occurred to him that day that "walking on air" was pretty much how he felt.

He wore that silly grin for most of the day, a sight that the cowpokes working with him didn't miss. In fact, while Eli mentally relived the sexual highlight of his life, the men kept poking each other and chuckling. They were all pretty surprised that Eli, a guy who'd *never* smiled before his marriage to the boss's granddaughter, now couldn't seem to keep a straight face or his mind on his work. And they knew where his mind was, too, by gosh and by golly, and who could blame him? That Melanie was one "mighty purty little gal" after all. Every man agreed on that point, which made it easy for them to understand why Eli had taken such a nosedive for Melanie, but what she'd seen in Eli had them all puzzled.

"He's the goshdurn foreman," one man said with a snort. "A lot of women like men in power. Now, I ain't never been partial to that type of lady, but—"

"You'd be partial to any lady that'd look at you twice," someone said, cracking them all up.

"Well, Eli ain't in power," another said disgustedly. "Garrett's the only power on this here ranch. And maybe Collin…a little bit. All Eli does is tell us what Garrett tells him to tell us."

That seemed to make sense, and since Eli just happened to be looking their way at that moment, they stopped their debate and went back to work.

They were in for another surprise, which came around two that afternoon. Eli, on horseback, rode up to them.

"Just keep working on that fence until quitting time. I'm heading in now." He rode away.

One old-timer took off his hat and scratched his head. "Well, I'll be danged. That's the first time Eli ever quit before the rest of us."

"That's 'cause he's in love," big Homer said in a falsetto voice. They laughed so hard over big Homer talking like a woman that some of them rolled on the ground.

No matter what Melanie tried to accomplish with makeup that morning, the bruise at the corner of her left eye had still been visible. As Eli had predicted, she had a shiner. Her sunglasses helped to conceal it, of course, but she knew if anyone really looked at her, they would ask questions.

She was lucky in one way, though. She'd gotten up too late to eat breakfast with the men, which had eliminated any raised eyebrows from that sector. Then she'd eluded Irma's sharp eyes by dashing through the kitchen and grabbing something from the fruit basket with a comment about not being very hungry.

Outside, there hadn't been a person in sight, and after eating her fruit while wandering around the deserted ranch—sighing hopelessly every few minutes because she'd made such a critical mistake with Eli last night—she finally went to the training field and worked with the fillies. Putting the young mares through their paces definitely helped her mood, and it wasn't long before she stopped worrying about herself and concentrated on the task at hand.

Around two that afternoon, she heard Collin call, "Hey, Mel!" from the fence line. Very glad to see him, she smiled broadly and walked over to join him.

"Hey, Collin," she said cheerfully.

"Irma said you'd been out here all day. I brought you a sandwich." Collin held a plastic-wrapped sandwich over the barbed wire, and Melanie accepted it eagerly.

"Thanks, bro. I guess I lost track of time." Unwrapping the sandwich, she took a big bite. "Mmm, good."

"Mel, what's wrong with your eye?"

Her heart sank, but she managed to answer in a normal voice. "Eli had a nightmare last night and I made the mistake of trying to wake him up when he was swinging his arms."

Collin's face froze. "Eli hit you?"

"Not on purpose, silly. He was devastated when he finally came awake and realized what he'd done."

"Sounds kind of peculiar to me," Collin said with a scowl. "Is that the truth, Mel, or are you protecting him?"

"Listen, Collin, if Eli had deliberately struck me, I would have yelled so loudly I'd have brought down the roof. Believe me, you would have heard about it the second it happened."

"I did hear something last night," Collin said thoughtfully.

"Probably just the wind," Melanie said nonchalantly, hoping to high heaven that Collin hadn't heard her and Eli making love. She'd made so much noise in Eli's arms last night it was embarrassing to even remember it. "So, what are you up to today? I haven't seen you or Granddad all day."

"We were in Elk Springs, talking to the accountant who handles Granddad's financial affairs. Mel, Granddad's going to buy the Whitehorn ranch."

"So he can give it to our half brothers?"

"All I know at this point is that he's buying the ranch. That's all he'll admit to. But why else would he want it?

Mel, I know this will probably disappoint you, but I'm going to Whitehorn with Granddad this afternoon.''

"Not again! Collin, I hate being left behind all the time. Why did Granddad even ask me here if he's never around?"

"I'm sorry, Mel."

"I know you are. How long will you be gone this time?"

Collin cleared his throat. "It could run into next week."

"But you'll be back for our rafting trip, won't you?"

"I can't guarantee it, Mel." Collin caught movement in his peripheral vision and turned his head to see what it was. "There's Eli now. Granddad's planning to ask him to take my place in the raft if we're not back. Neither of us wants you to miss that river ride, Mel."

She sighed. "I appreciate that, Collin. It's just that I was counting on you and I, you know."

"I'm sorry, sis," he said as they both watched Eli dismount near the horse barn and speak to Garrett who suddenly appeared by his side.

Melanie crawled through the strands of barbed wire and walked with Collin toward Eli and Garrett. Just the sight of Eli had put butterflies in her stomach. Recalling last night's feverish lovemaking had brought a rosy glow to her cheeks. Realizing that she could no longer use "refusal of conjugal rights" as the reason for an annulment had made her pulse race nervously.

Collin's laughter penetrated the depth of her concentration. "Sis, you must be a million miles away. I've said the same thing three times and I'll bet you still can't tell me what it was."

"You win the bet," she murmured with her gaze still locked on Eli. The closer she got to him the more disturbed he appeared to be. Why, he looked positively frozen in place…and even a little pale! What on earth were he and her grandfather discussing? She suddenly didn't want to know, nor did she want to explain her black eye to Garrett. She touched Collin's arm and stopped walking. "When are you and Granddad leaving?"

"Right away."

"Then I'll say goodbye now." Melanie began backing away, keeping an eye on Eli and Garrett to make sure they didn't spot her before she could make her escape. "Tell Granddad goodbye for me and…and I hope you both have a good trip." Ducking around the corner of a shed, she waved her hand at Collin. "Go on!"

"What's wrong? I don't get it," Collin said with a perplexed expression.

"A whole lot is wrong, but I have to work it out myself. Now go before Granddad sees you talking to this shed and catches on!"

"Melanie, he wants to see you before we leave," Collin said sternly.

She couldn't remember if they had ever had a dispute—anger over some childish disagreement before he'd left San Diego and moved to Montana—but she knew without question that cross words between them now would break her heart.

"Collin, you're my older brother and I love you," she said quietly, "but you must let me make my own decisions."

"I love you, too, Mel, but some of your decisions…" Collin shut his mouth and looked unhappy. He recouped quickly and muttered, "Aw, what the hell. I'll see you when we get back."

"Thanks," she said as he walked off, then she scurried around to the back of the outbuilding to stay out of sight until Garrett and Collin left. Within a few minutes, she heard their pickup start and drive away.

Eli had felt so good all day that he couldn't quite absorb the shock of the past ten or so minutes. Garrett had asked him to take Collin's place on the rafting trip with Melanie and he'd reluctantly agreed.

Melanie's sudden appearance in the tack room while he was putting away his saddle startled him. "Where have you been hiding?" he asked sardonically. "Collin said he couldn't find you anywhere." Eli set his saddle on a rack.

Melanie didn't like his tone. After last night she'd expected...well, she wasn't sure what she'd expected from Eli today, but it certainly hadn't been sarcastic disapproval.

"I was hiding behind one of the sheds," she said with a defensive thrust of her chin. "Do you have a problem with that?"

"No, I think that one is yours. My problems happen to be a little more serious than a game of hide-and-seek."

"For Pete's sake, do you think I wanted Granddad to see this?" Melanie yanked off her dark glasses. "I told Collin what happened and I'm not sure he believed me. What if Granddad thought you deliberately hit me? Some can of worms that would be."

Eli's knees got weak, not over what Garrett and Collin might have thought about Melanie's black eye, but because it was his fault. Stepping closer to her, he studied the bruise. "I could apologize a hundred times and it wouldn't be enough. Does it hurt?"

His nearness was stealing her breath. "Only a little," she said in a whispery, husky voice. "Don't worry about it, please. You didn't do it on purpose."

"No, but the result is the same." Very gently, he pushed back a curl that threatened to overlap the bruise.

"You said you were dreaming about swimming. The way your arms were going you must've been in a race or something."

Eli's face tensed again and he lowered his hand. "Something like that," he said grimly. "Which reminds me of another subject. Garrett said that he and Collin might not be back for that rafting trip and he asked me to go with you in Collin's place."

"Was that what you and Granddad were talking so seriously about? From a distance you looked rigid enough to crack open." She'd thought he might smile just a little over her silly remark, but his expression remained grim. And why, for heaven's sake, did his skin look so clammy? "Are you feeling ill today?" It might explain why he'd come back without the men as well as account for that sheen of perspiration coating his ashen skin.

"I'm not ill," he said flatly, almost rudely. "But I do have something to say to you and I might as well say it now and get it over with."

Her heart slammed against her ribs. Something was terribly wrong. Did it have anything to do with the chat she'd witnessed between Eli and her grandfather, which, getting down to brass tacks, had appeared as more of a conference than anything casual? Her intuition said yes, but she couldn't imagine what new problem had arisen to cause Eli to look so wrung out. In fact, did she even want to hear what it was? Could she deal with one more problem?

Whether she could or couldn't didn't seem to matter because she could see from the look in Eli's eyes that she was going to hear all about it. She braced herself for the worst although she had no clue as to what that might be.

"We're not going rafting," Eli said gruffly.

"Pardon?" She couldn't possibly have heard him correctly.

"I said we are not going rafting. I'm not going and you certainly aren't. Phone Sean Acton and cancel the outing."

Melanie was so dumbfounded that her brain actually stopped functioning for a few moments. When normalcy returned, it was armed with anger.

"I think we had better get something straight, Eli. Even if ours was a real marriage, I would not take orders from you. No one—man, woman or…or *husband*—will ever get away with ordering me around. If you don't want to go on that rafting trip, don't do it! But don't you dare try to stop me. Have I made myself clear?"

"You are *not* going, dammit! I'll phone Sean myself and—"

"You'll do nothing of the kind," she said in a lethally quiet voice, which was much more effective at setting Eli back on his heels than screeching at him would have been.

Looking at her beautiful face with the ugly bruise he'd inflicted upon her last night, he found his fighting spirit suddenly deserting him. He couldn't stop her from rafting down that river. She was right. *No one* could stop her.

"And I guarantee that you'll regret it if you try," Melanie added before turning her back on him and walking away. By the time she reached the house, she wasn't merely angry, she was livid with fury and outrage.

She went directly upstairs to her bedroom, took every stitch of Eli's clothes from the closet and bureau and put them in the hall. She really didn't give a damn where he slept from here on in, but it sure wouldn't be with her! This was it—the end!

And so began the cold war between the newlyweds. Melanie blamed Eli for discharging the first volley and he blamed her. They spoke to each other only when they had to—during meals, for example—and neither of them ever looked directly into the other's eyes.

What really got Melanie's goat was one of Irma's little kindnesses. She'd spotted Eli's clothes on the hallway floor before he did and gone ahead and moved them into the last unused bedroom in the house. Then she'd knocked on Melanie's door and told her what she'd done. "Every couple has spats, Melanie, so let's not embarrass anyone by forcing Eli to move back to the bunkhouse."

Melanie hadn't debated the point only because she liked Irma and wanted no disagreements with her, but it galled Melanie that when she went to bed at night, Eli was right down the hall. And she was positive that while she rolled and tossed and punched her pillow, Eli was peacefully sleeping. Unless he happened to have another dumb nightmare, that is. She still couldn't figure out why he'd been flailing his arms and acting almost demented over a silly dream about swimming. What was frightening about swimming, for Pete's sake?

Her eye healed in a matter of days, so the bruise had not gone very deep. But as the discoloration of her skin disappeared, Melanie began noticing a melancholy she had never suffered before. Even the longing for her father that she'd had while growing up couldn't compare to the emotional pain that seemed to be forever gnawing at her now.

Lying awake one night, with the house completely silent except for its usual nighttime groans and creaks, a tear leaked from her eye to the pillow, and that was when she knew. It was as clear, in fact, as if the words had been written out in neon on the wall of her dark bedroom: *You are in love with your husband! You love Eli!*

Panic seized her. "No," she whispered. "It's not true, it isn't!"

After panic came self-pity, and she turned her face to the

pillow and sobbed quietly. Her whole visit had been a bust. She'd spent precious little time with her grandfather, which was the reason she'd come to the ranch in the first place, and she hadn't even seen much of Collin. Instead, because they'd both been so busy trying to sort out her father's mess, they'd turned her over to Eli. This had brought about a marriage neither of them had wanted, and now she was in love with him, the big jerk!

So when she finally got back to San Diego and met with a lawyer, she would have to say, "I'm in love with my husband, but even though I have no legal grounds for such an action, I want an annulment." Or would she have to file for divorce?

It was all terribly depressing, and on top of that, she lied to her mother when Sue Ellen phoned one evening.

"Goodness, Melanie, you must be having the time of your life. I was sure you'd call again, and here I've not heard a word."

"Yes, Mom, the time of my life." *Lie number one.* "I've been meaning to call, but I've been so busy training the fillies and…and going riding myself and, uh, running here and there." That "running here and there" remark sounded pretty lame, so Melanie quickly added, "I went to Elk Springs with Collin last week, and we had a great time."

"That's wonderful. I'm so glad the two of you are spending time together. How about Garrett? Is he spending time with you?"

"When he can, Mom." *Lie number two, or was that number three?* "He's still going in circles about Dad's other kids, and I feel very sorry for him. It was so unfair of Dad to leave that mess for Granddad to deal with."

"Garrett always was a responsible sort and your father wasn't, Melanie. Mind you, I'm not judging either of them. What's past is past and best forgotten, or at least overlooked. My only concern now is for you and Collin. I don't want either of you getting shortchanged because of your father's indiscretions.''

Melanie was sitting at Garrett's desk in his office. The door was open and she saw Eli look in, then pass on by.

"Mom, I think the foreman wants to use Granddad's office for something."

"I seem to remember meeting him the day of Larry's funeral. Isn't his name Elliot, or something like that?''

"Eli. His name is Eli Forrester."

"Oh, yes. Quite a handsome young man, if I recall correctly. And very nice and well-mannered.''

"He's a stuffy, holier-than-thou, mule-headed know-it-all." *And I love him madly, and we're married, and I could wither up right here on Granddad's chair because I won't be in Montana very much longer, and I'll probably never see Eli again.*

"Really? Maybe I'm thinking of someone else. We met so many people that day."

"Yes, we did. I've got to hang up, Mom. Eli just looked in again. 'Bye. See you when I get home." Melanie put down the phone and said icily, "If you're pacing a hole in the carpet out there because you want the telephone or something else in here, I'm all through.''

Eli appeared in the doorway. "I didn't mean to cut your call short."

Melanie walked around the desk. "It was just as well. I was beginning to choke on the lies I was telling my mother anyhow."

"She still doesn't know about us?"

"Of course she doesn't!" Unnerved because this was the first time they'd been alone in a room since their altercation over the rafting trip, Melanie swept past him.

"You can't keep something as serious as marriage a secret," Eli said, and caught her arm just as she was about to go through the door, stopping her in midstride.

Instead of wresting her arm free from his grasp, she stood her ground and glared at him. "I can do anything I want to do, remember?" she drawled with heavy sarcasm.

Eli glared right back at her. "Yeah, that's the reason you let Garrett haul both of us to Missoula like sheep to the slaughter. You sure do talk tough when Garrett isn't around."

"So do you," she snarled. "At least I have an excuse. He's my grandfather. What's yours?"

Dropping her arm as though it had suddenly seared him, Eli backed away from her. She turned and ran from the office with tears of agony in her eyes and heard him yell, "I'm not a coward, Melanie!"

Such a thing had never entered her mind, but she couldn't let him have the last word. "If the shoe fits, wear it!" she yelled back, then rushed up the stairs to her bedroom, threw herself across the bed and cried until her eyes were red.

Chapter Fourteen

Though the effort proved futile, Melanie kept hoping that Collin and Garrett would come home. Her vacation days were dwindling; she had less than a week to go and she had the rafting trip on Thursday and she still hadn't visited her Aunt Alice.

On Wednesday she gave up watching the driveway for her brother and grandfather. Exchanging her jeans and boots for a skirt, blouse and pretty sandals, she fixed her hair and makeup just so and then took Garrett's car keys from their hook in the mudroom.

"I'm going to Elk Springs to see my aunt," she told Irma. "Not that there's anyone around who would care what I did."

Irma sighed sympathetically. "You look just beautiful, Melanie. I'm sure Alice will be very glad to see you."

"The only thing I'm sure of in Montana is that you are

consistently pleasant, Irma. Thank you for the compliment. I should be back in a few hours.''

Four hours later, Melanie was on her way back to the ranch and shuddering every time she thought of the ''visit from hell.'' Aunt Alice was the most bitterly unhappy person Melanie had ever been around. No matter what Melanie tried to talk about, Alice had managed to turn the conversation back to one of four topics: the terrible state of her health, the financial deprivation she had to live with because of her educated idiot of a husband, the disgrace heaped upon her head by her brother's scandalous reputation and, perversely, the inhumane suffering she'd gone through since Larry's death.

Melanie hadn't been in Alice's house twenty minutes when she realized that her aunt didn't know about her deceased brother's six illegitimate sons. She decided that she would very gently tell Alice about the safety-deposit box and its contents, but she would, of course, wait for a propitious moment to bring up such a difficult subject.

Two hours into her visit, Melanie changed her mind completely. After hearing the endless list of her aunt's health complaints, Melanie was positive that the news would shrivel Alice down to a tiny lump of burned-up coal. Melanie began making excuses to leave soon after, but it was almost two more torturous hours before she managed to get away.

Driving out of Elk Springs, Melanie finally felt free again. Alice's house reeked of oppression, and relative or not, Alice herself was the oppressor! How did her husband and son live with such a self-centered, negative woman? Nothing was right in Alice's world, which she herself had made very small.

''Dad was loony in his way and Aunt Alice is loony in

hers,'' Melanie muttered. ''Mom must know that about her. How come she never mentioned it?''

The car's engine coughed, and Melanie frowned. But it caught again and everything seemed fine—for another mile or so. This time, when the engine acted strangely, it was more of a sputter than a cough, and then it died completely. The power steering went out, too, of course, but Melanie managed to turn the wheel enough to get the car to coast onto the shoulder.

Looking around, she saw that not a house or car or anything else was in sight. She tried to estimate the remaining distance to the ranch. She was on a gravel road, but when exactly had she turned onto it? There was about twenty-five miles of gravel road after one turned off the asphalt highway, so it would really have helped her sense of distance if she had paid closer attention to the timing of that turn.

Upset over the dismal flop of the entire day, Melanie turned the key and willed the engine to start. It was then that she noticed the fuel gauge. Groaning, she put her head on the steering wheel. Why in heaven's name hadn't she checked the gauge before leaving the ranch? Like most big ranches and farms, the Kincaid spread had its own fuel supply. There was not a reason in the world for her to have run out of gas.

Melanie got out of the car and immediately picked up gravel in her sandals. Her lips pursed angrily, and she muttered, ''You stupid, stupid woman.'' If she was wearing her boots, or any kind of walking shoes, she would simply strike out for the ranch.

Her gaze fell on the fields enclosed by barbed wire on each side of the road. What were the rules around here? Did those No Trespassing, No Hunting signs mean that a stranded motorist dare not cross those fence lines to avoid hiking on gravel?

Without any warning, all the starch drained out of her. Stumbling back to the car, Melanie sat in the driver's seat and stared dully through the windshield. How much more trouble could she get herself into in this desolate place? she wondered.

"Eli, could I see you in the kitchen for a minute?" Irma asked.

"Sure." Eli followed her from the dining room, where all the men had gathered for the evening meal, to the kitchen, then registered the worried look on Irma's face. "Is something wrong?"

"I hope not, but Melanie went to town around noon to visit her Aunt Alice. She said she'd only be gone a few hours, and I phoned Alice just now and she said that Melanie had left around four. Eli, she should have gotten home before this."

Eli had been constantly on edge over Melanie's determination to go rafting ever since their big blowup. The fact that she'd kicked him out of her bedroom was a sore point, as well, but mostly the foul mood he'd been living with was due to a lack of sleep.

It was Melanie's fault and it wasn't. Eli could blame her for increasing the frequency of his nightmares with that senseless rafting trip, but the roots of those dreams went back to Carson's death.

Still, he'd been living as peacefully as was possible for him before Melanie had come along and mucked up everything, and he resented her for being irresistible and beautiful and so sexy that she haunted his days with at least as much anguish as the nightmares haunted his nights.

Now Irma expected him to rush to Melanie's rescue—if

rescuing was what she needed, which he doubted—and he was tired and hungry.

"Irma, she probably just stopped somewhere else," he said wearily.

"I think she would have phoned." Irma's eyes were admonishing. "Eli, she doesn't know this country. What if she took a wrong turn and got lost?"

"She could hardly get lost on the few roads between Elk Springs and this ranch, Irma." But Irma looked so beseeching and concerned that Eli gave in. "All right, I'll take a drive toward town."

"Thanks, Eli. I'd have gone myself if I didn't have a dining room full of men to feed."

Leaving the mouthwatering smells of Irma's good cooking behind, Eli slammed on his hat in the mudroom, then continued out the back door to his pickup.

Melanie had finally realized that impatience was a futile emotion, making her stomach and head ache and feeding upon itself until she wanted to scream. She'd forced herself to calm down. Someone at the ranch would eventually miss her and do something about it, and her sitting as tense as a coiled spring in her grandfather's car on this lonely road would not hurry the process.

Nevertheless, she was grateful when she heard the sound of a vehicle on the road. Still only a vague engine noise, but coming closer. She opened the door of the car and swung her feet to the ground. Standing, she listened intently and decided the vehicle was coming from the direction of the ranch.

Waiting for it to get close enough to see, Melanie acknowledged the beauty all around her—the spring-green fields and distant mountains looked like a picture-postcard. The sun was out of sight behind the Rockies, and the sky appeared to be lit by some special-effects equipment that flung spectacular pink and orange streaks dramatically across a silver-blue background.

It occurred to Melanie that she had never been in a more tranquil setting. There was a magic about Montana that she'd never felt in California. Of course, she was comparing apples and oranges, for she'd always lived in a city.

The vehicle was suddenly in sight, coming over a rise in the road and kicking up dust. It was a pickup truck and Melanie didn't have to see the driver to know who was behind the wheel. "Eli to the rescue," she whispered, wishing that someone else had noticed her absence and come looking for her.

But who else was there? Her brother and grandfather were much too busy worrying about six men they'd never met to worry about her! She was darned tired of being put on the back burner because of a bunch of guys who probably had no idea they even had a grandfather!

Eli was actually stunned to see Garrett's car up ahead, parked at the side of the road and obviously disabled. He hadn't once pictured Melanie having car trouble and, in fact, had visualized her fiddling around Elk Springs, maybe doing nothing more than seeing the town on foot, but taking her own sweet time about it and never considering that she might be causing someone at the ranch to wonder if she was all right.

He stopped his truck directly in front of Garrett's car, then got out. "What's wrong?" he asked gruffly.

Melanie stiffened. He couldn't even say a civil hello? "The car's out of gas," she said coldly.

Eli's jaw dropped. "You took the car without checking the fuel gauge? With a two-thousand gallon underground tank of gas at the ranch and a modern, easy-to-use pump, you drove away with a virtually empty tank?"

"Apparently so," she said frostily. "And all women aren't nitwits because I ran out of gas, so wipe that smug, superior, macho expression off your face."

"I've been here all of twenty seconds and you're already trying to pick a fight?"

"You were mad when you got here. What happened? Did someone tell *you* what to do for a change?" Melanie knew that was an unfair and undeserved accusation, but it hurt that he'd arrived angry instead of concerned.

"Someone's always telling me what to do," Eli snapped.

The cad was referring to their forced marriage. "Yeah, well, you don't always have to follow orders like a robot, you know."

"Like you did, you mean? Come on, get in the truck. I'll send a couple of the men back with some gas."

Melanie was suddenly battling tears. Why was she letting him make her cry? How did he have the power to make her cry?

Turning away, she climbed back into the car. "I'm not going with you," she said through the open window. "I'll wait here for someone to bring the gasoline."

Eli narrowed his eyes on her. "Why?"

"Because I want to!" she shouted. "Just get out of my face, Eli! I'm sick of your bad humor and better-than-thou personality. You're not half the man my grandfather is and you never will be! And stop acting as though you never ran out of gas, because in my estimation, old pal, old buddy, you never had any gas to begin with!" She rolled up the window.

Hopping mad over being the brunt of such an unjust tirade, Eli spun on his heel and returned to his pickup. He swore as he backed up and turned around that he wouldn't send anyone with the gas until morning. *A night in that car will do that little lady a world of good!*

But when he got back to the ranch, he went straight to the bunkhouse and asked two of the men to fill a five-gallon can with gas and take it to Melanie for Garrett's car, which was parked about fifteen miles away on Farley Road. He could tell they were curious about why he wouldn't take the gas to his wife himself, but he left before anyone could work up the nerve to mention it.

Melanie had a good cry, then dried her eyes and stared at the empty road ahead with an ache in her heart. Why did she and Eli constantly ruffle each other's feathers? They'd agreed to end their ludicrous marriage, so it wasn't as though they were miles apart on some crucial issue.

Well, her rafting trip tomorrow wasn't a crucial issue to her, at any rate, and it really was none of Eli's business. Why in heaven's name would he make such a fuss about it, rudely telling her that he wasn't going and neither was she? God save her from a marriage to any man who believed his word was law!

Melanie shuddered, then frowned a bit. Truth was, Eli was an uncommonly perplexing puzzle. In some ways, he was a big softy and as sensitive as anyone she'd ever known. Take the night that he'd struck her while she'd been trying to bring him out of an obviously terrifying nightmare, for example. Could any man have been more remorseful and apologetic?

But there was another side to Eli, a hard, secretive side. He would rather show people his soft underbelly than let anyone know that part of him. Or maybe she was the only one in Montana, or at least at the ranch, who'd seen *any* part of him!

Groaning, Melanie put her head back against the seat. God knew she didn't want to fight with Eli all the time, so why did she? And why couldn't he be nice to her? When she remembered their passionate encounters and how hungrily they'd kissed and made love, it didn't seem possible that those silly arguments could even damage such strong desire, let alone kill it.

There were no answers for such profound questions. No answers at all.

Eli heard Melanie come upstairs and go into her room. A few minutes later, he could detect the sound of the shower in her bathroom. About half an hour after the shower had been turned off and he was thinking she must be in bed, he heard Irma come upstairs and go into her bedroom. The house was then totally devoid of noises except for the usual creaks that old wood makes as it settles.

He hated the thought of a sleepless night, but the way his heart was pounding in terror over Melanie's rafting trip tomorrow didn't give him much hope of rest. Besides, he feared that if he did happen to fall asleep, he'd have the nightmare again.

"You're damned if you do and damned if you don't," he muttered.

At eleven o'clock he was still trying to figure a way to keep Melanie at the ranch tomorrow. At twelve he was angry at Garrett for assuming he would be happy to take Collin's place in Sean's raft. At one he was angry with himself for letting Garrett think for even a second that he was *willing* to take Collin's place, and at two o'clock he conked out from sheer exhaustion.

He awoke at five, sweating from a nightmare that had been much too explicit and close to home, and he immediately jumped out of bed. Yanking on jeans as he went, he ran from his room to Melanie's and walked in without knocking. She opened one sleepy eye and heard him say, "Don't leave without me. I'm going with you today."

* * *

They were almost at Sean's house, with Eli driving his pickup and Melanie sitting beside him. Melanie had been biting her tongue to prevent another argument, but she just couldn't keep quiet any longer.

"Why on earth are you doing this?" she asked. "You're so obviously in pain over this excursion that I can't imagine a reason for your changing your mind and coming along."

"You just said it. I changed my mind." It was difficult for Eli to even breathe normally, so the unnatural tone of his voice didn't surprise him.

"Eli, you're forcing yourself to do something that… that…" She stopped to frown. "Dare I say 'frightens you' without stepping on your ego?"

"Say anything you want. It's no skin off my nose," Eli mumbled.

His macho toughness and stiff-upper-lip attitude was more than she could take. "You're only doing this because Granddad asked you to, not because you want to and not because some magic beam from outer space zapped you and altered your negative opinion of river rafting. If you're really going along, then cheer up, dammit! And if you can't get that gloomy look off your face, then stay in town! I don't want your bad mood ruining my fun today."

"Your mood isn't so hot, either, so lay off mine."

"You are a…a grouch!"

Eli decided that *grouch* was a more palatable label than *coward,* and he let Melanie have the last word. His stomach felt queasy and he was afraid that he might have to pull the pickup over and let Melanie know just how terrified he really was. Not that losing his breakfast would forever stigmatize him in Melanie's eyes, but he'd rather not have her become even more curious about his behavior this morning than she already was.

When they reached Elk Springs, Melanie coolly told Eli how to find Sean's house. She was grossly annoyed and couldn't conceal how she felt. Eli had only come along because Garrett had put him on the spot, and since she sensed Eli's resentment so acutely, today could not be anything but a bust.

"This is a surprise," Eli said when he pulled into the Acton driveway and saw Sean's house.

"What did you expect, a hovel?" Melanie snapped, then opened her door and got out. Sean came outside and walked toward the truck. Melanie called, "Hi, Sean," and he returned the greeting with a warm, welcoming smile.

Eli climbed out and Sean did a double take. "Where's Collin?"

They all congregated at the front of Eli's truck. "He's on a business trip with Granddad," Melanie explained. "Sean Acton, Eli Forrester."

The two men shook hands and sized each other up. And then Eli said something that made Melanie doubt her own hearing. "I'm Melanie's husband."

Sean looked thunderstruck. "You're married?" he said to Melanie.

She felt thunderstruck. Eli and Sean were acting like two roosters in the same henhouse! She sent Eli a murderous look, but he didn't even flinch, merely waited with a grave expression for her answer to Sean's obviously stunned question.

"Yes, we're married," she said sharply, then added, "Is everything ready to go, Sean?"

"Uh, yeah, sure is. I...I'll take my truck with the raft and things, and you two can, uh, take yours. I like to put in at Perk's Landing. We'll leave the river at Lobel's Landing, and I've already taken a vehicle there to ride back in."

"Sounds like you've thought of everything. Thanks,

Sean. See you in a few.'' Steaming mad, Melanie climbed back into Eli's pickup and waited for him to get in. The second his door was shut, she said, ''What was that all about? The mess you and I have made of our personal lives is hardly any of Sean's business!''

Eli started the engine and gave her a don't-play-dumb-with-me look. ''He'd like to make *you* his business.''

She knew it was true. Sean had flirted with her at their first meeting, and from the look on his face today when Eli had made his little announcement, he sure hadn't expected her to suddenly produce a husband.

''What difference does that make?'' she said dully.

''Oh? Maybe you'd *like* him to make you his business?''

With an explosive anger, she turned on him. ''Let me tell you something, Eli. Right at the moment I'm not particularly fond of *any* man!''

''Least of all me.''

''No, not least of all you! *Any* man! Including my brother and grandfather! I took this trip to spend time with them, to get to know them better, and I've hardly seen Granddad except for the afternoon that he dragged you and me off to Missoula. Collin's done a little better, but the truth is that neither one of them cares whether I'm in Montana or Timbuktu. And I'm getting so I don't care where they are, either. I'm going home in two days and I'm never coming back to Montana, and you want to know something else? Nobody is even going to notice that I'm gone.''

''That's not true, Melanie.''

''Oh, what do you know about it?'' she said disgustedly, and turned her face to stare unseeingly out the side window.

Eli's stomach was churning worse than before. They were near the river, heading for Perk's Landing, and just the sight of that fast-moving water was horrifying. Along with that, tearing him up was the jealousy he couldn't have imagined before he'd felt it absolutely shredding his usual good sense in Sean's yard. At least he used to possess good sense, he thought unhappily. Before Melanie came along, he'd believed wholeheartedly that he had it in good measure. Was that a lie, too?

He parked next to Sean's truck at Perk's Landing, and he and Melanie got out and helped Sean unload the inflated raft and place it in the water with about half of it still on shore. It *was* awfully small, Melanie thought uneasily, nothing at all like the big raft she'd seen earlier with Collin.

Sean handed out life jackets. "Put them on," he said. "And if for some reason you fall in, point your toes downstream and try to avoid running into big rocks. Either of you do any rafting before?"

Melanie shook her head, but Eli said, "I have."

She looked at him with surprise. "You have?"

"Good," Sean said. "You can help out with the oars if need be. Okay, Melanie, in you go. Sit in the front. Eli, you sit in back and I'll row."

Eli was glad to have the back seat, which was no more than the rubber bottom of the rear end of the small raft, but he still felt squeamish and hoped no one would look back at him.

Sean rowed the raft smoothly and swiftly away from the shore. There were no rapids near Perk's Landing, so Sean took the opportunity to issue a few more instructions. "We're going to run into some three-plus rapids and one four-plus. There are no fives on Elk River, but the four-plus is close. Just do everything I say and we'll have a great ride. When I holler left or right, lean in that direction. We'll be moving fast and dodging some dangerous rocks, but don't worry. I've floated this river dozens of times."

Eli was having trouble catching his breath. His heartbeat was much too fast and he was sweating although the temperature was only pleasantly warm. He was risking his physical health and his very sanity for Melanie because he knew, he *knew,* something was going to go wrong today. He awaited it as a man must await his own execution, and the first time he saw Melanie reach over the edge of the raft to trail her hand in the water, he shouted, "For God's sake, Melanie, get back in the raft!"

Startled, she turned around. "What is wrong with you? I was only testing the water temperature." Eli was wearing a baseball cap and dark glasses—as she was—so she couldn't see all of his face. But the pinched lines around his mouth were perplexing. Good grief, if he was really afraid of water for some reason, why had he come with her? *She* certainly wasn't afraid. Even if they never saw a rapid, floating along on the river currents was wonderful. Sean rowed at times, mostly to steer the raft, she'd come to realize, because the river itself was controlling the raft's speed.

The first set of rapids was great fun. Laughing and yelling, Melanie hung on and loved every second of the ride. But when they were on smooth water again, she glanced back at Eli and saw him clinging to a strap for dear life and looking as pale as a ghost. The fun went out of her so fast she was taken aback. Maybe she shouldn't care if Eli enjoyed or hated rafting, but she did care. He was suffering, for Pete's sake!

She lied to Sean. "I don't think I like this. Can we turn around and go back?"

He laughed. "It would take a pretty powerful motor to buck this current, Melanie. Sorry, but we go only one way—downriver."

There was another set of rapids, and another. Melanie's concern for Eli grew, and she kept asking herself why he'd done something that made him so miserable. Yes, Garrett had asked him to take Collin's place, but had Eli really been worried about what Garrett might think or had he been worried about her?

Suddenly, she spotted something large and dark in the river. "Sean...what's that?" she yelled.

He hadn't seen it, and when he did, it was too late to avoid it. "Left!" he shouted, but the raft rammed into the log and upended, spilling everyone into the river. Melanie hit her head on something and blacked out. The current swept Sean against a huge boulder, breaking his arm, and he dazedly clung to the boulder and watched Melanie and Eli bob along past him. Then he concentrated on getting himself to shore so he could get help for them.

Eli realized that he was the only one who hadn't been injured. But that wasn't his most startling thought: he was no longer afraid! Not for himself, at any rate, and he turned over in the water and began to swim a powerful breast-stroke to catch up with Melanie.

When he did and saw that she was unconscious, he wasted no time in hooking his arm around her and heading them both to the nearest outcropping of land. He didn't let himself think about anything but getting Melanie out of that river. He wouldn't even permit concern about how badly she might be hurt to break his concentration.

After what seemed like hours but was really only minutes, they were in shallow water. Stumbling to his feet, Eli picked Melanie up and carried her to dry ground. Carefully laying her down, he was about to administer CPR when she coughed up some water and then opened her eyes.

"Eli," she whispered. "What happened?"

His emotions caved in then, and with tears streaming down his face, Eli gathered her into his arms and held her close to his heart.

"You're all right, you're all right," he cried hoarsely. "Melanie, I love you, and I had a horrible dream last night...or early this morning...about you and this river...and I couldn't let you go alone...and my brother Carson drowned in a canoeing accident and I should've been able to save him...but I saved you...my love...my wife...and I...I'm not afraid of water anymore and...oh, Melanie, I love you so much."

Chapter Fifteen

"Oh, Eli, I love you, too!"

"You really do?"

"Yes, I really do. Eli, help me out of this wet life vest, and take yours off, too. Oh, it's chilly, isn't it? The water was cold." Melanie glanced around. "Eli, where's Sean?"

"I'm sure he's all right. I last saw him holding on to a huge boulder. It wasn't far from the opposite shore. Come, sweetheart, we're in the shade here. Let's get in the sun and dry off."

They moved to a sunny place and sat with their arms around each other. "Say it again," Eli said softly.

"I love you very much. I...I think I fell for you at first sight."

"But you fought against it." Eli sighed. "So did I. I wonder why."

"Because it came as a shock. I never expected to meet the love of my life on Granddad's ranch, for goodness' sake, and you probably never expected that your boss's granddaughter would…would… Help me out here," she said with a smile.

"How about I never expected my boss's granddaughter to knock me for a loop?"

"That'll do for now." Melanie laid her head on his chest. "Oh, Eli, what you said about your brother breaks my heart."

"It broke mine into so many pieces, Melanie, I couldn't put it back together again. Then when I realized our parents blamed me…"

Melanie jerked her head up. "Oh, no, Eli, they couldn't have. Are you sure you weren't just so brokenhearted that you misunderstood their grief?"

Eli heaved a sigh. "It happened over four years ago. What was so painfully clear then is just a sorrowful blur now."

"Where is home, Eli?" she asked gently.

"Baltimore. After Carson's death and the trouble with my folks, I washed my hands of everyone and everything familiar. I ended up here in Montana, and now this is home." He took her chin and looked deeply into her eyes. "Could it ever be home for you?" After a second, he added, "It wouldn't have to be. I mean, as long as we're together, I think I could live anywhere."

"That's very generous of you, but I think we have to approach that problem logically and…and pragmatically. Eli, we both have jobs. Mine's in San Diego. Yours is here. I'm sure I could adjust to living in Montana much more easily than you could adjust to San Diego. Eli, are you laughing at me?"

"Not at you, sweetheart, never at you, but listen to me for a minute. The Forresters' wealth goes back to the first settlers in America. I have more money in banks in and around the Baltimore area than you and I could spend in ten lifetimes. We could live anywhere in the world and we'd only have to work if we wanted to.''

Melanie was staring openmouthed. ''You...you're not serious,'' she said in a tiny, shaky voice.

''Dead serious, sweetheart.''

''I *knew* you were different!'' she cried, startling him. ''But I couldn't have imagined that you were sneaky enough to be rich!'' She saw the panic in his eyes and rushed to console him. ''Eli, I was only teasing you.''

The panic vanished from his gorgeous blue eyes and was replaced by something hot and lustful. ''Yes,'' he drawled. ''I do believe your teasing was what nailed me to the wall, in the first place, sweetheart.'' He pushed her backward onto the grass and lay on top of her. ''What do you think? Are we going to be rescued right away or do we have time to drive each other crazy before the marines land?''

''Since I can hear the sound of a motor coming closer, and since people are probably worried enough about us to hurry up a rescue, I think we'd be wise to sit up properly and act like an old married couple so we don't shock the marines,'' she said with a pleased giggle. ''But you can sleep in my room tonight if you want,'' she added almost primly. Letting out a whoop of laughter, Eli tickled her ribs. ''Stop, stop!'' she cried. ''I give up. I'm all yours. Do with me what you will.''

''You're sure it's okay if I sleep in your room tonight?''

''Positive.''

''Okay, in that case we'll sit up nice and proper and wait for the marines.''

They held hands and looked at each other in wonderment until their rescuers arrived.

* * *

Eli phoned the ranch, expecting Irma to answer. But it was Garrett who said, "Kincaid ranch."

"You're back!" Eli exclaimed. "Garrett, there's nothing to worry about…I mean, the doctor said she'll be just fine in a day or so…but Melanie's in the hospital."

Garrett was instantly anxious. "Why? What happened?"

"We got dumped into the river by accident and Melanie hit her head on something. Over her objections, I insisted she see a doctor and took her to the emergency room. They said she has a mild concussion and they put her to bed. If no complications develop, she'll be released in the morning. She went through a battery of tests, and I think the whole experience wore her out. She's sleeping now, so I took this opportunity to call and let Irma know why we wouldn't be back tonight."

"Thank God you were with her, Eli," Garrett said emotionally.

"Yes, thank God," Eli agreed.

"You're staying there with her?"

"I'll be right here until they release her. She…she's my wife and I love her."

"I understand, son. Thank you for the call, and please let me know if the slightest thing goes wrong," Garrett said.

"I will, Garrett. Goodbye." Eli quietly hung up the phone on the stand next to Melanie's bed, then sat back in his chair and silently studied his sleeping wife. The love he felt for her was all-consuming, occupying every cell of his body. He'd truly not known that a man could feel so much for a woman. The future looked glorious. He would protect Melanie from harm, support her every dream and talent, stand by her side through thick and thin and love her till the day he died.

He'd known what was in his heart, what he'd so foolishly

been fighting against, when he'd seen her in that river, pale and unconscious. He'd saved her life, and in saving her, he'd saved himself. Freed himself from the shackles of the past and from fear itself.

The biggest miracle of all was that she loved him, too. Recalling their passionate confessions and plans on the riverbank, Eli smiled. He was still smiling with happiness when Melanie stirred and opened her eyes.

Leaning forward, he took her hand. "How are you feeling?"

She blinked at him as though attempting to focus her eyes. "Eli?" Her gaze darted around. "Where am I? Is this a hospital room?"

Eli froze. "You don't remember the rafting accident?" *Or what came after? Our beautiful declarations of love?*

"I...remember something."

"What, sweetheart? What do you remember?"

She looked at him oddly. "It's about...you. Did you save my life?"

"I pulled you from the river, yes." Eli got up. "I want the doctor to see you. I'll be right back." He hurried out and stopped the first nurse he saw. "My wife...Melanie Forrester in room 303...is having trouble with her memory. Could you please page Dr. Andrews and let him know?"

"Certainly, sir." The nurse went one way and Eli went the other. When he walked into Melanie's room again, he could tell that she hadn't moved an inch. In fact, she seemed to be staring into space. He sat and took her hand again, and she slowly brought her eyes around to meet his.

"Eli," she said, "I feel so strange. It's like someone took an eggbeater and mixed up my brain. Did...did you tell me about a brother?"

"Yes. My brother's name is Carson, and he died over four years ago in a canoeing accident."

Dr. Andrews came in. "Hello, Melanie. Do you remember me?" He began checking her eyes.

"You're Dr. Andrews," Melanie murmured.

"And don't you forget it," he said with a chuckle. After a few minutes, he turned to Eli. "She's just a bit disoriented, Eli. Nothing to be concerned about. I'm quite sure her memory will be back to normal within a few hours. Possibly sooner."

Eli followed him from the room. "She said that she feels like an eggbeater mixed up her brain."

"It won't last for long, Eli. Stay with her and talk to her if she wants to talk. But don't press her into conversation if she'd rather rest."

"Thank you." Eli returned to Melanie's bedside and sat back in the chair.

"Does the doctor think I'm wacky?" she asked dryly.

Her tone of voice made Eli feel better about her, and he grinned. "No wackier than usual."

She heaved an exaggerated sigh. "You're such a comfort." After a moment, she said, "So I'm disoriented."

"You received a mild concussion."

"And some bruises. Don't forget my bruises."

"Wouldn't dream of it. They're sort of a badge of honor, right? I mean, you rafted the Elk River and a scar or two is what every rafter needs to remind him or her of such an incredible experience."

"What a sarcastic voice! Obviously, you didn't enjoy the experience."

"Did you?"

"I think so, but I may have to do it again to know for sure."

Eli eyed her suspiciously. "You're feeling better, aren't you? More like your old self?"

"You know, my old self came up with the most remarkable picture while you were in the hall asking Dr. Andrews just how wacky I really was.''

''A picture of what?''

Melanie looked directly at him. ''It was a picture of you and me. When we were wet and soggy and thankful to be alive on the bank of the river, did we hold each other and talk about love and our jobs and your wealth and family, or is that whole scene a figment of my wacky imagination?''

''It happened,'' Eli said softly. ''It all happened, and I'm so damned glad you're remembering it now that I could do cartwheels around this room.''

She smiled. ''Go ahead. I'd love to see you turn cartwheels.''

Eli got up to plant a gentle kiss on her lips. ''You already know I'm head over heels because of you,'' he said. ''I'll show you the cartwheels another time.''

Melanie napped on and off the rest of the day. Each time she awoke she was more alert, and when the hospital staff served dinner, she was hungry and ate every bite. She was just finishing when Collin walked in.

''Collin! Oh, I'm so glad to see you. Eli told me you were back. Did Granddad come with you?''

''He's talking to Eli. Besides, the nurse said only one visitor at a time in this room.''

''That's silly. I'm perfectly all right.''

''Want me to go out to the nurses' station and raise hell because of the rules?''

Melanie grinned. ''You wouldn't do that if I said yes. You're nothing but a big tease.''

''Seems to run in the family, doesn't it?''

''Granddad doesn't tease. Goodness, I can't even imagine him cutting up.''

"He hasn't been the same since Dad died, Mel," Collin said quietly. "But he used to love a good joke."

"Did he buy the Whitehorn ranch?"

"Signed, sealed and delivered."

"And is he going to give it to our half brothers?"

"He never said. I know it's on his mind, but he didn't talk about it. My feeling is that he hasn't come to a decision about those guys yet. I have, though."

"You have? What've you decided, Collin?"

"They're Kincaids, same as you and me, and if Granddad wants them in the family, then I'll work with him to try to right Dad's wrongs."

"You make me proud to be your sister. I love you, Collin."

He leaned over and kissed her cheek. "Love you, too, Mel." He straightened. "I'd better get out of here so Granddad can come in. See you tomorrow."

An aide rushed in and removed Melanie's dinner tray. "Thanks," Melanie called as the young woman hurried out. When she looked up again, Garrett was standing there. Suddenly choked up, she held out both hands and said huskily, "Granddad."

"How come a person looks so small and helpless in a hospital bed?" he remarked as he moved close enough to take her hands.

"I'm not small *or* helpless, Granddad. Sit down, please."

Garrett complied. "Actually, you're looking much better than I anticipated. Your color is exceptionally good."

Melanie smiled. "That's 'cause I'm so happy. Did Eli tell you what happened?"

"He did indeed, which, in turn, makes me very happy. I've worried a great deal about my hasty and rather overbearing reaction that, uh, Sunday." Garrett cleared his throat and looked embarrassed.

"Don't you dare be embarrassed," Melanie said with an emotional catch in her voice. "My behavior shocked you, as well it should have."

"You were with the man you loved, Melanie. I interfered in something that was none of my business."

But I didn't know I loved him that day, Granddad. Melanie would have preferred being completely honest about it, but she simply couldn't give this wonderful old man one more burden or doubt.

"Collin said you bought the Whitehorn ranch," she said brightly.

"Yes, I did. Now I have to figure out what I'm going to do with it."

"Granddad, we've never had a chance to talk about this, or if there was a chance, neither of us took it. There's something I'd like very much to tell you. May I do it now?"

"Of course. What is it?"

"I know you've been worrying and fretting about Dad's other kids, about whether or not you should even try to find them for fear they might not appreciate hearing from a grandfather they don't know they have. Have you considered that some of them may know about you, Granddad? Or maybe only one knows and maybe he thinks that since his father never wanted him, neither do you.

"You must never count yourself as valueless, Granddad. I grew up yearning to know you and Dad. Now he's gone and that chance is gone, too, but you're not. You're alive and vital and a wonderful, ethical, moral man. Anyone would be pleased to have you for a grandfather, and those six young men deserve to at least meet you. Don't deny them that, Granddad. It's a gift that only you can give them."

Garrett's eyes had grown misty. "I slighted you so badly,

Melanie. All those years when we could have been in touch and weren't…'' Taking out his handkerchief, Garrett blew his nose. ''I'm sorry, child. Can I ever make it up to you?''

''Granddad, I've already put all that behind me. But ask yourself this. Five or ten years from now, are you going to be asking another grandchild to forgive you?''

Garrett smiled weakly. ''Honey, I might not even be walking this planet five or ten years from now.''

''I won't listen to that kind of talk. I could die before you, and so could any of those six grandsons. Granddad, I'm not saying you should give them anything tangible…such as the ranch in Whitehorn you just bought. That's entirely up to you. But give them something infinitely more precious—recognition and a little of your time.''

Garrett smiled at her through teary eyes. ''I know what I have to do now, just from talking to you. But I also know I can't do it alone. What do you think of my hiring a private investigator to help out?''

''Wonderful,'' she exclaimed. They smiled at each other, sharing a special moment. Later, when he was on his way out, she said, ''Granddad, I visited Aunt Alice while you were in Whitehorn. No one's told her about Dad's safety-deposit box, have they?''

''No, but I plan to do that first thing tomorrow morning.''

''I almost said something while I was there, but she…she's very hard to talk to.''

''I know, honey. Don't you worry your pretty head about it. I'll be taking care of everything from now on. You just be happy, okay?''

''I will be, Granddad, I know I will.''

It was getting late, close to eleven. The hospital corridors were silent except for the quiet movements of the nighttime nursing staff. Policy permitted a spouse to ignore regular visiting hours, and Eli sat comfortably next to Melanie's bed as they lazily talked.

He'd told her more about his family and a lot about his childhood, and she'd talked about growing up in southern California with her mother and stepfather. She'd told him about her job and he'd asked if she wanted to keep it. Her answer had been a question. "Are you going to keep yours?"

Then they both realized that they still had many decisions to make.

"I have to call my mother tomorrow and tell her everything," Melanie murmured.

"It's time I called my parents and let them know I'm still among the living," Eli said quietly.

Neither comment required discussion. They each had a family that couldn't be ignored. In Eli's case, his family could not be ignored any longer. He wasn't sure of the kind of reception he'd get when he phoned his parents, but he was finally prepared to find out. They should at least know that he was married.

"Mom's going to have a fit about my getting married without her," Melanie added ruefully.

"I doubt if my folks would care about that, but..." Frowning, Eli sat up straighter. "Melanie, you've said that before about your mother. Will she really be upset?"

"Eli, she's been planning my wedding since I was a little girl," Melanie said with a long sigh. "Yes, she's going to be *very* upset."

"Well, let's fix it so she's not."

"How?"

"By having a second wedding. As big a shindig as will make your mother happy."

Melanie thought a moment, then began tapping the tip of her forefinger against her chin. Looking at the ceiling, she said solemnly, "Now that I think about it, I never did hear a certain someone *ask* me to marry him."

"Are you back in teasing mode?" Eli asked with a laugh. "Or are you serious?"

"Maybe you should decide that for yourself," she said demurely.

Eli's smile faltered. He hadn't proposed, of course. They'd been whisked to Missoula so fast neither had known up from down. What were the odds of that kind of marriage lasting? What were the odds of a man and woman forced to the altar, as they'd been, actually falling in love with each other?

He knew what had to be done and he got up from his chair and sat on the edge of the bed. Taking Melanie's hand in his, he said, "Do you realize how lucky we are?"

"Yes, I do," she whispered.

"But you still want me to propose?"

"Only if you want a second ceremony."

The devilish twinkle in her eyes was a dead giveaway. She was toying with him again, the little minx!

"You're the one who would benefit most from a second ceremony, sweetheart," he said.

"Oh, no, darling. Believe me, *you* would benefit most. When my mother's happy, I'm happy, and whenever I'm happy, I guarantee that my husband will be walking on air."

His mouth fell open. "I've had that feeling before. Once before."

"Did you like it?" she whispered throatily.

"I *loved* it, just like I love you." He leaned over until his lips were but a breath away from hers. "Will you marry me again, my temptress, my sweetheart, my own true love?"

She sighed contentedly. "Of course I will. Did you ever really doubt it?"

* * * * *

MONTANA MAVERICKS:
WED IN WHITEHORN

*Silhouette's beloved MONTANA MAVERICKS
saga continues in a brand-new twelve-book series
with stories from your favorite authors! Welcome
back to Whitehorn, Montana—a place where rich
tales of passion and adventure are unfolding under
the Big Sky.*

*This enthralling series
will start in June 2000 with*

LONE STALLION'S LADY

by Lisa Jackson

*And look for one title
each month until May 2001.*

Turn the page for an exciting preview....

As Gina Henderson drove her rented Ford Explorer through the ranch land of western Montana, she glanced at her watch and smiled to herself. She was making good time from the airport and her job was just about finished. She'd helped Garrett Kincaid locate six of his son's illegitimate children. The only question that remained was whether Larry had sired a seventh.

She was willing to bet her life on it. There was that notation in the date book/journal Larry had kept this past year. It read simply: "Found out former flame had baby boy. Check into this. Could be mine. Timing seems perfect." It could have been idle scribbling, but Gina didn't think so; it wasn't Larry's style. No, there was a baby, all right, and she imagined, given Larry's track record for fathering illegitimate sons, the boy was a Kincaid. The date book had been stuffed into the box of Larry's personal effects, the one relating to all of his bastard sons. Gina had a feeling that another child had indeed been born, just in the last year or so, a seventh illegitimate son. Because of Larry's whereabouts in the past year, Gina would bet dollars to doughnuts that that baby was somewhere in the state, probably not too far from the town of Whitehorn. Well, she thought with the determination she was known for, she'd leave no stone unturned finding the kid.

Though of course she'd never met the man, Gina held a particular dislike for Larry; he'd been the antithesis of his father, Garrett. A hard-drinking, womanizing, gambling man, Larry Kincaid had swaggered through life without a bit of empathy, understanding or interest in anyone else. He'd fathered illegitimate children as if he were in some kind of contest, then pretty much ignored the offspring as well as the women who had borne them. Garrett, on the other hand, was decent and straitlaced, a man of strict morals, a man as steady and true as Montana, the vast land that spawned him.

All in all, she'd enjoyed locating Larry's lost sons…well, except for one. The hellion. But she wouldn't think of Trent Remmington now. She'd compromised her own set of rules by meeting him last month and lying about who she was and that thought still stuck in her craw.

She'd made a mistake of Biblical proportions on that one and nearly lost her heart in the process.

"Fool," she muttered, kicking off her sandals and driving barefoot. She reached into her open handbag sitting on the passenger seat. Squinting and avoiding a truck speeding in the opposite direction on this long stretch of highway, she dug into her purse, found her sunglasses and managed to slip them out of their case and onto her nose.

A few years ago, just out of college, she'd begged her brother, Jack, to let her work with him as a private investigator. He'd balked at first but finally agreed, and she'd sworn that she would never get involved with any of her clients.

It hadn't been a problem.

Until she'd met Trent. "Stupid, stupid woman," she berated under her breath and flipped on the radio. She listened to what little news there was, leaned an arm out the window and felt the hot wind pull at the strands of her hair. Acres and acres of rolling ranch land stretched as far as the eye could see and the wide Montana sky was a deep summer blue.

Fences sliced up the fields that were spotted with all shapes and colors of cattle and horses. She smiled at the sight of a Brahman calf with a tiny hump over its shoulders and wide, curious eyes watching as she passed. Spotted longhorns ambled along a creek bank and a frisky colt in another field lifted his tail like a banner and ran, kicking his black legs and shaking his head as he joined a small herd of Appaloosa.

The wide expanse was a far cry from the hustle and bustle of L.A. It was quiet here; probably too quiet for her. But a nice change of pace, and she was only going to stay for a while. Garrett had invited her to spend a few nights at the ranch as she peeked under every as yet unturned stone in her search for Larry's baby. She'd decided to take Garrett up on his offer. She'd always had a fantasy of spending a week on a real working ranch and now, it seemed, she was going to get her chance. Though she wouldn't stay a week; not when she knew that the rest of Larry's brood would show up soon and then she'd come face-to-face with Trent Remmington again.

Somehow she'd have to avoid that. Garrett had been making noises about her sticking around, meeting the sons and explaining her part in finding them all, but she intended to politely turn him down.

There was just no reason to stay.

She spied the turnoff to the Kincaid ranch just as Faith Hill's voice wafted from the speakers. Cranking hard on the wheel, she headed down a long lane of twin ruts. Tall grass grew between the parallel trails of sparse gravel, brushing the undercarriage of the rig. Potholes, now dusty, appeared and Gina smiled at the pure, raw grit of this part of the country. She spied a tractor chugging in one field; farther on, climbing to the sky, craggy mountains spired over rolling, pine-covered foothills.

Gina slowed as the lane curved toward a grouping of buildings at the heart of the spread. Stables were undergoing some kind of renovation; a bunkhouse stretched out near the parking lot while a weathered pump house, machine sheds and the like were clustered together around it. And the most stately building of all—a tall, rambling house that had once been white—faced the parking area. Once beautiful, it was slowly going to seed. Shutters missing slats sagged near windows, paint was beginning to peel and more than one windowpane had been boarded up. A wide porch skirted the first floor and a man was standing on the steps, a tall man with broad shoulders, dark hair and…and…

"Oh, God."

There, big as life, no, make that bigger than life, as Faith Hill sang about lost love and heartache, was Gina's own personal nightmare.

Trent Remmington was waiting for her.

And, from the looks of him, he was mad as hell.

Multi-*New York Times* bestselling author

NORA ROBERTS

knew from the first how to capture readers' hearts.
Celebrate the 20th Anniversary of Silhouette Books
with this special 2-in-1 edition containing her fabulous
first book and the sensational sequel.

Coming in June

IRISH HEARTS

Adelia Cunnane's fiery temper sets proud, powerful horse
breeder Travis Grant's heart aflame and he resolves to
make this wild ***Irish Thoroughbred*** his own.

Erin McKinnon accepts wealthy Burke Logan's loveless
proposal, but can this ravishing ***Irish Rose*** win her
hard-hearted husband's love?

Also available in June from
Silhouette Special Edition (SSE #1328)

IRISH REBEL

In this brand-new sequel to ***Irish Thoroughbred***, Travis and
Adelia's innocent but strong-willed daughter Keeley discovers
love in the arms of a charming Irish rogue with a talent for
horses...and romance.

Silhouette®

Where love comes alive™